FRANKI

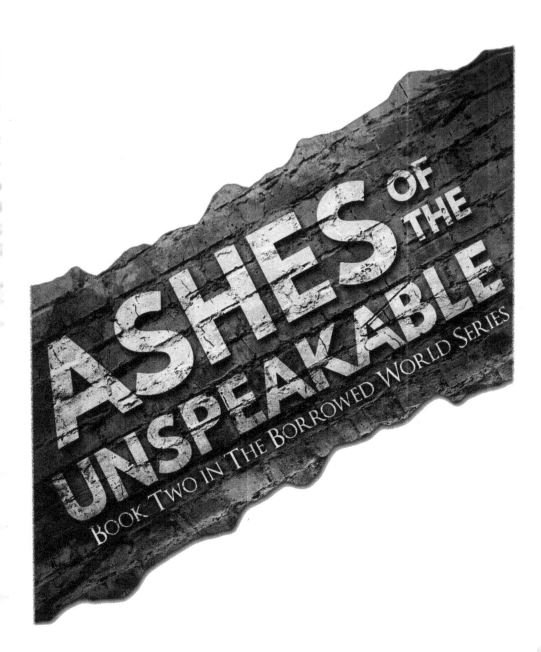

Ashes of the Unspeakable
by Franklin Horton
Copyright © 2015. All Rights Reserved.

ISBN-13: 978-1517442958
ISBN-10: 1517442958

Cover art by Deranged Doctor Design
Editing by Felicia Sullivan
Formatting by Kody Boye

ACKNOWLEDGEMENTS

Response to *THE BORROWED WORLD* has been overwhelming. It has especially been gratifying for someone who had pretty much given up on writing. I am grateful to the readers, the friends old and new, and the supportive online community who have all shared this experience with me.

I also feel a need to thank my old friend Jim Lloyd, owner of Lloyd's Barber Shop (yes, the *real* one). We have been best friends since elementary school and went out for barbecue in the Fall of 2014 to catch up on our lives. Jim asked me about writing, knowing that it had been a constant in my life since I was a teenager. I gave a long rant about my disgust with the publishing system, the fact that I had written multiple novels and still couldn't get my foot in the door. I told him that I hadn't written in ten years and probably never would again. In fact, the thought of writing made me ill.

"I thought you enjoyed writing?" Jim asked.

"Oh, I did," I said. "It's all I've ever wanted to do."

"Then why aren't you doing it?"

I didn't have a good answer, so I gave it one more shot.

It sounds simple, but it wasn't. I usually took my lunch break at work for eating (like most people) or going running (unlike most people). Instead, I started using it for writing, trying to get in three pages a day in that hour. Over the course of four months, I wrote THE BORROWED WORLD and I wrote it *entirely* on my daily lunch break.

I also want to thank some of the other writers who either inspired, motivated, or encouraged me at some level to write in this genre: Steven Konkoly, William Forstchen, A. American, and S.M. Stirling. I also want to thank Steven King and Cormac McCarthy for making writing seem like a worthwhile thing to do with your life.

There's also the team that made this series of books happen: my editor, Felicia Sullivan, who not only pares away the unessential but has been tremendously supportive and full of advice on independent publishing; the team at Deranged Doctor of Design who produce my graphics with top notch professionalism and efficiency; my coworker and proofreader, Anita Debord, who was recruited after finding every single typo in my last book; and Kody Boye, who produces the final files, always on short notice and without breaking a sweat.

I need to thank my parents, who had their work cut out for them in raising me. I was difficult as a child and probably still am. Lastly, there are the best things that ever happened to me -- my wife Jane, my son Elliott, and my daughter Arwyn, who have continued where my parent's left off, trying to shape me into a halfway respectable and socially acceptable human being.

Thank you all.

PROLOGUE

It had only been a few days since a coordinated terror attack, believed to be the work of ISIS operatives, hit the United States. Except for a few isolated pockets, America no longer had electricity. What had once been a unified national electrical grid now lay in tatters. One and two-man terrorist teams armed with explosives and mortars had destroyed massive transformers at critical junctures in the grid and it had started the fragile electrical infrastructure crumbling like the dried husk of an insect. The attacks were simple but devastating. There were only two places in the world that made replacements for those critical transformers that had been destroyed and both were an ocean away. With each transformer having to be built specifically for its location within the power grid, and with each taking up to a year to build, it was unknown how long it would take to restore power to everyone.

Communication networks had also been designated targets. GPS worked. Cell phone reception was sporadic. Sometimes you could get texts out, but it might be hours before they went through. Or it might not go through at all. As propane generators began to run out of fuel, the remaining functional cell towers would begin dropping like flies. Then all that would remain would be the human network of rumors and stories passed from person to person.

Other terrorists in the group destroyed weakened and neglected dams. This actually took very little effort at all on the part of the attackers. Structures that were known risks, long overdue for repair or replacement, collapsed easily under mortar attacks. Billions of gallons of water were released onto millions of unsuspecting citizens. Many homes were washed away, collapsing as they were swept off their foundations. Other homes remained intact, their frightened inhabitants watching helplessly from windows as they spun away on the dark waters. Nashville, Tennessee was only one of the major cities devastated by flood from a breached dam. The death toll was unknown, with estimates only placed at *massive*.

The lack of fuel was the crippling blow. Nearly all of the major refineries had come under attack. One man with one mortar at each of those refineries, and now most people in the United States did not have access to any fuel for their vehicles or generators, nor would those who relied on oil for heating their homes be able to get it this winter. Those who sat in flooded cities awaiting rescue would be waiting for a very long time. First responders quickly discovered there was just not enough fuel remaining to do everything that needed to be done. Nor was there enough to save everyone that needed saving.

As the magnitude of the attacks became apparent, the government issued orders to restrict fuel sales to the public. First responders, police, and the military could obtain fuel for emergency vehicles but no one else had access. Gas stations along major highways had larger underground tanks that held more fuel, so law enforcement officers were dispatched to those points to guard that supply. Shootouts erupted in this process and lives were lost on both sides. Across the country, men in business suits were breaking into strangers' storage buildings to siphon gas from lawnmowers, simply trying to get home from work. Ordinary folks were killed either trying to get fuel or to protect their own fuel against those wanting to take it.

Those unfortunate enough to be caught any distance from home were forced to abandon their vehicles. With no fuel and no prospects for getting more, their vehicles became useless to them. Rest areas and highway exits quickly became populated with stranded and confused travelers. With the growing crowds came crime, violence, and unrest. Nowhere on or around any highway was safe.

In an attempt to defuse this growing refugee problem, FEMA responded by creating camps along interstate highways. They ran buses along the interstate to pick up the desperate vacationers, the starving business travelers, the long haul truckers, and anyone else just plain unlucky enough to be caught out in this disaster. Law enforcement at all levels was working to clear crowded interstate exits and force people to use the FEMA camps. It was the only way they saw to restore order. The plan was that once people were at a camp, FEMA would work toward getting those folks back home. They acknowledged it could take months to get the logistics worked out. A person might be shuttled from camp to camp, slowly getting closer to home with each relocation, but eventually they would get there. Or so it was promised.

For some, this did not seem like much of a solution. The very idea of FEMA camps had a lot of negative implications attached to it. Folks were concerned that they would become like internment camps and that the residents would never be allowed to leave. Those travelers legally carrying concealed weapons were afraid they'd be forced to give them up if they went to the camps. They were right.

Although many people on the East Coast weren't yet aware, parts of the American West were left in poisonous ruin. Mortar attacks on two nuclear power plants had led to breaches that discharged radioactive waste into the atmosphere. The scale of those disasters grew worse every day, contributing to the inability of FEMA and the government to get a handle on things. The government was crippled by the scale of the attacks. FEMA was pulled in so many directions that they were rendered ineffectual on all levels. Their intentions to help people in the eastern U.S. get home were watered down by their efforts to rescue Americans fleeing the nuclear disasters out west.

The lack of information was one of the most psychologically devastating aspects of the disaster. Americans had grown used to a constant intravenous feed of news and information. They watched disasters unfold like sporting events, glued to the televisions or the internet, absorbing every facet of the suffering of others. They watched wars, earthquakes, elections, and movie award shows with equal fascination and equal disinterest. They'd become dependent on it. Now, the total lack of information created an ominous cloud that hung over the nation and increased the generalized anxiety experienced by each and every person.

Everyone wanted to know what was happening.

Of course, had everyone known what was happening at a national level, they would have found no comfort. Despite what religious groups and the paranoid thought, it was not the end of the world. This was not *the* doomsday event of legend and lore. It was, however, an event that would change the face of the nation. For a long time, it would be the end of the world as they knew it. The government was still there, they just couldn't speak directly to the people. They also couldn't do a damn thing to help them.

Even if they had been able to speak to the citizenry, what would they say? Would they tell them that, without power, the nation faced a greater than ninety percent mortality rate over the next year? Would they warn folks in the northern cities that they would probably freeze to death over the coming winter, if starvation and disease didn't get them first? Would they tell folks that there would probably be no more trucks of food showing up at grocery stores? Would they admit that law enforcement would have little impact on the coming waves of crime, violence, and social unrest?

Would they tell people that they would soon turn on each other?

Would they tell them that it had already started?

CHAPTER 1

Lloyd's Barber Shop
Crawfish, Virginia

Jim Powell awoke, disoriented, and immediately reached for his pistol. When his hand went to his side and did not fall on his holstered weapon, there was a moment of panic and he tried to sit up and locate it. His attempt to sit up was met with a pain and stiffness so intense that it took his breath and nearly made him cry out. He bit back an agonized groan. The pain brought clarity, though, and as he gasped for the breath taken by the pain, he realized where he was. He was in his friend Lloyd's first-floor apartment in Crawfish, Virginia. He was in a sleeping bag in the floor, scattered among a half-dozen or so other sleeping bodies. They were all people he knew.

He was safe.

He had awoken on this particular floor more times than he cared to admit. Usually it was after a drunken night of live acoustic music, cheap cigars, and whatever booze was at hand. Though he didn't have a hangover this time, he was experiencing a worse type of pain. The previous day gradually came back to him, and he recalled the details of his injury. He had been clotheslined from an ATV that he was driving on the Blue Ridge Parkway. He'd nearly been decapitated by a trap sprung on him by the last survivor of a group of lowlifes he and his co-workers had encountered on the road. Had he not had his arm raised to point at a landmark, the barbed wire strand would have caught him by the neck and likely killed him. Instead, it only made him *wish* he was dead. His spine felt as if someone had attempted to twist him into a pretzel.

He carefully probed his head and could feel a pronounced knot on the back of it, and a large scrape on his scalp that had scabbed over. It hurt to touch it, so the logical thing to do would have been to *not* touch it, but injuries are like magnets and Jim kept poking at it. The muscles of his arm, shoulder, and back were tight and very sore. He knew that beneath his shirt his upper body probably looked like an old banana – all brown, yellow, and black. He preferred not to look.

ASHES OF THE UNSPEAKABLE

The wire had dislocated his shoulder, forcing him to jerk it back into place by himself. He was hoping that was truly a once in a lifetime experience. It was that special. As much as he wanted to get home to his family, he was not sure if he would be able to carry a pack today with these injuries. He would have to see how his body loosened up once he got moving.

He removed his phone from its case on his belt. He powered it up and waited for it to go through the boot process. He'd been charging it with a portable solar unit while he walked, but with no signal here at Lloyd's, he'd turned it off last night to conserve power. He didn't need it to make a call right now, he needed a different kind of connection.

When the phone finished booting up, he selected the photo library and started thumbing through pictures. There was one of him in a tandem kayak with his son and daughter when they were little more than toddlers. There was another of his daughter clutching a long Northern Pike in her hands, a nervous smile on her face as she stared at its pointy teeth. There was one of his son looking sweaty and exhausted, resting on a stone bridge on the carriage roads of Acadia National Park after a long bike ride. There was another of him and his wife taken at a friend's cookout several years ago. There were always fewer of the two of them together since they were usually the ones taking the pictures. They'd always meant to remedy that situation, but it never worked out.

The pictures made Jim well with emotion. He was sure that this was made worse at the moment by his physical pain and sense of desperation. He needed to be at home looking out for his family. He worried constantly for their safety. He *had* to get home. Before he could do that, he first had to get up from the floor. He had to make himself get to his feet and restart his journey home.

He attempted to extricate himself from his sleeping bag. It took some work with the pain hitting on all cylinders. It was more than stiff muscles. His back felt as if nerves were being ground to pulp between his vertebrae. He would have cursed but the pain took his breath and left none to spare for profanity. Once free of the sleeping bag, he finally got to his feet. That took more awkward maneuvering and he was hoping that no one was awake to watch when a cramp struck his calf muscle. He carefully hobbled around, attempting to stretch the cramped muscle and make this new pain go away. It was the icing on the cake. In this morning of suffering, he felt as far from his family as he'd ever felt.

His backpack lay in the floor above his sleeping bag. Propped on top of it, he could see his Beretta 92 in its holster. He had started this journey home with a smaller backpack full of what he called his Get Home Gear, however, he was now carrying a larger Gregory backpack. He'd found it on the Appalachian Trail, dropped by an escaping ATV rider after one of his group had killed the man's partner. The men had attacked Jim's camp in the middle of the night but they'd been ready for their attackers. They suspected the pack had originally been stolen from an Appalachian Trail through-hiker. The pack and the gear inside was not of the type likely to belong to the low-life that dropped it in his escape. They assumed that the hiker who had originally owned the pack was dead. Jim was fairly certain that the men responsible for the hiker's death were dead now, too. He suspected they were among the numerous men he'd seen die these past few days. It had been that kind of trip.

There were only three in his group now – himself and two co-workers. They had made their way this far after being trapped in Richmond, Virginia, in the aftermath of the sweeping ISIS terror attacks. Their party had been larger at the beginning of the crisis, and as the scale of the attacks became clear to them that morning in Richmond, they had decided as a group to try to make a run for it. They thought they could make it home by car, but at a travel plaza not far outside of Richmond the harsh reality of their situation came crashing down on them.

They had turned off the interstate for fuel and a restroom break only to find a sign indicating that fuel sales were restricted to a few gallons per customer. In the moments between their arrival and their attempt to buy fuel, state troopers had arrived to halt *all* fuel sales and to guard the pumps. This news had been devastating to the large crowd that that had formed there waiting for their opportunity to refuel. An altercation between a disgruntled customer and a trooper quickly escalated and turned deadly. Gun shots rang out.

When waiting customers pulled their own concealed weapons to protect themselves, rounds flew in all directions. A stray round had caught Lois, one of Jim's coworkers, in the head, and she was dead before she hit the floor. Though he and Lois had not gotten along at all, at the same time, he'd never wished death on her.

They were forced to abandon one of their cars there since it was blocked in by a vehicle. They'd also been forced to leave Lois' body behind in their scramble to escape the scene without further casualties. When they attempted to exit the truck stop parking lot, they got into an altercation with another stranded traveler intent on carjacking their vehicle. The man shattered their driver's window and was drawing back to shatter Gary's skull with the same tire iron when Jim reacted. He flew out of his door, leveled his pocket-sized .380 concealed-carry pistol across the roof of the car, and dropped the man dead in the road.

It was the first man he'd ever killed. Between the brutality of watching Lois die and seeing Jim kill a man, most of his group was in a state of shock. They didn't even realize he had a gun with him. It was, in fact, a violation of his company's policy to have a gun with him in a company car, a policy Jim had always ignored. What those coworkers didn't know either was that Jim's gun was not the only gun in the car. Gary was armed, and Jim had a second, larger pistol in his Get Home Bag in the trunk of the vehicle.

A little further down the road their fuel ran out and they were forced to start hoofing it down the interstate, leaving their company car abandoned on the shoulder. Tension was already developing in the group at this point. In Jim's mind, the situation taking place was crystal clear. He knew what was happening. He'd read about this type of thing and suspected they were experiencing what was known as a *collapsing systems failure*. Others in the group had blinders on and assumed that this was all simply a really, really bad day at work and things would be okay tomorrow. Jim thought they were idiots and may have mentioned it once or twice. People skills were not his forte.

After several miles of walking, they'd reached a crowded interstate exit where they were able to get a meal and hole up in a dark, powerless hotel. The local cops maintained a roadblock to prevent mobs of travelers from entering their town. This was becoming the case all along the interstate highways in every state throughout America; stranded travelers were becoming distressed and creating trouble for roadside communities. The local sheriff had shown up that evening at Jim's exit and made an announcement that FEMA was going to start running buses up and down the interstate the next morning to deliver people to recovery camps, then *eventually* on to their homes.

Two of the folks in Jim's group – gullible people in his opinion –

preferred to trust in FEMA to provide for their needs and get them home. Gary, Jim, and a coworker named Randi were less trusting about turning their fate over to anyone else, particularly the government. Early the next morning, their group of three set out on foot to avoid being caught in the FEMA roundup. Though it had not been an easy trip, they consoled themselves with the thought that they were getting closer to home every day. Yesterday, they reached Crawfish, Virginia. The town was home to Jim's oldest friend, Lloyd, and the group had stopped there hoping to get some rest and resupply before continuing on their way.

*

Jim found his shoes, unfortunately relying more on his sense of smell than sight. Such was the consequence of walking too many miles with too few showers. Shoes in hand, he limped toward the kitchen, weaving his way through the still bodies. Lloyd wasn't married, and it would have been apparent, even to a stranger, that this house did not have a woman's touch. Lloyd's building was nearly 150 years old and his storefront apartment had at various times been a doctor's office, a law office, and a movie theater. It was decorated with musical instruments, old bottles, and other antique junk. Lloyd lived in the past. Not even his own past, more like his grandfather's or great-grandfather's past. Unlike Jim, Lloyd was not a child of the 1960s and 1970s but by his own choosing, a child of the 1930s. It made him an interesting person to know.

In the kitchen, Jim found one of Lloyd's musician friends making coffee in a stovetop percolator, an appliance Jim had not seen in action since his childhood. The natural gas must still be flowing in Crawfish. The man making the coffee was thin with black hair that stuck out in all directions. Jim wasn't sure if it was from sleep or some funky hairstyle. He wore a green t-shirt that said *Fear the Banjo*.

"I've heard a lot about you, Jim" he said. "Lloyd is always talking about the adventures you guys used to have as kids."

He reached out to shake the man's hand. "Those adventures extended well past childhood. Trust me on that."

"I'm Masa," the man said. "Lloyd calls me Tojo."

"He calls all Asian people by that name," Jim said, shaking his head. "Aren't you offended?"

Masa placed the lid on the percolator and slid it into the burning stove eye. "Nah, it's just how he is," he replied. "He's equally offensive to all races – especially his own."

"So what are you doing here in the U.S.?" Jim asked. "I think I remember Lloyd saying that you were from Tokyo."

"I am. We were all headed to the Galax Old Fiddler's Convention. I come every year," Masa said. "A couple of years ago, Lloyd told me that he always had a group come to his house before the festival to play and get geared up. This is the first year I've been able to make it."

"And what a year you picked."

"No shit." Masa sat down at the table.

Jim made his way across the room, shoes in hand, and stiffly sat down across from Masa. He struggled with his shoes in an unforgiving wooden ladder-back chair. Even Lloyd's newest furniture appeared to be at least fifty years old.

"I got down here a week before the festival," Masa said. "We played music here every night and drank lots of alcohol. Then we packed up, bought tons of food for camping at the festival, bought cases of beer and liquor for drinking at the festival, and we hit the road."

"I take it you didn't make it?"

"No," Masa replied. "We got to the first gas station about twenty minutes up the road and stopped to fill up for the trip. We pulled in at the pump right when they were hanging signs on them saying that there was no gas for sale."

"I know the feeling," Jim said. "That completely sucks."

Masa shrugged, lit a cigarette, and inhaled deeply. "Yeah, but it would have sucked worse to have gotten all the way down there and been trapped at Galax. Trapped on a fenced-in fairground full of hillbillies, can you imagine? They'd be clubbing each other over the head with instruments and eating the dead."

Jim shook his head at the image knowing it was probably the way it would have played out.

"Since we didn't get any farther than that, we turned around and came back here. We've been playing and drinking ever since. I think we already drank all our booze. Sometimes people wander in from the town and bring us food or some of that moonshine and listen to us play. It's been fun, in a post-disaster kind of way."

"It's not been fun on our end," Jim said. "Too much worry, too much violence. I've got family at home that I'm trying to get to and it feels like it's taking way too long to get to them. You know, the worst part about this whole disaster is the lack of information. I grew up in the 1970s and we were blissfully ignorant then. There was thirty minutes of local news and thirty minutes of national news each night. If they didn't talk about it then, you didn't need to know about it."

The percolator began boiling, a sound that roused a sense of nostalgia in Jim, reminding him of beehive hairdos and long cigarettes. "You guys hear any news here at all?" he asked.

"Nothing reliable. Every person that came by Lloyd's shop had some story about who did this or what was happening. Half of them say it's your own government. None of it sounded very probable. I never knew this country had so many conspiracy nuts. We don't have so many in Japan."

"A true conspiracy nut would say that's because your government killed or imprisoned them," Jim said, only half joking.

Masa put out his cigarette and stood. "How about breakfast? We've still got coolers full of camping food that has to be eaten before the ice melts."

The idea of fresh food sounded great to Jim. The mere thought of it made him instantly hungry. "Let me get some of that coffee and I'll help."

*

An hour later, the whole house was up and everyone was gorging on paper plates heaped with bacon, eggs, biscuits, sausage, and gravy. People were crammed onto 1940s sofas and odd wingback chairs with shiny, threadbare upholstery in the dark and musty room. Jim took in the assortment of people, noting that there wasn't a lot of difference in the appearance, or smell, between this group and the through-hikers they'd encountered on the trail. Knowing that this group of musicians stank despite having lived in relative comfort for the last few days, Jim assumed that his own smell and appearance must be far worse than he imagined.

"This is great," Gary said. "I'm so sick of candy bars and trail food. Once I make it home, I hope to never eat another candy bar in my entire life."

"That's harsh, dude," Masa said. "Snickers are the fucking bomb."

"Try living off them for a week and tell me that," Gary said.

Over the meal, Gary, Randi, and Jim discussed their plans for the next stage of their journey. Jim's body continued to send signals that all it wanted was to lie back down. He attempted to convince his body that this was not a possibility. He hoped that moving around would loosen him up enough that he could travel. Under different circumstances he would concede defeat, take it easy for the day, and give his body a chance to heal, but this was a different world and time was a luxury he did not have. Depending on what his family was going through, a delay of a day, even an hour, could mean the difference between someone's life and death.

There was no way he could relax when he didn't know what was happening to his family. Days ago, when this journey started, there was a sense of exhilaration that he was taking his fate into his own hands and starting this journey back home. Others in their group had opted to wait for a FEMA bus and allow themselves to be taken to a camp along the interstate until they could be transported home. Jim, Randi, and Gary had not felt comfortable with that idea, instead choosing to walk.

As the days dragged on and he still wasn't home, Jim began to experience both mental and physical symptoms that pressed him forward with ever increasing urgency. Mentally, he was so worried about his family at this point that it consumed nearly every waking thought. Physically, that worry manifested itself as an anxiety that clutched his chest like a claw. Each passing day turned up the volume on his worry by one more notch.

He could whine and say that he didn't know how much more he could take, but he'd learned a long time ago that the degree to which a human could experience suffering was nearly infinite. Ask any tortured prisoner. Ask any parent who has lost a child. There is no merciful insanity that shields you and whisks you away to a better place. There is no respite. There is no rescue.

Gary was experiencing his own set of aches and pains as well. Yesterday, Jim and Randi thought they'd lost him when he took a handgun round to the chest. It turned out that he was wearing light body armor that had stopped the round. They didn't even know he had the body armor. The impact left him with a nasty bruise to the chest and some sore ribs. Randi had had a round graze her cheek, nearly taking off her head. The whole group felt beaten, abused, and debilitated.

"I'm with you, Jim," Gary said. "I feel like shit, but feel like I need to be moving in the direction of home, even if I have to crawl there."

Randi agreed. "Let's get back on the road and get another day closer. What's the plan?"

They'd come this far utilizing a Get Home Plan Jim had developed over several years in preparation for a disaster hitting if he was away from home. He traveled to Richmond, Virginia, so frequently in the years after 9/11 that it was hard not to think about how he would get home if disaster struck. He liked to think that a little paranoia could save a life. His plan had been to use the Appalachian Trail to get off the main roads and back home safely. By design, the trail avoided major metropolitan areas, which was exactly what Jim wanted. By the time his group left the trail for good, they would hopefully be within thirty miles or so of their homes.

Lloyd was eavesdropping on the conversation as he stuffed his face. At this stage of his life, less interested in impressing people, he'd more completely submerged himself into his character, adopting a depression era mode of dress. He wore dark pants and a collarless white shirt with a felt hat and suspenders. Jim was used to a lifetime of Lloyd's odd manner of dress and paid no attention to it anymore. People that didn't know him would often pause for a second look, like he'd escaped in costume from a theatrical troupe.

"I might want to go with you," Lloyd said. "I've got no family here and I'm worried about my parents."

Lloyd's parents still lived in the same town where Jim lived. They were both retired and probably needed help about now if they didn't have any preparations made. If Jim had been home, he could have checked on them.

"You're welcome to join us," Jim said. "If you can keep up. The terrain is challenging, to say the least. You musicians live kind of a sedentary lifestyle and I know you're not used to anything physically demanding."

"Shouldn't be a problem," Lloyd said. "I have good shoes and a strong woman to carry my stuff." He nodded in Randi's direction and winked at her.

She was not impressed. "One more crack like that and this strong woman will be carrying your stuff in a jar, if you know what *stuff* I mean." Randi scissored her fingers together in a snipping motion.

Lloyd winced and crossed his legs.

Two of Lloyd's musical entourage stood and dumped their paper plates in a nearby garbage bag. One was Frank Hollister, whom Jim had met several times over the years, and the other was Steve Wright, whom Jim knew from previous visits. They were both from York in the U.K. and came over each summer to play the Old Time music festival circuit with Lloyd. They called their group *Frank, Lloyd, Wright.*

"We're thinking we'd like another nip of that moonshine," Frank said in his crisp English accent. As a frequent pub musician back home, he had a beer belly and a permanently red face. His beard was a thick red-gray mass that sprouted from his face in all directions. He was a fiddle-maker by trade and regarded by all as a damn fine musician.

Steve Wright nodded and grinned in agreement, obviously ready for a nip. While a drinking man like his buddy Frank, his appearance stood in stark contrast to the other man. Steve was rail thin with greasy black hair that was tied back into a long ponytail. He made his living as a busker, playing the sidewalks of York for tips. He was truly a man that lived for the day and the future could be damned. The current disaster meant nothing to him, really. As long as he had a fiddle and a drink he was content.

"Sorry, boys," Lloyd said. "You drunken sons-of-bitches drank it all yesterday."

The men were crushed, their wilting posture saying more than words ever could have.

"I might know where we can get more," Lloyd offered.

Their spirits lifted instantly.

"Claude, the car dealer from up the road. You remember him?"

The two Englishmen nodded enthusiastically.

"He usually keeps some for guests. We can probably trade him out of some."

"With what?" Frank asked. "What would he require in trade?"

Lloyd pointed to the old trunk that he used as a coffee table. It was a vintage steamer trunk from the 1800s. "Clear the junk off top of that."

Gary removed the ashtrays and empty bottles from the top of the trunk and carefully set them on the floor. When he was done, he flipped the latches and raised the lid of the trunk. A smile broke out on his face when he looked inside.

Jim stood up and walked over to look inside. "Damn. Where did you get all these?"

The trunk was nearly full of handguns of all types, and boxes of ammunition, some obviously vintage judging by the ragged packaging, scattered through the trunk with the guns. Jim reached into the trunk and moved a few around. Some of the guns were wrapped in oily rags, some were zipped into proper pistol cases, and still others were loose and piled atop each other. As a gun lover, Jim was appalled at the carelessness of Lloyd's weapon storage system.

"I'm a barber," Lloyd explained. "Everyone knows the town barber. When someone needs cash, they come to their barber and ask if he wants to buy something they're selling. Sometimes it's a car or truck, a tractor, a musical instrument. Sometimes it's car parts. Sometimes it's guns. I've got a whole closet of rifles back there too."

At that, Gary and Jim glanced at each other. They had complained to each other several times on this trip that they sure would appreciate having a long gun of some type. The limited accuracy of pistols at great distances had restricted their ability to take out a threat from a position of cover the previous day. They'd been forced to expose themselves to gunfire to get close enough to shoot back with any accuracy. With a good rifle and a well-placed shot, the issue could have been resolved with less risk to their group.

"So you're like a pawn shop?" Randi asked.

Lloyd shook his head. "Not exactly. I make them an offer and they can take it or leave it. I don't want to hear what the item is worth or what they have in it – I don't give a shit. I never pay much for anything, because I'm not desperate, they are. If it's a gun, they have to give me a box of shells with it. That's my rule. Guns always sell better if they come with ammunition. And unlike a pawn shop, there's no promise that you can come buy it back from me when your circumstances are better. Once you sell the gun to me, it's mine. I might sell it back to you, or I might not. I might sound like an asshole, but those are my rules."

Lloyd stood up, threw his paper plate in the garbage, and walked to the trunk. He dug around, pulled out a Harrington and Richardson snub-nose .38 and a worn box of shells, then handed it to Frank.

"Offer him this for two gallons," Lloyd said. "Don't take less."

Frank frowned. "I thought you said he only kept a little moonshine for guests. You think he really has two spare gallons lying about?"

"He does," Lloyd assured him. "He has thirsty guests."

Frank turned to Jim. "Would one of you gentlemen be so kind as to lend us the use of your quad bike? Frankly, I'm too fat and hungover to walk."

"Do you know how to operate one?" Jim asked. He wasn't familiar with the term quad bike, but was assuming Frank meant the ATVs they rode in on.

"Yes. I've worked on farms back in England quite frequently and our farmers find them as useful as your farmers do."

"Then certainly, Frank," Jim said. "They're parked around back."

"Gentlemen," Steve said, tipping his hat, "we shall return momentarily, hopefully with intoxicating spirits. Please tune your instruments."

Lloyd was shaking his head as the men departed. "Crazy English bastards."

"They're funny bastards," Jim said.

"They certainly are," Lloyd agreed.

The men heard the ATV start up out back and accelerate, then it pulled around the front of Lloyd's building. Suddenly, there was a shout. It was hard to understand the words but it sounded like a shout of warning or alarm. Jim stood up to investigate and a loud gunshot broke the quiet of the morning. He flinched and ducked back from the picture window he'd been approaching. A second shot quickly followed.

Lloyd waved him off. "Don't worry, those crazy bastards must have loaded that pistol. I guess I should have specifically told them *not* to shoot the gun while they were delivering it across town. You'd think they would fucking know that."

Gary was getting up, concern darkening his face. "I think that was a shotgun blast. Not a pistol." He drew his Glock.

Jim reached down to his own hip for his pistol but for the second time that day it wasn't there. He had a moment of panic before he realized that he'd left it sitting on the arm of the couch where he'd been eating. The damn thing kept poking him while he tried to eat. He took a couple of quick steps back in that direction, grabbed his Beretta, and headed toward the front door, checking to make sure a round was chambered. When he reached the door, Gary was already there, staring around the edge of a vintage window shade. Jim took the other side of the door and peered out. The glass was old and distorted, with small bubbles scattered through it, but he could see well enough to get a clear picture of what had happened.

"Oh shit," Gary muttered.

Jim saw the two Englishmen lying on the ground beside the overturned ATV. It was still running, one rear wheel still spinning. About twenty feet away, an elderly man in coveralls was pointing a shotgun at the fallen men. Beside him stood the hulking banjo-toting man in a diaper that they had passed on their way into town the day before.

"Who the hell is that?" Jim asked.

Lloyd reached the window about that time. "Damn it!" He shouldered Jim out of the way and flung open the door, running out of the building before Jim could stop him.

Gary and Jim looked at each other, wondering what they should do. They were torn between the safety of their position and looking out for the man who'd sheltered them last night. Jim sucked in a deep breath. Lloyd was his oldest friend. He took a quick look out the door, then ran and took cover behind a car parked along the street. The car stood as a barrier between him and the shooter, but the old man didn't appear to notice that Jim had come out. He had no reaction at all.

In a moment, Gary was at Jim's side. They crouched by the front wheel, leveling their pistols across the hood at the armed man, hoping there was enough engine block to provide some protection if he turned the scattergun in their direction. If Lloyd hadn't been there, Jim would have shot the old man by this time. On the sheer merit of the scene before him, he knew the man deserved to die. The old man had shot the Englishmen in cold blood. They were good people.

Lloyd stood distraught in front of the old man, pointing and yelling at him. "Gerald, you fucking idiot! *Why*? You killed two of my friends. They were guests in my house! What the hell are you *doing*?"

The old man squinted at him as if could not recall who Lloyd was or why he was there. The old man was dark and wrinkled, wearing bibbed overalls and a dirty flannel shirt that swallowed his diminutive figure. Tufts of white hair poked from beneath a crumpled cap advertising Red Man chewing tobacco. He did not lower his shotgun, keeping it pointed in the direction of the fallen men.

Lloyd turned his back on the old man and walked over to his prone friends, dropping and checking them. He touched them, shook them, begged his maker to restore them, but it was not to be. They were dead as disco. A pool of blood steadily grew and encircled them. Lloyd was devastated. The men had been his friends for a long time.

"Why did you kill them?" Lloyd asked, turning back to the old man, his voice cracking with emotion. "I've always been good to you, Gerald. Who gave Lawrence there his banjo?" Lloyd was pointing, indicating the giant intellectually disabled man standing beside the shooter. He wore only a diaper, cowboy boots, and t-shirt. His large paw gripped an old banjo by the neck. He must have been in his mid-fifties and looked like a banjo-toting cherub, with his diaper and shape.

The man, apparently Lawrence, held his banjo up to show Lloyd and smiled broadly. "You gimme it." When Lawrence smiled again, Jim could see that every tooth in his head was missing.

"Didn't know they was your friends, Lloyd. Didn't really mean to kill them," the old man said, his voice like cold water over stones. "Tried to ask them a question and they started to drive off. I'm too old to chase them so I had to shoot them."

Lloyd shook his head in disgust. "What question was so damn important that you killed my two friends over it?"

The old man considered this, his shotgun still raised and pointed towards the bodies as if they might rise and need to be shot again.

"That four-wheeler they were riding belongs to my grandson. He didn't come home yesterday. My family went looking for him and now they ain't come home, neither. I'm feeling like something bad has befallen them. I intended to ask these two sons-of-bitches what they knew about it, but they went and got all froggy on me. Tried to drive off like they had something to hide."

Those words hit Jim like a ton of bricks. This was *his* fault. The old man was a relative of the people that his group had clashed with over the past two days. It had started when they met up with some hunters on the Appalachian Trail. One of their group had gotten all high-and-mighty with the hunters that they were damaging the trail by illegally using their ATV there. Jim deescalated the situation, but he was still left with an uneasy feeling that they'd see those hunters again so they left a decoy camp that night and slept deeper in the woods.

While most of the group was sleeping, the hunters returned in the middle of the night, shooting into a tent and then setting it ablaze. Randi killed one of the men but the other got away. In the aftermath, the dead man's family came looking for Jim's group and killed a young couple that had been traveling with them. In that fight, they were forced to kill their attackers and hide their bodies on the side of the road. After patching up their wounds, Jim and his friends took the ATVs and used them to reach Lloyd's place. It now appeared that this may have been a mistake and that this mistake may have killed two innocent people.

Jim stood up from behind the car, his Beretta leveled on the man. "Tell me about the people you're looking for."

The old man turned to Jim and squinted. "I don't know you, son."

"You don't," Jim agreed. "You probably don't want to, either, so don't turn that gun in my direction."

"Or what?"

"Or I drop you where you stand."

The man kept the shotgun pointed away from Jim, but a fury grew within his eyes. "Other night, my grandson didn't come home. Yesterday, the rest of my people went looking for him. They didn't come home, neither. Then Lawrence, my son here, saw one of our four-wheelers coming into town with someone else driving it. I come to find out why. That's it yonder."

"Those men had nothing to do with it," Jim said. "You murdered innocent people."

"Ain't no one innocent," the old man said. "I've been on this Earth long enough to know that fact."

"Your people weren't innocent. They died trying to kill us. We fought back and they died. It was their fault. Their choice."

The man's body shuddered as if he could not control his physical response to the news that had been dropped upon his shoulders. His family was dead. "I've lost everyone. You killed them all."

Lloyd stepped toward him. "Gerald, you haven't lost everyone. You've still got that boy that needs you. Who's going to take care of Lawrence if you die here? You know he can't take care of himself. You told me once that the only reason the Lord put you on this Earth was to take care of Lawrence."

The old man's eyes never left Jim's. "I might just have to kill you."

"You'll die if you try," Jim warned.

"He's going to shoot," Gary whispered.

"Stop it!" Lloyd yelled at the old man, his frustration at the breaking point. "Stop it! You've already lost everyone, you dumb bastard. Tell him,

Lawrence, tell him to put down that gun and go home with you."

Lawrence looked toward his father and spoke softly, oblivious to the seriousness of the situation but becoming scared by all the yelling. He stuck out his hand toward his father. "Go, Daddy. We go home."

"Everybody calm the fuck down!"

It was Randi. No guns moved, but all eyes moved in her direction. She stepped out from Lloyd's apartment and slowly walked between the cars, into the street. She had her hands out in front of her, showing that they were empty.

"You all are scaring him," she said, approaching Lawrence, smiling at him.

"What do you know about it?" the old man spat.

"I've worked with people exactly like Lawrence every day," Randi said. She continued moving closer to him, closing the twenty feet between them.

"Do not get near my son!"

Randi held her hands up. "I'm only trying to help."

The old man laughed bitterly. "Every time somebody said they were there to help, they ended up trying to take my boy away from me. Nobody ever helped him but us. He's my responsibility."

Randi continued to get closer to Lawrence. "I just want to take him somewhere safe. I want to get him out of the middle of all these guns. You don't want to see him get hurt."

The old man swung his gun toward Randi, his finger on the trigger. All it would take would be the slightest of flinches and Randi would be dead. "I told you once. Do not touch my son!"

Gary couldn't take it anymore. "Get back here, Randi. He's going to kill you."

"It's okay," Randi said. She was not talking to anyone but Lawrence now, her voice low. She made eye contact with him and smiled. She took another step and reached out her hand to him. "It's going to be okay."

The old man was quivering with anger. His face was red, tears rolled from his eyes as if squeezed from his core by an immense pressure. "I told you..."

"He's going to do it," Gary said. "He's going to do it."

The old man shifted his aim from Randi, raised his gun toward his disabled son, and pulled the trigger. Buckshot sprayed the man-child from mere feet away, the concentration of pellets shredding completely through his neck and exiting in a cloud of gore. Randi was enveloped in the gruesome spray and fell backward.

Lawrence collapsed instantly, his spine severed and his head rolling awkwardly to the side. Without pause, the old man continued an awkward rotation toward Jim, racking the pump on his shotgun to chamber another round.

He was not fast enough. There was no way that he could have been with both Jim and Gary already holding him in their sights. If his first shot had been in Jim's direction instead of his son's, he might have had a chance. Jim sent three 9mm Hydro-Shock bullets into the old man's center mass before his rotation was complete. He didn't intend to shoot him that many times but the wiry bastard wouldn't drop. Gary fired as well, not counting his shots but aware that there were several. The old man was dead before his body hit the ground, his old Winchester 97 clattering away onto the paved street. Blood seeped from his wounds, mixing in the dirty street with the blood of the dead Englishmen.

Gary holstered his Glock and sprang around the car, rushing to Randi's side. She was spitting and wiping blood from her face. Gary took off his shirt and wiped the blood from her eyes. She grabbed the shirt with both hands and began wiping her mouth. When she was able to see, she opened her eyes to the gory scene before her, then exploded into sobs. Lawrence's body lay at her feet, the wound gaping at her, the blood soaking into her pants and shoes. She began kicking violently, trying to scoot away from the pooling blood.

"Is she hit?" Jim asked, joining Gary.

"I don't know yet," Gary said. "I can't tell." He put his hands under Randi's arms and dragged her back to the sidewalk, out of view of Lawrence's body.

"Are you hit?" Jim asked.

Randi was gasping, unable to cry, talk, or breathe. Her eyes were wild, manic, those of a trapped animal.

"Randi!" Jim snapped. "Are you hit?"

She finally held up a hand in a gesture that indicated they should give her a minute.

The normally unflappable Lloyd had not yet been exposed to anything like this. He'd spent the first week of America's collapse in a drunken stupor playing "Sally Ann" and telling lies. He'd not seen the violence that had wracked the lives of normal people caught up in this disaster. He dropped to his knees in the street – cursing, crying.

"I didn't see that coming," Gary said. "I knew he'd shoot at you and I was waiting for it. I didn't think he'd kill his own son"

Jim crouched at Randi's side, placing a hand on her shoulder. Though her breathing was calming, tears still burned their way from her eyes, washing grisly paths down her blood-spattered face. "Are you hit?" he asked once more. "We need to know."

Randi began patting her body. She looked down her shirt. "I don't think he hit me. It's not my blood."

"Thank God," Gary said. "I don't know how he missed you."

"It was close. I felt it," Randi said. "I've got to get out of these clothes, get cleaned up."

Jim and Gary helped her up and she walked toward the door to Lloyd's apartment. She turned around and looked at the scene. "I won't shed another tear the entire way home. I know the rules now. You can be completely innocent and it won't make any difference. It doesn't fucking matter."

Jim couldn't think of anything to say. He knew that he was selfish. Selfishness was at the very heart of survival. He was grateful to have another day.

However, this was not a proud moment. The world was changing around them and it was becoming a place where a man would kill his own son so that he would be free to try and kill you. When Jim replayed the situation and tried to understand how things might have turned out differently, it was hard to make any other decisions than those he'd made at the time. Each day had been built upon the one before it. Decisions he'd made days ago would affect things that took place weeks from now. All he could do was keep going and hope that there was a day when things got getter.

He felt vaguely uncomfortable that he understood the perverted logic of why the man did what he did. It was uncomfortably similar to when his own grandfather was dying in a hospital and he took him the gun that he used to end his life. Love wasn't always about hugs and warmth. Sometimes it was about exposing yourself to the infinity of pain and darkness. Sometimes it was about opening up your own well of blackness and letting it spill out upon the world.

Jim had gotten through the first days of this journey drawing on the strength of his grandfather and the stories he knew of him. He was a different breed of man who had lived a hard life in West Virginia, growing up early and having to work in a man's world when he was little more than a child. Over the course of his life, he'd killed several men, telling a much younger Jim that each of them had needed killing. Jim could hear his grandfather's voice whispering in his ear for him to *harden the fuck up*. Jim had been hearing that since he left Richmond and those words had gotten him this far. Hopefully they would get him home.

"Let's get out of here, Gary," he said.

"What about him?" Gary asked, looking toward Lloyd still kneeling in the street.

"Lloyd, you coming with us?"

Lloyd looked up slowly. "Is this what's out there? Is this what people are doing to each other?"

Jim wasn't sure Lloyd really wanted the answer so he did not give one.

CHAPTER 2

Lloyd's Barber Shop
Crawfish, Virginia

Everyone pitched in to move the bodies from the street. Lloyd had a stack of old moving blankets in his garage and they used them to wrap each body. It was gruesome work and more than one of them spewed their breakfast into the gutter. The whole thing was a pointless misunderstanding, but how did that change anything?

They piled the bodies in the bed of Lloyd's truck, which still had enough fuel to take the bodies somewhere. Lloyd really didn't know what he was going to do with them yet. He wanted to give the Englishmen a proper burial; he wasn't sure about the others.

In the end, Lloyd chose not to leave with them. Jim had explained to him that the violence he saw this morning was only a taste of what the world had to offer.

"You may see that every day," Jim cautioned. "Or worse."

Lloyd did not like the sound of that. "I just want to be left alone to play the banjo. I think I'm going to wait things out here and see what happens."

"Things will probably get worse," Randi said. "I'm trying to stay positive, but I keep getting disappointed."

"If things do get worse, I'll worry about it when it happens. Maybe I'll pack up then and head to my parent's house."

"If you do, find me," Jim said.

Lloyd insisted on giving them some of his food, despite the fact that he was staying behind. Jim tried to talk him out of it but Lloyd would not listen. He packed two large coolers into their trailer of gear, then slipped in another box of packaged and canned food.

"I appreciate it, Lloyd," Jim said. "This will give us enough for the final push home."

"You'd do it for me," Lloyd replied. "All I ask is that you check in on my parents when you can. Make sure they're safe."

"I will."

After some discussion, their final plan was to leave town on the ATVs.

Jim studied the *Virginia Gazetteer* that he carried in his pack and found a large network of fire roads and forest service roads in the area. They could travel those for a good distance. The other option they'd discussed was to get back on the Appalachian Trail at the nearest juncture and continue on foot. Walking the AT meant increased safety and a degree of isolation from the unrest of the open road, but it was slower. Though driving the four-wheelers meant covering more ground in a day, they would be using roads and trails that may be more highly traveled, possibly exposing the group to threats. The four-wheelers also made noise, which drew attention. They ended up choosing a route that would always be within a day's walk of the AT in case they ran out of fuel or broke down. That way they could return to the safety of the AT when they had to.

Lloyd was not convinced that their plan had merit. He wanted them to use one of his vehicles – an old Dodge Dart with a 318 engine –and use a run and gun approach. The car looked like a granny-mobile, but Jim knew from terrifying personal experience that the car was light and extremely fast. Lloyd thought that they should book down the interstate at top speed and crash through road blocks while shooting wildly out the window. Jim explained to him that this was not *The Dukes of Hazzard,* but instead something more closely resembling martial law, at least on the interstate highways. They would probably be killed by cops or soldiers if they attempted that approach.

While they made their final preparations, Jim asked Lloyd if he was carrying a gun. "You need to have it on you all the time. Do not be caught without it. You saw a taste this morning of what it's like out there."

Lloyd looked at Jim like he was an idiot. "Of course I carry a damn gun. What kind of hillbilly do you think I am?" He raised his shirttail to expose a leather basket-weave holster. Inside was a nickel-plated revolver with black handles. It looked like an antique.

"Can that thing even fire a round?" Jim asked. 'What the hell is it?"

Lloyd removed the gun from the holster and presented it to Jim. "Smith and Wesson .32 caliber from 1903. A rock solid weapons platform."

Jim handed the gun back to him, not completely convinced. "I hope it shoots. It's not even heavy enough to be thrown as a weapon."

"You worry about yourself," Lloyd said. "I'll be fine. Don't be bad-mouthing my hardware."

A siren chirped outside. There was no doubt about what this meant.

The cops were here. Someone had heard the shooting.

Jim groaned. "I guess we should have gotten out of here faster."

Lloyd went to the front window and looked out. "I know this guy. He's a town cop. As mayor, I'm practically his boss. This won't be a problem."

Jim had his hand on the butt of his pistol and Lloyd noticed. "Let me talk to this guy. You can't be shooting everybody. And don't put your hand on your gun. It makes you look like a threat."

"I *am* a threat."

They filed out of the building and onto the front sidewalk, Lloyd in the lead. A single cop stood leaning against his car. "Morning, Wild Bill," Lloyd said.

"Morning," the cop replied. "And don't be calling me that."

"What can we do you for?"

The cop looked the group over. "These more musician friends of yours, Lloyd?"

"Not all of them. Some are friends from back home."

"You all shoot anyone this morning?"

An interesting way to ask that question, Jim pondered. It was similar to the way a small town cop may ask someone if they'd seen any deer that morning or if the fish were biting. It was casual and conversational.

"There was a little trouble," Lloyd said. "And yes, some people died."

The cop nodded at Gary and Jim, standing side-by-side in front of the door to Lloyd's apartment. "I'd be inclined to think if there was killing done, that one of you fellows did it. Lloyd here ain't got the stones for killing. Might have been the woman, though I doubt it. Women usually only kill men they love."

Jim opened his mouth to issue a sarcastic reply when the cop drew his gun and leveled it at him.

"What the hell?" Lloyd brayed. "Has everyone in this town lost their damn minds?"

The cop didn't take his eyes from Jim. "That would be a *yes.* Everyone *has* lost their damn minds. Everyone up and down the highway, everyone from sea to shining sea, has gone bat-shit crazy. I'm working the roadblock by the interstate this morning when someone called up there with a radio and said there had been a shooting in front of the mayor's place. They said you all were hauling bodies out of here in a pickup. You think that ain't some crazy shit? Who's lost their mind now?"

27

"I did some of the shooting," Jim admitted.

"Finally, we're getting some-fucking-where," the cop said, smiling. "Tell me more."

"Hold on, Bill, there's more to the story," Lloyd explained. "Gerald and Lawrence were up here. Gerald accused my English buddies of stealing one of his family's four wheelers. He killed them before we even came outside. Then he killed Lawrence and was going to kill us. Jim here shot Gerald before he could shoot the rest of us."

"That's quite a story," the cop said. "Am I supposed to believe that Gerald killed his own retarded son after dedicating his whole life to taking care of the boy? Why the hell would he do that?"

"I don't give a shit what you believe," Jim said. "That's what happened." He'd about had enough of people getting between him and home. He was ready to kill this cop if he had to. He'd crossed a line in his head, a line where the only rule was *get home*. He'd accepted that he might have to kill this man.

The cop walked over closer to Jim, standing directly in front of him and glaring. "I might fucking shoot you right now for your attitude. You think I got time to deal with your shit? This town is falling apart around me. We're running out of gas, running of out of food, and I'm running out of patience. Before you open that mouth again, you better remember that I'll kill you before I take the time to haul you to jail."

"I can't let you do this, Bill."

Both Jim and the cop turned their heads. Lloyd had his old .32 leveled at the cop, the hammer drawn, his aim steadier than Jim thought him capable of, based on how Lloyd had been dealing with the rest of the morning.

"Put… that… *down*," the cop ordered.

"No fucking *way*."

"You wouldn't shoot a cop," the cop said, although he did not sound the least bit confident about it.

"You see, that's part of the problem. I don't really see you as a cop anymore," Lloyd said. "I see you as some asshole who shows up at my shop wanting a free haircut because of his gun and uniform. Did you know that everybody in this town hates you? Me included?"

The cop ignored the question. "So how does this end? Because I got other things to do. I can't stay here all day dicking the dog with you people."

Lloyd looked over at Jim for a second, then back to the cop. "My friends are going to leave. You and I are going to stay here and look at each other until they're gone."

"They can go," the cop said. "I don't give a shit about Gerald and his son. I don't give a shit about your friends. I just want everyone to play nice and follow the rules for as long as possible. Put down the gun. I do *not* like a gun pointed at me, especially some antique piece of crap like that."

Lloyd smiled and shook his head. "Sorry, I don't think I trust you to keep your word. We'll stay like this until they're good and gone."

"Lloyd, you could change your mind and come with us," Jim said. "It's not too late."

Lloyd considered this briefly. "I may catch up with you somewhere down the road," he said. "That's all I'm saying about it. We're wasting time here and you all need to go."

Jim shifted and the cop followed him with his gun. "Don't you *move*."

Lloyd fired his weapon and a bullet ricocheted near the cop's foot. It was a surprisingly well-placed shot, unless he'd actually been aiming at the cop and missed, which was completely possible. In either case, the cop flinched. "Go ahead and drop your gun," Lloyd said. "You apparently can't handle the temptation of having it there in your hand."

"Okay, okay," the cop said, leaning forward and placing the weapon down gently.

"Masa," Jim said. "You take care of yourself."

"I'll be fine," Masa said. "Somebody's got to teach this hack how to play the banjo."

"Then we'll be going."

"Hey, Randi?" Lloyd called as she started to walk away.

She turned in time for Lloyd to give her a big wink. "You miss me, you know where to find me."

Randi rolled her eyes, then she and Gary scurried around the corner toward the rear of the building. Jim looked back at his oldest friend once more. He really didn't want to leave him behind. He opened his mouth to offer another suggestion and Lloyd cut him off. "Get the hell out of here."

Jim shut his mouth, shook his head, and followed his coworkers around the corner. By the time he got behind the building they had their machines running and were sitting atop them.

"Let's go!" Randi yelled.

Jim mounted his machine, started the engine, and accelerated down a back street, away from town. He listened for a gunshot but if one came, he didn't hear it. He wondered how long it would be before he learned how this played out, if he ever learned at all.

CHAPTER 3

Russell County Jail
Lebanon, Virginia

At the Russell County Jail, authorities had a tough time deciding how to handle the inmate crisis they were facing. Certainly the same pressures were being experienced by other jails, prisons, and mental health facilities around the nation. The question was how to humanely care for the persons in their charge when resources began to dwindle and staff stopped showing up for work. That was the question, and no one seemed to have the answer.

It was inevitable they would face this dilemma. Inpatient and correctional facilities were usually prepared for short-term disasters, such as power outages, ice storms, and blizzards. They kept a little extra food and used generators to provide emergency power. Very few had preparations for disasters that might stretch into years. Despite the most detailed emergency planning, the institutions could not expect staff to continue showing up for work when they had no fuel to drive and when their own families were facing personal hardship from food shortages, lack of medical care, and the inability to communicate with their loved ones.

Russell County officials pondered this while prisoners sat in dark, stinking cells. With no electricity, there was no ventilation, and temperatures quickly became stifling. Two days into the disaster, the municipal water supply began to fail when hilltop water tanks could not be pumped full. The stainless steel toilets in the jail could no longer be flushed. Rather quickly, they were used beyond their capacity and overflowed, filling the cell floors with a putrid sludge that prisoners had no choice but to walk in. The smell rose and escaped the cell block to permeate the hallways of the courthouse. Certainly the men suffering in these conditions were not choirboys, but to what length should a person be made to pay for their bad decisions? When did it go from mere punishment to torture? After all, these were local people. These were someone's sons and daughters. They were voters.

No more trucks arrived to restock the pantry shelves in the jail kitchen. Jailers had to cut the number of meals from three a day to two. The cooks scrambled to see what they could scrape together from items that remained on the back of pantry shelves. One day they had waffles for both meals because they had a surplus of mix. Another day they had powdered eggs and hard biscuits that were made without all the required ingredients. Jail officials realized that there would soon be a day when meals went from two a day to one. That day would arrive sooner than later. With fewer deputies showing up for work, there was the ongoing concern that under these conditions prisoner frustration might boil over. Understaffed as they were, the single jailer on duty might be overpowered, taken hostage, or killed.

To avoid any potential blame or liability, the federal justice authorities decided it was best to make no decision on the matter at all. They relegated the decision on how to manage the prisoner crisis to the state level. In Virginia, a formula was developed in Richmond to serve as a preliminary filter to determine which prisoners should be released. All non-violent offenders were released. Persons with drug possession charges, warrants for parking tickets, and unpaid child support were turned out by the tens of thousands across the state. For violent offenders, it was established that all persons having committed a violent crime could be released if they had served at least eighty percent of their sentence.

For all remaining cases, the parole board within the state prison system would attempt to meet and review each case to see who would be allowed to go free and who would have to remain locked up in the rapidly disintegrating conditions. No one was sure if members of the parole board would even be able to attend a meeting under current circumstances. There was also talk within the prison system – and this was definitely not discussed publicly – that any prisoners on death row would not be leaving their facility alive. They would likely rot in their cells, slowly starving to death, or the prison may choose to conduct an expedited execution. No one wanted to take responsibility for releasing the worst criminals back into society, and decided that execution would be more humane than starvation in a dank prison cell.

On the local level, at the county and regional jails, the decision on who to release from local facilities was being made by the sheriff and the commonwealth attorney. They were the folks with direct knowledge of who was being maintained behind bars. Most of the offenders in the local jails were non-violent offenders. The number of prisoners locked up dropped quickly when the facilities were purged of those there on drug charges, drunk driving charges, and theft charges.

For those still incarcerated after this measure was applied, there were fewer options. One option was what was known as Greyhound Therapy, derived from the practice that public mental health workers sometimes resorted to with very difficult cases who wouldn't get better and wouldn't go away. The idea was that you would buy the person a one way bus ticket to a very distant location, knowing that the person couldn't afford to get a ticket to come back. Then they would become someone else's problem.

This would be akin to the sheriff dropping someone off at the county line and telling them to never come back, which was exactly what was done in some of the cases. Wife-beaters and other persons who had committed acts of violence that the sheriff determined made them undesirable within their own community were loaded onto transport vans. They were driven to the Kentucky state line under cover of darkness and dropped off with the assurance that they would be shot and their bodies disposed of if they ever returned home.

It was not a hollow threat. There were two child molesters in the jail and they were given a one-way drive that did not result in them being released into another state, though the men spent the drive trying to convince themselves that this was the fate that awaited them. Contrary to their hopes, in a region full of abandoned, flooded coal mine shafts there are plenty of efficient ways that justice could be served. The methods required neither lawyers nor courts.

Two deputies frog-marched the child molesters through dew-soaked weeds to a padlocked enclosure. One of the deputies scoured his pockets for a brass key. He tucked his mag-lite under his arm so he could use both hands to work the rusty lock. When the shackle sprang open, he shoved the chain-link gate back and it swung open, clanking against the high fence. Before them was the long-abandoned shaft of a man-lift, an elevator used to lower coal miners deep into the mine. The mine was worked out, empty of coal, and the man-lift long gone. All that remained was a locked fence around a deep pit. On newer mines, the pit would be capped. On some of the older mines, these open pits were still around if you knew where to look.

The deputy played his light down into the pit and saw oily black water about fifty feet down. When the pumps were pulled from the mine decades ago, groundwater gradually filled it to the level of the water table. The men in his care whimpered and prayed. They begged. The deputies walked them to the edge of the pit. The men began to apologize and offer excuses. The deputies did not want to hear them. They had both worked the individual cases which resulted in these men being arrested. They had talked to the child victims, heard their vile stories that sickened them, then had to go home from work that evening to their own children, unable to get those stories from their head. It wore on a man, gave him nightmares. It was the reason why these particular deputies had volunteered for this duty, hoping to purge their heads of the memories.

Over the rising pleas of the chained men, one deputy raised his Glock 22. The other deputy quickly followed suit. They counted. "One... two ...three."

The shots erupted in the night, the scene briefly lit by the flash of the gunshots. Each shot caught its intended recipient at the base of the skull, severing the spinal column from the brain. The men were dead before they fell. One toppled freely into the pit, the sound of his splash ringing off the hard pit walls. The second man required a good kick to send his dead body into the void. The deputies gladly obliged.

*

Among those turned out of the Russell County Jail with the non-violent offenders was a man named Charlie Rakes. Charlie was a local boy, born and raised. The tale of his life in Russell County up to this point would have been one of crime, cruelty, and mayhem. It would have been a public service for his mother to have stayed home from the beer joint that night in 1966 and avoided conceiving him entirely, but she didn't. Thus, there was Charlie, a stain upon the moral fiber of the community and a blight upon its soil.

Charlie was a violent man, but it was to his great fortune that his current admission to jail was not the result of a violent offense. He'd been violent before and he certainly intended to be violent again in the future. In fact, he'd lain awake at night in his jell cell thinking about it. Unable to read with any comprehension, he had nothing to pass the time but his dark fantasies, thinking of the people he'd hurt simply because they'd pissed him off at one time or another. He'd rarely been caught for his acts of

34

violence. It was the stupid stuff that got him locked up, mainly the fact that he had sticky fingers.

He'd first killed a man in 1989 after smoking weed with him under a bridge. It was a black man who was trying to sell him some of the same weed they were smoking. They had a fire going from driftwood and Charlie realized that everyone else he knew had left the riverbank and gone home. It was only him and the black man. The fact that he was a black man would be totally irrelevant were it not for the fact that, in an area of little racial diversity, the man's presence instantly set Charlie on edge and made him suspicious. After they finished the joint, Charlie began to feel the very pronounced and unusual effects, and the man informed him that the weed was laced with PCP. Charlie panicked. He'd heard nothing but horror stories about so-called Angel Dust.

Charlie's ability to process was minimal in the best of times. He was a TRS-80 in a Pentium world. Impaired by the drug, a single thought coalesced in Charlie's mind. The man in front of him was the devil. The devil was here to collect his soul for all the bad shit that he had done. Charlie was screwed. He watched the man's face in the firelight, flames flickering in the reflection of his wet eyes, on the surface of his teeth when he smiled. A fear gripped Charlie so deep that he felt urine running down his leg and into his shoe. He had never been so scared in his entire life.

Charlie stumbled into the dark, found a brick, and caved in the man's skull. He pulped the man's head, and continued until it was unrecognizable. Splattered in gore, he rose from the body, panting in the firelight like a demon himself. He rolled the defaced corpse into the river, erasing all evidence of his crime. As far as he knew, no one had ever found the body.

Last year, he'd taken to following church prayer requests on Facebook so he could see who was suffering from cancer. Unable to master this technology himself, he'd convinced his sister-in-law to do the work for him. She'd find the names and addresses, and Charlie would hide out near their homes and wait for them to leave for doctor appointments, and then break in and steal pain medications. He thought it was a pretty good system.

Most recently, he had been busted for stealing from people's storage buildings and selling the loot to buy drugs. Most of what he stole was sold for only a fraction of its actual value. It didn't matter to him; it was all free money to him. If he only got five dollars for a three hundred dollar chainsaw, it was five dollars he didn't have yesterday.

The sheriff knew the nature of men like Charlie Rakes. He'd been in law enforcement long enough to read him like a book. This was a man who never learned from incarceration. He was a criminal and he would always be a criminal. Going to jail was nothing for him but a cost of doing business. Business owners sometimes had to put up with frivolous lawsuits. Garages had to deal with bounced checks. Farmers had to deal with the weather. And Charlie Rakes occasionally had to go to jail.

With there being no hope of teaching Charlie a lesson through incarceration, the sheriff really had no choice but to let him go. The sheriff was not aware of any of Charlie's violent crimes that may instead have prompted him to drop Charlie off at the state line as he had others of this undesirable criminal class. He knew of nothing in Charlie's history that justified him being shot and his body hidden. So even though he despised Charlie, he had no choice but to let him go.

"You're a lowlife," the sheriff told him as he opened Charlie's bars for the last time. "But I don't know what the hell else to do with you."

Charlie could not stifle an ear-to-ear grin.

"Don't look too happy or I might change my mind," the sheriff warned sternly. A deputy returned Charlie's possessions to him, then escorted him to an outside door and opened it.

"Try to behave yourself, Charlie," the sheriff said. "The rules are going to be a lot simpler until things get back to normal. You start being a pain in the ass and someone will kill you dead."

Charlie met the sheriff's hard gaze but said not a word. He knew when to keep his mouth shut.

*

Charlie didn't have a place of his own. He'd rented a trailer for one hundred dollars a month prior to getting locked up. It had all the amenities you'd expect of a hundred dollar trailer, which was exactly none. It was little more than a long camper that dated from the 1960s. The outside was painted in a thick coat of brown paint. Inside, the floor was spongy and an old car wheel sat in the stove to hold pans near the broiler element. A blue tarp lay on the roof with old tires holding it down. The trailer was miserably hot in the summer and freezing in winter. Still, it was home, and Charlie had lived there about six years. It was where everyone knew to find him, including the law, and that was his downfall. Once he got locked up, he couldn't pay the rent anymore and lost the place. It was hard to sell enough stolen weed eaters from jail to pay your bills.

His brother lived in a trailer park in the country outside of town. His wife was the one who hooked Charlie up with sick people off Facebook. He'd have to make his way out there and see if his brother could put him up for a little bit. He'd never measured the distance but assumed it to be seven or eight miles to the trailer park where they lived. He could walk it in a day if he had to but he hoped to hell he wouldn't have to. Walking was for kids and drunks, and he felt too tired to be one and too sober to be the other.

There weren't any cars moving that he could see. He'd been in jail for eight months this time and only knew the current state of the world through secondhand reports. The world was strange with no moving cars. It was a much quieter than he remembered. Less hectic. He did not have to worry about stepping into the road and being hit by a coal truck. He moved from the sidewalk to the center of the street and looked both ways. Not a car moving anywhere. On this empty road he could walk wherever the hell he wanted, so he turned north and started walking.

In about a mile and half, he approached the outskirts of town. Over the course of his walk, he'd passed people walking, children playing, and men moving about engaged in various tasks. No one paid much mind to him, the presence of a man walking up the middle of the road being more common now than it was a week ago.

He noticed a lot of businesses were closed. The fast food places he passed had signs in the window that read: CLOSED, NO FOOD. He saw a convenience store that was still open. They had a sign indicating that there was no fuel available, but he could see that they still had an inventory of candy, magazines, and some odd food items. He saw an old can of peas, a can of deviled ham, potted meat.

He walked up to the door of the BP station and peered inside. With no lights on, the store didn't appear open but a man that Charlie didn't recognize sat on a chair behind the counter. Charlie cleared his throat. "Got any Tahoes?"

The clerk was morbidly obese and about Charlie's age. He had long hair and a hillbilly beard.

"Ain't got any smokes," the man said. "They went fast."

"What about roll-your-owns? Drum? PA?"

"No Prince Albert, but I got Drum. Surprised it ain't all gone yet."

"How much?"

"I'll take thirty dollars."

"*Thirty dollars*?" Charlie replied. "I reckon you *would* take thirty dollars. That's three times what is used to be."

The man chuckled, shaking his entire body. "In my daddy's day it was a dollar," the man replied. "Inflation, you know."

Charlie stepped through the door. "I ought to whip your ass and take it, you smart-alecky bastard."

The man drew a stainless revolver from beneath the counter with a casual movement. He thumbed back the hammer and pointed it right at Charlie's face. Charlie froze and looked at it, spat in the floor, and walked out.

A little further down the road he encountered a teenage boy driving a golf cart. The boy was driving it in a lane like a car while Charlie walked the middle of the road as if he owned it. Charlie stuck his thumb out like he was hitchhiking, grinning like a good-natured rube. The boy was about fourteen, as best as Charlie could tell.

"Sorry, dude, I'm only going a couple of streets over to check on my grandmother. She's about out of food. My dad said I had to go straight over there and back."

Charlie smiled. "That's nice of you to check on your grandma." He looked over the golf cart. "This here is what a man needs," he said admiringly. "It run on gas or batteries?"

"Gas," the boy said. "It gets pretty good mileage. You can drive all day on a tank of gas."

"That right?"

The boy never saw the fist coming. Charlie struck him in the side of the head with a blow like a pile driver. The boy was stunned. Before he could react, Charlie grabbed him by his long hair, dragging him from the seat. The boy staggered in a circle, restrained by his hair. Charlie hit him three more times – sharp blows to the head that pushed the boy to the edge of consciousness. He fell, crying and trying to cover his face. Charlie started kicking, aiming his blows at the boy's head, his back, his groin, whatever he could reach.

When the boy no longer attempted to get up, Charlie got in the golf cart. The boy quivered and cried, his face covered to ward off any more blows. Charlie watched him for a second, disgusted that the boy had no more fight in him than that. He studied the floor for a second, found the gas pedal, and accelerated out of town.

At twenty-five miles an hour he drove toward his brother's trailer. The drive was scenic. Having not seen much of the world since entering jail, Charlie enjoyed the warm breeze, the sunlight playing on leaves, and the squirrels and chipmunks that flitted into the road. He swerved at a few but didn't connect. In one of those maneuvers he almost turned the cart over. It scared him and for the rest of the drive he followed advice his granny had given him that he'd been unable to apply to the larger context of his life: he attempted to straighten up and fly right.

CHAPTER 4

The Cave
Russell County, Virginia

Pete sat back from the table, folded his hands over his stomach, and smiled. "I've been thinking about this and I guess I'm technically a caveman now," Pete said. He was enjoying the fact that his family now lived in a cave.

Ariel frowned at her mother, obviously disturbed by the thought. "Is Pete really a caveman, Mommy?"

"Of course I am," Pete crowed. "Look where I live. Can't you smell me? Best of all, that makes you a cavewoman."

Ariel tightened her lips. "I am *not* a cavewoman." She saw herself as more of a rising tween sophisticate, although that mode was harder to adopt with no television, no internet, no cell phone, and no places to go and be seen.

"If we stay in this cave you'll have to put a bone through your nose," Pete said. "Then you'll look like a cavewoman too." He began laughing at his fuming sister, unable to restrain his glee.

Ariel grabbed a nearby stick and drew back to whack her brother with it. Ellen intervened, grabbing the stick and tossing it back into the wood pile. "If you don't want to be a cavewoman then don't act like one. Beating people with sticks is how cavewomen act, not sweet little girls."

Ariel scowled and stomped off. Pete laughed.

It did seem as if they really were becoming cave people, though. One of the things that had sold Jim on this long-neglected farm was the large cave at the back of the property with a good spring flowing from it. Utilizing equal degrees of both foresight and paranoia, Jim saw the cave for its potential as an emergency shelter. As a young Boy Scout, his troop had gone to the Lost Sea Caverns in Sweetwater, Tennessee. At the time, in the 1970s, the cave was still designated as a nuclear fallout shelter. There was a steady supply of fresh water and large chambers that would hold thousands of people. The government stocked it with pallets of survival crackers.

ASHES OF THE UNSPEAKABLE

Ever since that day, Jim had maintained the thought in the back of his head that he'd one day like to own his own cave. This cave had several things going for it. There was a gentle spring flowing from the mouth of the cave, but the water flowed to the side of the entrance. That meant you could enter the cave without having to walk through the water. It had a dry floor in the first large chamber. Some spring caves have submerged floors and Jim was pleased that this was not the case with his cave.

Over the years, as he came upon the time, materials, and spare cash, he'd made improvements to his cave. He cleaned up a lot of the loose rock on the floor of the entrance chamber. The rocks that he couldn't move by hand were pulled out of the way with a winch and pulley so that he could create some floor space. He rented a jackhammer that he could run off his generator and used that to further shape the interior to suit his needs. With his generator and a concrete mixer, he'd formed up small areas of the floor and over time managed to pour a decent concrete floor in the main entrance chamber. This made walking through the main part of the cave much easier and contributed to the sense that it was actually a room and not just a hole in the ground.

A couple of years later, he came across a deal on some rejected cinderblocks from the local block plant. He got them cheap and was able to purchase enough to wall up the entrance to his Hobbit Hole. It took a lot of cutting and chipping to make the perfectly uniform blocks fit the random curvature of the cave mouth. He drilled holes with a large hammer drill into his concrete floor and into the rock walls at the sides of the entrance and epoxied rebar pins into the holes, using them to anchor his cinderblock wall to both the floor and sides of his cave. Longer pieces of rebar ran down the hollow cores of the block and tied them all together when he grouted the block cores with concrete.

For a door, he bought a used commercial grade steel door with steel jambs off Craigslist. The jambs were filled with mortar when he installed it, which tied the door frame to the block wall very securely, making it very difficult to remove. The door itself was installed on ball bearing hinges that carried a lot of weight. In his paranoia, Jim imagined that there might be a day when this door was all that protected him and his family from violence. Not trusting the door itself to block heavy rifle rounds, Jim had installed a second crude steel door on the inside. He ordered heavy hinges that were customarily used for installing iron gates at a property entrance. He tied those hinges to his block wall with strong expansion anchors. The door was made of square tubing and quarter-inch steel plates that Jim tack welded onto each side. When the door was swung into place behind the commercial steel door, a simple hasp held it closed. After all, it was only intended as a ballistic shutter and not as the actual door.

Once he managed to secure the entrance to his cave to his satisfaction, Jim worked toward making the interior more hospitable. Caves were by nature damp, but there were things that could help combat this. One such thing was to install heavy mil plastic against the ceiling in the entrance chamber. He held the plastic in place by using a powder-actuated fastener tool. It was essentially a gun that you placed a hardened steel pin into, then used a .22 rimfire blank to propel the pin into rock, concrete, cinderblocks, or mild steel. It was a very useful tool. Jim placed large vinyl washers against the plastic sheeting as he held it to the ceiling and fired the pin through the washer. That helped distribute the weight of the plastic over a larger area, preventing the pin from tearing through the plastic.

Once he'd covered the entire ceiling of the entrance, the steady stream of dripping groundwater that had been bouncing off his head now ran off to the sides of the room. Next, he focused on putting a low budget solar system in place. He bought two solar trickle chargers for around twenty dollars that kept two used boat batteries charged. The 12-volt boat batteries powered a few automotive lights that hung from the ceiling. It was a crude system but it worked, providing enough general light to find your way around the place. When people needed better lighting, they could use headlamps or lanterns.

While the underground temperature in the cave was generally around 58 degrees, the entrance received more outside air and could become quite cold in winter. For that reason, Jim made an enormous wood stove from an old heating oil tank and installed it in the cave. It definitely didn't meet any EPA efficiency standards but you could feed four-foot logs into it and heat it cherry red. A chimney constructed of thick steel casing from a water well directed the smoke outside.

Ellen fed wood into the stove to knock off the dampness, following Jim's advice to use the driest wood they had because it produced the least smoke. The smell of wood smoke carried, though there was nothing she could do about that.

The woodstove had a homemade water jacket made from a clean steel drum. It was a primitive system, utilizing pipes and buckets to add hot water to the drum and to extract it. Close to the woodstove was the bathroom. It had actual walls constructed of pressure-treated lumber and lined with corrugated steel panels for privacy. A pipe from the hot water jacket allowed a person in the bathroom to add water to a large plastic tub for washing. There was a camping toilet in there but it was the last resort for most of them. Jim had built a primitive outhouse near the mouth of the cave and they all preferred it to the camping toilet.

The whole family thought the cave was a neat place to visit but no one had ever wanted to live there. Well, maybe Pete had. Jim had pitched the idea to Ellen that it could serve as a tornado shelter for the family during those rare tornado warnings that they had in this region. Ellen had known that in his ever-present paranoia, Jim had built this to be their bunker. Now, despite her reservations and eye-rolling, that was exactly how the family was utilizing it. They needed a safe, nearly impenetrable home and this was it.

Jim's parents were not very excited about it. They did not like sleeping on cots. They found them uncomfortable and the cots exacerbated the effects of the mild arthritis they both experienced. They also did not like the damp, the wood smoke smell from the fire, nor the sense of impending danger. They wanted to go home. Ellen saw it every day, but she knew that they would not leave her and the children. She greatly appreciated that and, for that reason, sought to make their stay as comfortable as possible.

In light of the growing threat from the unprepared and demanding folks on their road, Ellen had resolved to move their entire operation to the cave. It was no small undertaking. By entire operation, she meant everything of value to them in their current circumstance. She wanted to leave nothing at the house that could be stolen. She was concerned about the house being burned to the ground out of some sense of revenge, and decided it was simply not safe to leave anything there.

It was critical that they keep the existence of the cave secret. She did not want the people from the trailer park or anyone outside of the family to know about the cave. As part of this operational security, they made an effort to only load items from the side of the house that was not visible from the road. Even so, Ellen constantly scanned the countryside with binoculars to be certain that they were not being watched. Still, there was no guarantee. When she was at the house she felt exposed and vulnerable.

She had never felt like that at her home in all of the years they'd lived there.

Pops and Nana were at an age where the heavy lifting and carrying were difficult for them. They assisted with the unloading at the cave but most of the loading at the house was done by Pete, Ariel, and Ellen. They had prioritized their trips and made lists to make sure they didn't forget things. Ellen had initially looked at their retreat to the cave like a big camping trip with a lot of guns. Then, as those items were all safely relocated to the cave she expanded her net and added more items. Her goal was to eventually have all of their gear in the cave or hidden in caches throughout the property. She wanted to leave nothing in the house that they'd miss or cry over.

Their first trip had focused on guns, ammunition, and tactical gear. Most of that was centrally stored in the house so it didn't take a lot of digging to find it all. One trip to the gun safe and she was able to place all of the pistols into a storage tote for transport. She packed all the rifles into their appropriate cases or wrapped them in blankets. A trip to the gigantic steel Jobox in the basement and she was able to grab all the ammunition, magazines, and spare ammo cans. Of course, that trip was not as easy as it sounded. The Jobox storage locker probably held eight hundred pounds of ammunition. That required a lot of trips up and down the basement steps with milk crates and plastic buckets.

Ellen was concerned about taking all the guns with her into the damp cave environment but she didn't want to leave them behind. She recalled that Jim had once explained to her a method of making caches for guns and ammunition from 4-inch and 6-inch Schedule 40 PVC pipe. Gluing end caps onto the pipe would make a nice watertight connection that would protect the firearms and allow her to hide a few in strategic locations around the farm, just in case. In the meantime, she'd have to make sure that they regularly cleaned and oiled every firearm so that the dampness did not have a chance to affect them.

It was interesting to Ellen to note the transformation taking place within her son. She'd been extremely worried about him over the past day or so. He'd been forced to shoot two men who were approaching the house in the middle of the night. They were not strangers to them, but men who'd been part of a larger group that had threatened Ellen earlier that day. Pete had killed one of them and wounded the other. Ellen had finished the injured man off with a fatal shot after he began making threats. These were not days when you could leave a wounded enemy alive. That mercy would come back to haunt you. In the end, the decision would haunt you either way.

Despite her grieving over the lost innocence of her son, Pete had been handling things better since that day. He'd been withdrawn on the morning after the shooting, though had since come to terms with his actions. She was not sure if it was the result of a conscious decision on his part or if the whole event had broken the last tenuous thread that held him to childhood. Either way, he was adapting to their new life in this new world. Gone were the baggy sweatpants and tank tops he'd worn since warm weather had returned. Nearly Jim's size now, Pete had taken to wearing his dad's cargo pants and a camouflage shirt as his daily uniform. On his belt he carried a multi-tool and his dad's SOG Seal Pup knife. He'd adjusted Jim's desert tan tactical vest to fit him and was wearing it all the time. Pete filled the multitude of pockets and pouches with mysterious gear and Ellen had no idea what it all was or why he needed it. She did know that he'd asked to carry a pistol in the cross-draw holster attached to the vest and she'd nixed that idea. Maybe in time, but not yet. She was not ready to let her little boy strap on a gun when he got up in the morning.

Pete had been a Boy Scout and wanted to eventually become an Eagle Scout. As such, he'd always been interested in camping and survival. Perhaps having to shoot two men brought the seriousness of their plight home to him and he now realized that he needed to rise to the occasion in his father's absence. He understood now that survival was about more than camping out in a field and cooking s'mores over a fire. It was about keeping your family alive and that was exactly what he was going to try to do. Rather than Ellen having to prod him now into assisting with the move to the cave as she would have had to do barely a week ago, Pete was practically taking over the logistical effort. He'd developed his own list of *Things Daddy Would Want Us To Take* and he made sure they got loaded into the truck.

Over the course of one extremely long day, the family shuttled most of the critical items to the cave. By the end of the day, they'd moved all the "must haves" and most of the "we'd like to haves". Somewhere over the course of the day they lost track of how many trips they'd made. When they finally settled down to dinner, they were all exhausted. Jim's mother had prepared diner for them while Pete, Ellen, and Ariel made their last trip of the day.

The dining room was a corner of the entrance chamber of the cave. It had a concrete floor and was close to the woodstove. With a roaring fire going in the stove and a battery-powered Coleman lantern hanging over a folding camping table, it was comfortable. Another folding table nearby held the family's propane camping stove/oven combination. Nana had used that stove to cook up some food items that needed to be used. There were pork chops that had been in the freezer and had thawed out. There were potatoes that took a beating in the move, and corn that had been fresh before the power went out that needed to be eaten. Nana had made homemade biscuits and cooked them in the camp oven. Something about the smell of biscuits cooking sealed the deal. This was their new home.

CHAPTER 5

The Valley
Russell County, Virginia

Charlie Rakes wasn't sure what he'd expected to see at the trailer park where his brother lived, but the country he'd driven through was nothing like the country he remembered. Certainly the terrain was familiar; however, the behavior of the residents was not the same. Summer in the country usually had farmers out riding on tractors, tending to hay, planting, or working cattle. There would be trucks with Farm Use tags driving into town at fifteen miles per hour. There would be slower traffic from tractors with orange safety triangles bolted to the back of the cab. Charlie saw none of this.

Even the trailer park was not the same. There were no kids on bikes, no people sitting on porches, and no one in the yards working on vehicles. Trailer parks were one of the last places where you still saw men with a chain hoist and a tripod of logs swapping the engine out of a vehicle, but no one was out.

Charlie was not sure if anyone was home or not. The whole place looked abandoned. If that was the case, he wasn't sure where he'd go from here. Any chance of finding his brother would probably be shot and he'd be on his own. He turned the golf cart into his brother's driveway and brought it to a stop. He watched and waited. He saw nothing.

Perhaps the machine had not been loud enough to draw the attention of anyone inside. Charlie examined the dash and steering column. He found a button with a horn icon and pushed it. There was an anemic toot and Charlie studied the trailer for a reaction. Finally, he saw a curtain move, then pull shut again.

A moment later the door flung open and Charlie's sister-in-law emerged from the trailer, a tangle of kids bursting out the door behind her. They all tried to squeeze through the door at the same time, and Charlie had to smile. He didn't know much about kids, never having been around any besides these nor having had any of his own. He reckoned that he liked these kids about as well as he liked anything else on this Earth. They were

49

damn entertaining sometimes. They were his blood, and that meant something even if familiarity was lacking. The kids oozed around their mother and passed her, then clambered onto the golf cart and mobbed him. Charlie watched the door of the trailer expectantly as he wrestled the army of children.

"Where's Sammy?" he asked.

His sister-in-law, Angie, didn't answer. She began pulling her brood from Charlie one-by-one. "You all go play next door," she said. She turned to the oldest, Robert, who had hung behind. "Keep an eye on them."

Charlie wasn't sure, but thought that oldest boy would be about seventeen or eighteen years old now.

"I'm so glad to see you," Angie said, her worry spilling free. "I think something's happened to Sammy."

A dark wave rolled over Charlie and the playfulness he'd felt with the children was gone. "What are you talking about?"

Angie put her hand on the roll cage of the golf cart and leaned closer. "He ain't come home. He left night before last and hasn't come back."

"Left to do what exactly?"

Angie shrugged. "You know things are tight around here. By the end of the month we don't have nothing left. When these attacks happened, we didn't have money to go stocking up on food like some people did. Then when the power went out we lost our water."

"How have you been getting by?"

"Well, some folks left to go stay with family. Once they did that, the rest of us broke into their trailers and took anything that was left, but none of them had much. The men were hunting some before Sammy disappeared. Doing some fishing too. But there's others back in here that's better off than us."

"What's that mean?" Charlie asked. He was a little aggravated by this whole turn of events. He wasn't sure what he'd expected but he didn't think things would have sunk this far this fast. He'd expected to be able to share his first cold beer in months with his brother, but there wasn't any beer and there wasn't any brother.

"There's some folks back there that have livestock," Angie said. "We butchered a cow once but the man that owned it figured out it was us. He came up here with a gun and started threatening people."

"Did he now?" Charlie asked. Nothing stirred his anger like people threatening his family.

Angie nodded. "Then Sammy and one of his buddies found another house up the road where they thought they heard a generator. There's several folks living there and they have food. We've smelled them cooking."

"Did you see if they'd share anything?"

Angie nodded again. "We asked nicely. Greedy bitch turned us down cold as kraut. Wouldn't give us a damn thing."

"Bitch, you say?"

"Yeah, a woman," Angie said. "Sammy said she has a husband but no one has seen him since all this mess started."

"You still ain't said what happened to my brother," Charlie said.

Angie leaned in a little closer. "Him and his buddy went up there to see what those people, had. Maybe borrow a few things, if you know what I mean."

"Borrow?"

Angie nodded. "A few things, depending on what they had. Neither one of them ever came back."

"Did you go looking for them?"

"Of course we did. We ran all up and down this road looking for them everywhere. No one admits seeing anything."

"What about the woman?" Charlie asked. "Did you talk to her?"

"Yeah, we talked to her. We told her we were coming on her place to look for him whether she liked it or not, but she had a gun and told us she'd shoot the first one to step onto her land."

"And you believed her?"

"It was a big old army-looking gun," Angie said. "She looked like she knew how to use it. My oldest, Robert, climbed her gate and started over top of it. She drew down on him and I thought for sure he was dead."

The mere thought of someone, especially a woman, threatening his kin with a gun made Charlie's blood boil.

"So you don't know anything for sure. What do you *think* happened?"

Angie was silent a moment. She released her grip on the roll cage and leaned back from the machine, looking out across the empty field beside the trailer park. Her eyes filled with tears. "Some folks heard shots that night."

Charlie could guess the rest of the story and knew it was probably true.

He knew that his brother was dead or else he'd be here taking care of his family. Nothing would stop him from that. It hurt his heart.

"How long since you and the kids ate?"

Angie looked embarrassed. "It was before Sammy left," she said.

"That oldest boy ain't been out looking for food?"

She shrugged. "No, not really. He ain't a go-getter like his daddy. He's kind of stayed around the house, I guess."

Charlie and Robert would be having a talk shortly about a man's responsibilities to his family.

*

The sun low at his back, Charlie Rakes strolled up the paved road through the valley. His only food of the day had been a hard biscuit for breakfast washed down with bottled water. He felt guilty for his hunger, considering that his brother's family had eaten nothing for two days. He didn't know why that oldest boy had not been out scrounging for something – a rabbit, a squirrel, a catfish. Charlie and his brother were already men at that age. That boy knew nothing except for the world of video games and dreaming of fast cars he'd never own. The more Charlie thought of it, the more he felt the boy deserving of an ass-kicking for not stepping up to the plate. When he returned, he'd make a point of letting the boy know that the gravy train had stopped. He could contribute or go his own way in the world.

The sole of his cowboy boots scraped on the asphalt and kicked the occasional stray gravel. Approaching a curve that stirred a vague familiarity, Charlie looked for the mailbox that Angie told him he'd find. There it was.

Henry Sullivan.

The mailbox was made of thick steel pipe with a round door welded onto it. Charlie admired it for a moment, certain that it had been the end result of too often replacing a weaker version that had met its maker at the end of a baseball bat.

Cattle wandered about the field behind a fence, and the world was so silent that the sound of their chewing carried to him across the distance. Occasionally one would snort, swish its tail at a fly, and then return its head to the grass. The sound of a chain rattling in the barn answered the one question that pressed at Charlie's mind – where would he find Mr. Henry Sullivan.

Charlie wanted to avoid the driveway and the sound of gravel beneath his feet so he crossed the fence nearest to where he stood. It was a good stout fence of welded wire four feet high. There was a single strand of electric fence at the top but Charlie assumed it to be dead with the loss of electrical power in the area. When he straddled the top wire he found his assumption to be incorrect. The fence was solar powered.

As the bare wire grazed the hole worn through the inner thigh of his jeans and met flesh, Charlie felt a sensation that was beyond his limited language skills. He understood what had happened and knew that separating himself from the fence was the only way that he could end the pain. He attempted to spring free of the fence, much in the same way that a cat attempts to jump when startled, leaping both in no direction and all directions at the same time. The result of this awkward bounce was that Charlie dropped on the wire once more with the full weight of his body, both nearly castrating himself and at the same time reintroducing the bare flesh of his thigh to the high voltage fence wire. This second wave of pain produced a near instinctual reaction in which Charlie sprung free of the live wire but, at the same time, captured the foot that he intended to land upon in the grid of the fencing, causing him to land hard on his head and shoulder.

As a lifetime drinker, thief, and general miscreant, Charlie was no stranger to taking a beating. It came with the territory. He rolled around on the ground for several minutes, the wind completely knocked from him, his array of pain so wide and multi-faceted that he didn't know what to clutch first. Throughout this experience, he did, at some remote region of his brain, maintain awareness that he was in a situation where he should keep quiet, which he managed only through enormous effort.

When he regained his ability to breathe, he pulled his foot free of where it hung in the fence. He paused for another moment, then rubbed his hand on the side of his face, feeling for blood where it struck the ground. His vision was scrolling to the side, then resetting and scrolling again, much in the same way as he'd experienced on some of the worst drunks of his life. He expected that he probably had a concussion. Though his shoulder was extremely sore, and would remain so for days, he did not think he'd broken his collar bone, his arm, nor his wrist.

When he was once again able to stand, he did so slowly, making sure that no one had seen his awkward dismount and was waiting for him with a rifle. He saw no one. He knew from Angie that this man Henry was armed and he wanted to make sure that the man had no opportunity to go for his gun when they had their *discussion*. His fall had ignited a rage in him. His body hurt from head to groin and he knew that it only hurt because he had been forced to come here, forced to deal with this man who had no Christian charity in his soul.

Charlie closed the distance between himself and the barn. He heard hammering inside, a large hammer pounding steel. He moved slowly, peering through the door, exposing as little of himself as possible. An older man with graying hair and a beard was hammering on a tractor attachment, attempting to fasten a hay spear onto the tractor's three point hitch. The hay spear was a long steel spike of nearly four feet. Henry could use this spear to back his tractor into a round bale of hay, stab it, and then use the tractor to lift and move it to where it was needed.

The fact that he had fuel to use a tractor proved to Charlie that the man had hoarded resources at the expense of his neighbors. He had cattle, he had fuel. Who knew what else he had? All the while, Angie's children had nothing.

Charlie found himself walking toward the man as he hammered, trying to align two parts so that they could be fastened with a six-inch steel pin. Charlie's steps were slow and deliberate in the fine dust of the barn floor, making no sound at all. He stood behind Henry, his breathing all but stopped, his hate an engulfing, burning fury.

He exploded toward Henry, clasping a strong hand onto each side of the man's head. Henry had no idea what was happening and was stunned beyond reaction. Charlie's hands drew Henry's head back before he could stop it, then burst forward with a ballistic energy, impaling Henry's head on the thick steel hay spear. There was a crunch as the sharp tip penetrated, then scraping when Charlie forced the head forward. Henry kicked spasmodically, but Charlie held the man's head in place as the body responded to the ever diminishing signals – twitching, writhing, blood pooling at his feet like oil.

Charlie staggered backward, his own anger spent, and he released the man's warm skull. He gasped and croaked. It seemed as if he could not suck in enough air, as if he'd been holding his breath since this morning.

He collapsed into the dirt, staring at his creation.

The things we do for family.

He took a few minutes to collect himself and settle his breathing. He couldn't take his eyes off the macabre pendant that hung in front of him, shifting and settling occasionally. Killing Henry Sullivan had sated some of the fire burning inside him, extinguishing some of his anger, making him forget the dull ache of his groin. His job was only half done, though. He had come here to remove a threat and to gather resources. In order to gather those resources, there was more work that had to be done. Henry had a wife.

On Henry's body, Charlie found a leather pancake holster with an older model Colt .38. He checked the cylinder and found it to be full of dull brass casings with an old-style lead hollow point bullet. Charlie thought the rounds were probably thirty years old. He swung the cylinder into place, made sure it snapped closed, and went to the barn door that faced the house. He peered out. From a kitchen window, there carried the sound of dishes bumping and scraping together, dulled by water. Someone was washing dishes.

The barn was visible from the Sullivans' kitchen window, so Charlie went back across the barn and left through the door he'd come in. He took a roundabout track through the taller weeds of a pasture, circumventing the view of whomever was doing dishes. In a moment, he arrived at a carport, flattened himself against the brick wall of the house and listened. The door to the house was open, a white screened storm door all that stood between him and the inside of the house.

With his left hand, Charlie reached for the black door handle and depressed the button to open it. There was a click and the latch opened. Charlie pulled on the door slowly, hoping that the door would maintain silence and allow him to enter quietly. There was the slight whooshing sound of the pneumatic door closer yielding as he pulled it open. When the opening was wide enough, Charlie slipped through, the buttons of his shirt catching on the edge of the door as he went by. The floor of the mud room was a dark wood parquet with several olive green rugs lined up to catch the debris a farmer might bring inside on his boots. Charlie crept toward the opening that he expected led in the direction of the kitchen. He could no longer hear the sound of dishes. Maybe she was drying.

Charlie paused at the opening. He could see that he next needed to make his way down a short hallway. He could see the corner of a kitchen cabinet through another opening down the hall. He stepped into the hallway, now on a red carpet so plush that he knew it would maintain silence even if he were to spring into cartwheels. He relaxed his breathing. He took another step, his foot sinking into the carpet. He was less than eight feet from the kitchen now. He involuntarily held his breath, his adrenaline picking up. He took another step and a woman sidestepped into the hallway in front of him. Charlie froze, nearly startled enough to let loose his bladder. She was fiftyish, crouched slightly, and had a gleaming chef's knife raised in her hand.

"What the hell are you doing in my house?" She took a step toward him, drawing the knife back, preparing to thrust, to gut him like a pig.

Charlie took a step back, then remembered the gun in his hand and raised it. She appeared not to have noticed the gun in his hand before this point. There was a flicker of recognition, of realization, then acceptance. He looked for fear and did not see it before he raised the gun stiffly and fired a round into her chest. She fell backward, the knife dropping silently onto the thick crimson carpet. A deep sucking moan left her body. She was not dead. Charlie stepped closer and shot her in the face, not out of anger but in a vain attempt to erase the penetrating stare that bored deep through him, both accusing and condescending at the same time.

He backed out of the hallway and sat for a moment in a soft blue recliner, its back covered with an old quilt to keep Henry from soaking it with his sweat. The world was completely quiet now. There was a large picture window to Charlie's left that lit the room, showing Charlie the lifeless television set, the large white bible, the framed family pictures. In those pictures Charlie saw a boy. The family had a son. Other pictures showed the son, older now, with a wife and child of his own. He scanned the room and saw no toys. The son's family was not staying here at this house, but they could be close. They would come out here at some point, looking for the man. He would keep that in mind.

*

When Charlie drove the old Dodge up to the trailer park, his brother's family streamed out to meet him, a little less hesitant than they'd been when he showed up earlier in the day. That Angie and Robert recognized the truck Charlie was driving was apparent, though they said nothing. They had long ago realized that they were part of a family structure where such questions were not asked. The sudden appearance of items that had not been there earlier, and which the family clearly did not have the means to purchase, was accepted as normal to them. Questions led to beatings. It was an early lesson.

Charlie leaned out the window and addressed his family. "I've got to go deliver a message. I'll be back in a few minutes. Pack any shit you'll need for the next couple of days. We're moving."

He pointed at Robert. "Get in the truck, boy. I need your help."

Robert hesitated and looked at this mother, wide-eyed and afraid.

"You better go," she whispered. "Don't make him mad."

Though Robert's look betrayed his anger at his mother's weakness, he said nothing else, just went to the truck and climbed in the passenger side. Charlie backed up and turned the truck. As he did, the missing tailgate clearly displayed two stiffened forms piled in the back, encrusted in blood. Her children turned to her, eyes full of questions they all knew better than to voice.

"Well, you heard the man. We got work to do."

CHAPTER 6

FEMA CAMP
Near Lexington, Virginia

Rebecca and Alice were quickly finding that FEMA's plan for getting them home was not all it was cracked up to be. On the same morning that Jim, Gary, and Randi left the interstate exit on foot, the two women had waited in the hotel room until they saw people begin to congregate outside. They gathered their belongings and gladly bid farewell to the stifling, putrid hotel where they'd spent the night. While Rebecca still had her suitcase in tow, Alice was carrying Randi's. Alice's had been left in the vehicle they'd abandoned at the truck stop after their co-worker, Lois, had been shot. Randi had left hers in Alice's care when she departed with the guys.

When they left their hotel room and entered the hallway, it was very dark, with a small amount of indirect light coming from a window somewhere down the hall. The temperature inside the building was in the eighties, steaming a foul reek from the besoiled carpet that seemed to bond with their skin as they walked. Clumps of toilet paper littered their path, clearly indicating that not all guests had used the bushes to relieve themselves last night. Neither woman could blame them. The atmosphere outside last night was heavy with danger.

Outside, the two women sat on the shoulder of the road amidst the abandoned vehicles, leaned back against their suitcases and waiting on the promised buses. The day was hot and they both felt dirty. Two days of heavy sweating and no shower was taking a toll. They were professional women, unaccustomed to appearing in public in such a state. Alice could not help but recall the words that Jim had used with her several times. *This is a different world*, he'd said. She was starting to believe him.

Rebecca wiped the oily sheen from her forehead, then wiped her hand onto her pants. "I feel like a refugee."

"I was thinking the same thing."

"I guess technically we do qualify as refugees now," Rebecca said.

Alice nodded grimly. "This is making me think about those people in the New Orleans Superdome after Hurricane Katrina. How miserable they looked."

"Those people Jim kept going on about?" Rebecca asked, although it was more of a sarcastic dismissal than a question.

"Yes, those people. I know how they must have felt now and I don't like it. Seeing them on TV, it was easy to dismiss them because we see so much disaster footage. Now I'm *in* the disaster footage and it completely sucks."

Rebecca snorted the dismissive laugh she used so often in meetings. "What, you feel your suffering is wasted if there's no one here to preserve it for posterity? Should I snap a quick picture of you?"

"That's not at all what I mean. I'm merely saying that Jim may have had a point. Maybe we do live in a bubble, thinking things will always be okay, when really we're always on the brink of disaster. Most of us can't live our daily lives each day knowing that, so we create a little illusion and live inside it."

"You've drank the fucking Kool-Aid, Alice. I think Jim's craziness must have rubbed off on you."

Alice looked sharply at Rebecca, trying to figure out where this constant cruelty and dismissal stemmed from.

"Now I know why people have such a hard time getting along with you. I tried to mediate when we were all together because that's what I'm used to doing. That's what I do at work. If it's only the two of us here and you continue to be so *condescending* to me, I don't know what to think about that. I'm seriously thinking of moving on without you. I don't know how long it's going to take to get home but I don't want to spend it dealing with your attitude."

Rebecca frowned, mumbled a lukewarm apology, and they didn't say much else. For two hours they silently watched miserable people wandering about aimlessly waiting for the buses to arrive.

When the buses finally came, there were four of them, all matching tour buses, and they came to a stop at the bottom of the exit. When the brakes were set and the engines turned off, people clamored toward the buses, shoving each other, kicking and cursing. There were cries of pain when people fell or were stepped on. Mothers yelled for children pulled from their grasp. Elderly couples tried to hold each other's hands and stay together.

The door to each bus swung open and an armed soldier appeared in each. The soldiers blocked each bus entrance, shouldering their weapons and aiming them at the crowd. Everyone froze. Parents gathered their children into their arms and hovered over them. Alice and Rebecca, unsure of the wisdom of being caught in the trampling masses, had remained at the back of the crowd.

The presence of the armed soldiers quickly brought order. When the crowd had finally grown silent, a man in a windbreaker with a FEMA cap stepped from one of the buses and raised a megaphone to his mouth.

"Good morning, folks," he said. "I know everyone is anxious to get to safety but we need to take care of some business first. I want to make sure everyone knows the rules. Don't be alarmed by the soldiers. They are here to maintain order and make sure no one gets hurt."

There was a groan from the crowd, some mumbling, and a lot of cursing. The crowd apparently felt they'd done nothing but wait all day and they weren't anxious to do more.

"First, I want to assure you that everyone will be able to get out of here today so there's no need to rush. I have more buses at my disposal and if you fill these, I can have more here shortly. Second, I need everyone to load in an orderly fashion with no pushing and shoving. We don't want any injuries. If you cannot obey the rules, I have soldiers who will place you under arrest and you will be processed as a prisoner when we reach the camp. Prisoners are maintained in a separate locked facility that is much less comfortable. If you want to remain with the party you are travelling with, then you need to follow the rules. Does everyone understand?"

There was a reluctant murmur of assent.

"Next, I need you to know that no weapons, drugs, or alcohol are allowed past this point. If you have any of those items, including pocket knives, I want you to toss them to the side before you get on the buses. No one will be keeping track of what you throw out here. No one is going to give you a ticket for pulling out a bag of weed or an illegal weapon. But you will be searched before being permitted into the general population at the camp. If you reach that point with contraband, you will be processed as a prisoner and kept under locked conditions. Are we clear on that?"

"Did you hear him say 'general population'?" Alice mumbled to Rebecca. "That's what they call inmates in prison. I don't like the sound of that."

Rebecca didn't know what to think of any of it. She had a sick feeling in the pit of her stomach that she had bet on the wrong horse.

"How soon before we can get to our homes?" a woman shouted.

The FEMA man smiled. "You'll get answers to all your questions when you are processed into the camp. Those issues are all being worked out as we speak. For now, let's work on getting you folks to some better accommodations. There will be food, water, and showers waiting for you."

The words brought forth an agreeable murmur from the crowd and served their intended function – there were no more questions, no more delay. The crowd boarded in an orderly fashion with the promise of food and showers completely silencing any dissent.

*

The FEMA camp was on a remote section of interstate somewhere near Natural Bridge, Virginia. There was a cluster of buildings that had originally been warehouses for a defunct interstate trucking company. FEMA had procured the buildings for their emergency camp, transforming them into a bustling city. There were more armed soldiers and FEMA men with megaphones waiting when they got off the buses. Lines of steel barricades herded them toward long military tents. The sides of the tents were rolled up to reveal tables and lines of people with luggage in hand. Beyond the tents were the warehouses, people moving in and out of them. A white tent with a Red Cross emblem stood beside one of the buildings and a crowd was gathered around it as well.

While their cavities were not searched, everyone was wanded with a metal detector and forced to walk through body scanners. Their luggage was electronically scanned, and a bored soldier quickly tossed the contents by hand to see if anything dangerous had escaped detection. Once they were deemed safe, the *campers,* as they were called, moved to a further stage of processing where demographic data was collected. FEMA staff, appropriately badged and labelled, collected name, date of birth, social security numbers, next of kin, home address, where they were coming from, and the names of other members of the party they were travelling with.

The last question addressed each stranded traveler's final destination.

Where were they trying to get to? Travelers were encouraged to answer this carefully because once they reached their destination it may be a while before they found a way out of there. In other words, if you were traveling to visit Aunt Mabel in Pennsylvania you should list your home as your intended destination and not Aunt Mabel's house, unless you intended to spend the next several months – or even years, potentially –with Aunt Mabel. The question was simple for Alice and Rebecca. They both wanted to get to Russell County, or at the least as far down the interstate as Abingdon, Virginia. If they could get to Abingdon, they could walk home. It would be a long walk at a little over twenty-five miles, but they could do it, even if it took them two days. They assumed that Jim, Gary, and Randi were probably doing that right now.

The two women were issued colored plastic bracelets, similar to the admission bracelets you would get at a concert or festival. There were a variety of colors being issued; Alice and Rebecca both got blue bracelets. It was explained that the color of your bracelet indicated your direction of travel. It was like a routing slip and contained a bar code with all the demographic information from their intake interview encoded into it. A blue bracelet indicated an intended direction of south on Interstate 81. Green indicated north. A yellow bracelet indicated your destination was the Interstate 77 interchange at Wytheville where another camp was supposed to be set up. If Interstate 77 was your destination, you would be reprocessed there and receive another bracelet indicating your next exchange. Similar bracelets marked folks as being bound for the Interstates 40, 64, 26, and 75.

"I feel like a UPS package," Alice told the FEMA lady who issued her bracelet.

The lady smiled.

"Any idea how long we'll be here?" Alice asked. "We only live a couple of hours from here."

The lady's smile vanished and she sighed. Alice was obviously throwing a question at her that she was tired of hearing or unable to answer. "Right now, all buses are being used to pick up stranded travelers and get them here to safety."

Reading between the lines, Alice continued. "So what you're basically saying is that no routes are running right now to deliver folks home?"

"That's correct." The lady's posture and tone indicated that she was braced for the onslaught of Alice's anger, which must have been the typical reaction.

Used to reading people as a Human Resource Director, Alice did not respond in the expected fashion. As a practical problem solver, she read a couple of steps forward and knew that this answer meant that even as close to home as they were, she and Rebecca would be there for a few days.

"Can I volunteer for anything?" she offered. "Do you all need help? I'd like to have something to do to keep me busy."

The lady's shoulders relaxed and her friendly demeanor returned. "Definitely. There's a volunteer desk set up just inside the emergency housing unit. The metal buildings over there," the woman clarified. "They used to be warehouses. Now they're lined with cots. Someone at the volunteer desk will find a job for you."

"Thanks, honey," Alice said. "You have a good day."

The lady beamed back. "You too."

When Rebecca followed close behind her, Alice slowed down so they could speak. "If we are going to be stuck here a couple of days I'm going to volunteer," Alice said. "I'll go crazy if there's nothing to do. Are you interested?"

Rebecca laughed that irritating, sarcastic laugh again and rolled her eyes. "I'm not interested in helping them out. If the government let this mess happen, fixing it is their problem. Not mine."

Alice shook her head. "I don't understand you, Rebecca. If we're stuck here in this camp, isn't it *our* problem too?"

Rebecca started walking away in a manner that made her attitude clear. Alice was dismissed.

*

After spending several minutes at the Volunteer Desk listing off her career accomplishments and her job duties, Alice was assigned work at the intake tent. She would be processing other new arrivals into camp. Other than the constant nag of worry about how her husband and son were doing back at home, Alice found the job to be agreeable with her background and skills. She was good at keeping people on-task and collecting the required information without getting bogged down in answering the numerous questions that people threw at her. In her line of work it was called *redirection.*

The most interesting part of the job was hearing the news that people brought in. Most of the people came in with experiences that were similar to what her own group had gone through. Some of the folks had been stranded at exits, as they had. Others came in with stories of highway rest areas, roadside gas stations, truck stops, and even tourist attractions. There were no good stories. Everyone's experience was similar: fear, desperation, worry, hunger, concern for their families, and an overwhelming desire to get back to the familiarity of home and their old life. While the job prevented Alice from spending the entire day dwelling on her own problems, it certainly exposed her to the misery of others.

Alice knew now, despite her initial rejection of Jim's way of thinking, that the home she returned to would not be the one she left. She would not walk into a house where her family was distracted by electronics. Her husband would not be watching television. Her son would not be playing X-Box. If home was in the same condition as the places she'd seen recently, they would not have power. That meant that all of the refrigerated food she'd bought for her family to tide them over while she was out of town would probably be bad now. All of the meals that she had prepared in advance and frozen so that they could easily reheat them would be going bad.

With no electricity, their heat pump would not work. Her husband suffered badly from seasonal allergies and they relied on the heat pump all summer to keep pollen from infiltrating their home. He would have had to open the windows in this heat and she knew that he would be congested and his eyes swollen. She didn't recall if they even had any allergy medicine in the house since they so relied on the heat pump to keep him from being exposed to allergens. When they bought allergy medicine, it was only because the previous package had run out. They never had an extra box on hand. It was always assumed that they could go buy another.

Her husband did not like to use gas pumps. No real reason other than that he simply didn't like pumping gas. He always waited until their vehicles were nearly empty before refilling them. If that was the case now, as she assumed it probably was, then they would be limited to what gas they had on hand. That would probably not be enough to refill their vehicle for multiple supply runs. Her husband had a one gallon gas can that he used for filling their lawn mower. It was usually empty because her husband filled it only when the mower was empty, and immediately poured the contents into the mower. They never had gas sitting around. They lived about six miles from town. That would be a long walk. She wondered if her husband could ride the lawnmower that far.

Their water supply came from a well, which she knew was two hundred and sixty-five feet deep, typical in her neighborhood. Without power, there would be no water at her home. There was a farm pond nearby, maybe a half mile from her house, but that water would not be drinkable. She had grown up on a farm with a gravity-fed spring water system. Her father had been proud of it, having grown up in a house with no running water. To Alice, the gravity-fed system represented poverty and she was proud to have been able to afford a deep well. She could not escape the worry that her family might be going through without water now. How were they cooking? How were they flushing toilets?

Her only consolation was that her husband was a practical country-boy. He'd been raised on a small farm and had worked on other farms growing up. He was industrious. They also had camping gear. Their son was in high school now, old enough to help. Hopefully, between the two of them, they could keep themselves alive until she got home.

After three days doing intakes, hearing more horror stories than she could absorb, the feeling that she needed to get home as soon as possible had risen from a gnawing feeling to a devouring ache that she couldn't escape. As she got to know her co-workers over those three days and heard their stories, she began to develop some friendships. She became privy to small bits of privileged, non-public, information, such as the daily population of the camp. That number continued to grow over her time there, and it became clear to her that no one was leaving this camp. Folks came in, and no one was being shipped out.

She realized and understood the mission. FEMA's goal was to collect all the stranded travelers and make sure they were taken care of. What she didn't understand was if a bus was going thirty miles south on the highway to pick up stranded travelers, why couldn't folks wanting to travel south hitch a ride and get that much closer to home?

There were several official answers. For one, if they dropped you off too far from your home you would be back in the situation that led you here in the first place – stranded, with no resources or supplies. You would end up at another exit, rest area, or lingering on the outskirts of a town that would not let you past its borders. It had become clear that no one wanted starving hordes traveling down the interstate raiding all the towns for supplies. It was inevitably going to lead to bloodshed, if it hadn't already. Alice's group had twice run into law enforcement blockades set up intentionally to keep travelers from entering nearby towns and attempting to steal the limited resources of the residents.

While the average camper was not privy to the comings and goings of the buses, FEMA felt there was no need to restrict this information from the staff working the intake desks. Those front-office staff needed to know the plan for their own scheduling purposes. They would need to have adequate intake personnel stationed at those desks when folks arrived. They couldn't do that without being privy to the game plan. Since most of the intake personnel were strangers to one another, discussing the comings and goings of the buses was one of the few common topics they had for discussion.

"Going to be a slow afternoon," one would say. "They sent two buses to the zoo today. Word is there's a few stranded folks there but nothing like the crowds at the truck stops."

Alice absorbed this information and began to formulate a plan. Her desperation continued to grow each day. She had noticed that, as a volunteer, her movement throughout the restricted areas of the camp drew no attention. She was allowed into the staff commissary for a cup of coffee or snack on her breaks. She was allowed to visit the supply tents for more routing bracelets, batteries, or for an ink pen.

From her observations, she knew that some of the supply tents stored what the FEMA folks called Ready Bags, which some of the staff called Go Bags. They were small backpacks containing a three day supply of food, bottled water, and a few emergency supplies. She had watched some of the camp staff leave with the bags. She didn't know if these were FEMA folks or from some other branch of government, but it appeared their function was to help locate the pockets of stranded people in advance of buses being sent to retrieve them. These folks always took these Ready Bags with them when they left, and often a few extras to distribute if the situation was desperate enough.

If she could get her hands on one of those bags and find a way out of this camp, she might have a chance of getting home quicker. In the back of her mind, amidst the fear and worry, was a panic that told her that her family may not be able to remain in their home if they could not obtain water. If they left, would she be able to find them? With no cell phones and no working landlines, how would she ever track them down? The thought was like ice water in her veins.

CHAPTER 7

Mount Rogers National Recreation Area

Speeding from Crawfish on the ATVs, Gary, Randi, and Jim made decent time. They felt like they were flying on the machines after days spent trekking steep mountain trails on foot. As much as Jim enjoyed hiking through the woods, it was different in a disaster. This trip was clearly not about hiking, it was about getting home to his family as quickly as he could. It had been some time since he'd been able to get a text through. He charged his phone daily on his folding Anker solar charger, strapping the unfolded charger to the back of his ATV so that it could charge while he drove. His expectations were low. This mountainous section of the state had only sporadic signal before the crisis. Now, he expected that this was not simply a case of poor reception but that cell towers were losing power and beginning to fail. The generators were running out of fuel. It was one thing to not know what was happening to his country, but not knowing what was happening to the people that meant the most to him was eating him alive. It was a desperate hunger that tore at his heart whenever he thought of them.

He was worried about leaving Lloyd behind. Lloyd was his best friend from childhood. He knew him well, and he knew that when Lloyd told them to leave, he meant it. That's what Jim had to keep telling himself. Lloyd knew the cop and they would work through this. Then Lloyd could do what he wanted. If he wanted to get to his parents' house in Russell County, then he'd show up there at some point. Knowing him, he was just as apt to go back inside with Masa and play music until his building fell in around him.

Much of the Crawfish area was surrounded by National Forest. Using the topographic maps contained in his *Virginia Gazetteer*, Jim had plotted a route last night before passing out on Lloyd's floor. He was glad he had taken the opportunity to do that at that time since the peace of the morning had deteriorated pretty quickly. Using Forest Service roads, Jim had come up with a plan to get them as far in the direction of home as he could.

The Forest Service roads were often merely crude tracks cut through the forest. Some of them weren't even gravel, but simply earthen shelves sliced into the shoulders of steep mountains with bulldozers. The Forest Service used them for logging, fire control, and search and rescue operations. There weren't many people out on these roads at the best of times. They were most often accessed by hikers, hunters, mountain bikers, and wildlife. Jim's fingers were crossed that at the point they ran out of drivable road, they would be near the Appalachian Trail again. He'd planned for that, but plans didn't seem to mean much anymore. Shit kept happening. The more he saw of how civilization was behaving, the more certain he was that using remote trails was the only safe way home.

For a brief moment, he'd wrestled with Lloyd's idea of a "run and gun" approach. Lloyd had been determined that he could take one of his old, fast cars and haul ass home on the highway, shooting anyone who got in the way. It was the West Virginia bootlegger in Lloyd's blood that made him think like that. Jim understood it perfectly, sharing some of those roots. The problem, as Jim knew and Lloyd didn't, was that the people in their way would severely outgun them. It would not be deputies with Glocks and shotguns, it would be federal troops with SAWs and .50 caliber sniper rifles. One .50 caliber round through the block of Lloyd's 318 Dodge engine and they'd be dead in the water.

Jim knew that, regardless of how far they made it on these machines, in the end they'd be walking the final approach home. As they got closer to home, the terrain became rougher and the mountains steeper, with fewer paved roads. What roads there were became pinch points where the group could easily be ambushed, robbed, or killed if they tried to travel them. Jim wasn't going to get this far from Richmond only to be killed in his backyard. They would go as far as they could on the ATVs then start hoofing it again. ATV, then AT, then a day or two of walking familiar fields and ridgetops to get themselves home.

To Ellen. To Pete. To Ariel.

*

By the end of the day, they'd jostled and jolted their way up the slopes of Mount Rogers. The last miles had been brutal on the back of the machines and Jim felt like his organs had been colliding together like pool balls.

70

Mount Rogers was a wilderness area that had once been a massive cattle farm with thousands of acres. Even now there were cattle grazing the high-elevation pastures atop the mountain. The group's destination was known as "the corral" and was exactly what it sounded like. It was a corral where the ranchers gathered their cattle to take them to market. Since the corral was now a stopover destination for Appalachian Trail hikers, some improvements had been made to the area. One of the most impressive features was an outhouse. It didn't take much to impress a hiker: a cold Mountain Dew, an ice cream cone, an outhouse. All were a sight for sore eyes. Besides the outhouse, the corral had a really good spring and lots of camping space within the flat, fenced corral. It was only accessible by the rugged mountain road that the cattle haulers used and by the Appalachian Trail.

Jim's group had only passed a single traveler on the wilderness roads all day, a skittish man in camouflage with a puny Whitetail deer tied across the cargo rack of an ATV. The deer was about the size of a Collie. Concerned initially that Jim's group was the law catching him with an illegal deer, worry flashed across the man's face. After a better look and perhaps a few moments of increasing situational awareness, he realized that they weren't law enforcement and maybe that meant they were something worse. The man punched the throttle and accelerated wildly away from them.

When they finally reached the corral, it appeared vacant except for an old camper with peeling paint. There were no cattle anywhere in sight, no tents, nor any hikers. Jim rode closer to the camper and could see that a padlock was threaded through a hasp on the door. He had seen this same camper here on his last hike through this section. Supposedly it belonged to the cattle company that held the grazing lease. The ranch hands stayed in the trailer when they were up this way tending to the cattle, though there was no visible evidence that anyone had been there recently.

"Is that a bathroom?" Randi asked. She was pointing toward a fairly nice wooden building with a metal roof about fifty yards away.

"It is," Jim told her.

She didn't waste any time. She pressed her throttle and fired off in that direction without another word.

Gary turned off his machine and stared at the camper. "It would be nice to stay in this camper for the night."

Jim turned his machine off, and looked at the sky. There were dark clouds in the distance and the breeze was picking up. It could mean rain overnight. He sure missed the weather app on his phone. Weather apps had made people less able to forecast changes in the weather from the natural signals around them. There was a whole generation coming up who would not know how to read the signs of a coming storm. If technologies did not return soon, average folks would have to relearn the ability to forecast weather.

Gary got off his ride and pointed to a padlock on the door. "You think there's a key hidden somewhere?"

Jim looked at the lock. It was a basic Master padlock. In an action movie, someone would have fired a shot into the lock and popped it open. In reality, it wasn't that easy. There was a chance that deflected lead from the bullet would end up in someone's leg or foot, and the possibility that a gunshot would deform the lock to the point that it would never open again.

Jim looked up under the camper and quickly spotted a discarded beer can.

Exactly what he was looking for.

He ducked under the camper, retrieved the can, and extracted his multi-tool from its case on his belt. He unfolded the scissors, punched a starter hole in the side of the can, and trimmed out a square of aluminum about two inches by two inches. He trimmed out what looked like a T-shape, except the top was the full two-inches wide and was about 3/8 of an inch thick. The main trunk of the T-shape was short, only about an inch long, and was rounded on the bottom.

He took the padlock in his hand and wrapped the aluminum strip around the u-shaped shackle of the lock. The aluminum was thin enough that the rounded trunk of the T was able to slip down into the mechanism of the lock alongside the shackle. He folded the long top strips of the T around the shackle until they met, then pinched them together to use as a handle. When he twisted the aluminum strip, it rotated around the lock shackle. The bit of can that penetrated down into the mechanism of the lock acted as a wedge, slipping between the mechanism and the notched shackle, freeing it. The lock popped open and Jim removed it from the hasp.

"Where did you learn that?" Gary asked.

"If I told you, I'd have to kill you."

"No, seriously?"

"You Tube," Jim replied. "It's a padlock shim."

"I'm going to have to learn to make those. Can I have that one?" Gary deposited it inside his billfold like it was some precious object. Jim saw the flash of credit cards in Gary's billfold. Under current circumstances, the padlock shim was indeed likely to be the most valuable thing in there.

The trailer was old, the door ill-fitting. When they opened it, the hinges groaned from neglect, and a stagnant smell reached their nostrils. It was old sweat and mildew, baked into wood. It was unlikely the trailer ever got aired out properly.

Inside, the windows were dirty, but enough light penetrated that Jim could see the interior clearly. There was torn upholstery on the built-in seating. The color was burnt orange, which gave him an idea of the age of the trailer. There was evidence of mice, and dead bugs made for a crunchy carpet. Jim noticed that the floor sagged beneath his feet and felt a little spongy. People often tested bad floors by bouncing on their toes to see how much the floor gave. Jim was certain that a move like that would drop him through this floor like a rock through a wet paper towel.

Gary came in behind him and flipped open a cabinet door. There was some canned food, Styrofoam plates, and some charcoal starter. He pulled out a can of Hormel chili and examined the label.

"Says it expired about three years ago," Gary said.

"I'd eat it in a pinch, but we're good on food."

"I think I'll pass," Gary said, replacing the can in the cabinet.

In one corner, there was a stack of camp chairs. A couple of blue water jugs were lined up beside them. There was a milk crate with kindling for a fire, and an axe stood in the corner.

"I could sleep here," Gary said.

Jim nodded. "Me too."

He turned and walked back out. "Let's unload our gear. We'll probably need to leave some stuff here because we won't be able to take the trailers any farther. The trail gets real narrow beyond this point. We'll probably even have to cut some fences to get these machines through."

"How about I empty my trailer and use it to go get some firewood?" Gary offered.

"Sounds good," Jim said. "While you do that, I'll see what we have that needs to be eaten before tomorrow. After dinner we can consolidate some gear. I'm not sure how much further we can ride the ATVs, but every mile helps."

They heard an engine fire up and Randi drove toward them wearing an ear- to-ear grin. "I never thought I'd be so damn happy to sit in a stinking outhouse," she said after she parked her machine. "That place up there is uptown compared to most of what we've had the last couple of days. No need to worry about poison ivy, bears, or snakes. Just pure comfort."

Jim had to laugh. "I might have to pay that place a visit myself. You're building some pretty high expectations."

"You better ask first. I'm not sure I'm willing to share my outhouse."

Gary started setting gear out onto the ground and had his trailer empty in a few minutes. After he drove off to collect some wood, Jim caught Randi up on their plans for the night. She helped him unload his own trailer and he pushed it around behind the camper, planning to leave it there. Maybe it would serve some purpose for someone else on down the road. He spread out a blue tarp and they piled their gear on it, checking for redundancies. With the relatively high storage capacity of an ATV with a trailer, they'd not had to be as selective as they'd been when they were toting the gear in their backpacks. Now they had to do a first stage reduction, narrowing the gear to only what they could fasten to their luggage racks. Jim assumed that at some point tomorrow they'd be doing a further reduction and going back to backpacks and gear they could carry. He dreaded it because it meant each mile would take that much more work.

The expendable items that Jim planned on leaving behind were mostly gear that they'd picked up from the people they'd fought on the Blue Ridge Parkway. The majority of those items had already been in the trailer when they took it, and there were the coolers full of the food that Lloyd and Masa had given them. They'd left some of it behind for Lloyd but there was still plenty. They would eat what they could tonight and load up some carbs for the next couple of days. There were some extra blankets and tarps, some knives, assorted camping gear, and extra rope. Jim would probably leave most of it behind in the trailer as payment for breaking into the place and using it for the night. Maybe the food would help the next folks that came upon the camper.

"Did you look in this cooler?" Randi asked, opening the cooler that had come from Gary's trailer.

Jim shook his head. "I didn't load it. Lloyd did."

She turned the open cooler to Jim. It was full of beer sloshing in icy water.

"Oh my God, that's a pretty sight. That may be the last icy beer for hundreds of miles," Jim said. "I'll take one of those."

"I heard the sloshing, but I thought it was soft drinks," Randi said. She pulled out two and extended one in Jim's direction. He took the bottle and held it against his throbbing abdomen, right over his stapled hernia scar. It was the closest thing he had to an ice pack.

"Do I need to leave you alone with that?" Randi asked, giving him a strange look. "You look like you guys are kind of hitting it off."

"Hernia," Jim mumbled. "Give me a break." He raised the bottle, twisted the cap loose, and stuck it in his pocket. An old habit. After a hot, dusty day of being bounced over rocks and scraped by branches, the beer was just what the doctor ordered. He started with a sip but it turned into a long draught that lasted until the bottle was drained.

Randi was still standing with her unopened beer watching him. "Thirsty?"

Jim nodded, looked at the beer in her hand. "That mine? You're not drinking it."

"Fucking try it and see what happens," she warned.

He went to the cooler and grabbed another, opened it, and drank this one slower. "I'm rehydrating. I've read articles that say that beer makes an excellent recovery beverage after a strenuous workout."

Randi opened hers and, not to be outdone, drained it in a single swallow. She pitched the empty up under the camper then grabbed another for herself.

"Rehydrating?" he asked.

"Definitely."

*

By 7 p.m. the temperature was cooling in the high country but it felt nice after the heat and sweat of the day. They had a roaring fire going in the fire pit in front of the camper. They didn't need it for the heat, but fire served multiple purposes in the backcountry. Besides its use for cooking, the smoke from the fire kept the bugs at bay, and the glow served to temporarily lift the cloud of gloom and foreboding from their journey.

They pulled the folding camping chairs from the camper and sat around the fire, cooking their dinner. The food in the cooler was purchased for Lloyd's camping trip to the music festival, not for backcountry travel, so they ate it first. It was neither light nor suitably packaged for travel and some of it required refrigeration. There were hot dogs, good deli chili, coleslaw, canned baked beans, and bags of potato chips that they knew they had to eat because the chips had no hope of surviving their trip. It was a dirty job, but they forced themselves to eat every last potato chip they had. Despite their gluttony, Jim didn't think there was even a shred of guilt between the three of them.

Randi and Jim had each had several beers by this point. Gary had joined them for one, even though he didn't drink.

"It's not a beer, it's a recovery beverage," Jim assured him. "You need to rehydrate."

Randi nodded seriously in agreement.

Gary conceded reluctantly. "Since it's practically medicinal, I guess I don't see any harm in it. Besides, I think anyone who's had the kind of week I've had deserves a drink. I guess you've noticed that I've even let a curse word or two slip out."

"I noticed, Gary," Randi said. "Beer and cursing? Welcome to the dark side."

When darkness fell and dinner was over, the loneliness set in on them like the arrival of fog. They all fell silent, sipped whatever they were drinking, and watched the fire. Night birds called; the fire crackled; bats swept into their circle of light to devour the insects that watched the fire with them. In the distance, a lone coyote called, mourning alongside them. Others joined in, yipping.

The business of the day and of setting up their camp had distracted them. For a moment they'd nearly forgotten their plight. Only for a moment. For that time, they were three friends sharing a dinner over an open fire, then an instant later they were back to being three acquaintances separated from their families, not sure if they'd even make it home, and not sure what would be waiting on them when they got there. Turn your back on reality even for a moment and it will sneak up and body slam you.

They had planned on sleeping in the camper but no one made a move to get up. The night air was comfortable, while the interior of the camper was humid and stale. Jim expected that at some point it would become too cool and he would need to drag out his blanket but for now he couldn't move to do it. He looked around and saw Gary and Randi both had their eyes closed. They were all beat and sleep was preferable to sitting there missing their families, stewing in their own somber juices. The fire was dwindling. He decided that he needed to muster a last burst of energy and throw a log or two on it. While he was up he would dig out the blankets and toss one across his traveling companions so they'd be there if they needed them. For an obnoxious jerk, he could be a pretty nice guy sometimes. The thought almost made him smile.

He grabbed his backpack from the tarp and laid it down beside his chair, deciding he'd dig for the blankets after he took care of the fire. He grabbed a three foot piece of oak deadfall from the pile and carefully laid it across the coals. Out of nowhere, there was explosion. Burning embers showered his face and grit filled his eyes. He could smell hair burning. He fell backward, slapping at his face, unsure of what he was trying to put out. Had the log exploded? Was there something else in the fire pit? An aerosol can? What the hell had happened?

Jim fell backward over one of the camping chairs, fighting to open his eyes, feeling defenseless with his vision impaired. The scratching and burning was so intense that he couldn't focus on anything. He barely cracked his eyelids and saw the glow of the fire. There was a flash of relief when he realized that he was not blind. He did not seem to be on fire at the moment either, which was also a relief. His hands rubbing at his eyes touched raw, burned skin. He knew it should hurt – that it would hurt later – right now he was too stunned to notice.

Then Randi was over him, yelling, leaning to put a hand on his shoulder. She was speaking to him when there was another sound. This one was clearly a gunshot.

He grabbed at Randi's arm and pulled. "Down!" She dropped alongside him.

"What's wrong?"

"My eyes," he hissed. "I can't fucking see!"

He felt a pain that seared completely through his skull when the beam of her flashlight hit him in the face. "Shit!"

"Sit still," she ordered, brushing at his face.

There was another gunshot, this one shattering a camper window.

"There's no time," he said. He squinted toward Gary, who'd rolled out of his chair and was flattened out on the ground from what little Jim could see.

"What's going on?" Gary yelled.

"I don't have a fucking clue, but we've got to get out of here."

Jim shaded his eyes and crawled in the direction of his bag. Another shot rang out and he heard the soft thud of a high velocity round hitting his backpack. He grabbed the carry handle on the top of the bag and quickly began crawling backward, dragging the bag and trying to get out of the circle of firelight where he made such an easy target.

"Run! Get out of the light!"

Jim backed into Randi at the edge of the firelight and kept crawling, shoving her. "Go! Get back!"

"My stuff," she said. "My pack."

"Fuck your stuff. Go!"

Randi sprang to her feet and took off running into the darkness. Jim tried to follow, slinging his pack over one shoulder, but he couldn't see well enough. He was staggering and off balance. He ran into bushes and over rocks.

"Jim!" Randi whispered from off to one side. "Hold onto my shoulders."

He placed a hand on each of her shoulders and followed awkwardly behind her. They quickly realized that they couldn't move too fast or their feet would tangle. There was another shot but it didn't sound close. He hoped it wasn't close to Gary. He started to call out to him but realized that he didn't know where their enemies were or how many of them were out there. They needed to keep quiet and not give away their positions.

"Did you see Gary get away?" Jim asked, stumbling behind Randi.

"He grabbed his pack and ran into the dark with a gun," Randi said, her breathing labored. "He was going the other way."

Jim could hear voices behind them now. There were at least two men shouting back and forth, and they were not far away. He tried to jog, pushing Randi, but she couldn't see in the pitch black night any better than he could and they fell several times. Branches crackled in the darkness.

"We need to slow down," Jim said. "We're making a racket and we're going to end up impaled on a branch. We need to hide until morning."

He slowed his pace. He heard a twig snap behind him, and it was the only warning he got before he was tackled from behind. His spine bent and hyper-extended in ways it was not designed to move. With the heavy pack on his back, he was not able to react. He could not regain his balance and he went flying, slamming into Randi. She screamed, then went sprawling away across the wet grass and leaves. Jim was on his stomach when the first of the blows came. It was a heavy fist that struck the side of his head like a sledgehammer. His first thought was not of the pain but that this was a really bad spot to be hit. Concussions came easier when hit from the side. So did unconsciousness.

There was another blow in the same spot. Same hammer.

He was fucked.

He fought to stay conscious. There was a pause as his attacker turned on a headlamp. Jim could see the glow of the light as his face was pressed into the grass. The blows to his head had made his eyes water, helping clear them slightly. He knew that it was too little, too late. With this pack on his back and an attacker sitting atop it, he could not maneuver. He could not reach his knife or his gun. He was completely at the mercy of his attacker. He was going to die here and he would never reach his family. They would never know how hard he tried to get back to them.

Will my death sentence be their death sentence too? he wondered.

The attacker's weight shifted. Whoever was atop him drew in a ragged gasp. Jim didn't know if he was drawing back for another blow or it this was to be the knife strike that would finish him off. This thought was interrupted by a bloodcurdling cry. It was not a shriek, but a soul-ripping roar of pain – the deepest, most animalistic expression of hurt that Jim had ever heard. Knowing that this may be his only chance, he shifted his hips and got a hand under his chest, exploding upward and throwing his attacker from his back. The man put up no fight, falling to the side without protest.

In a flash, Jim had his SOG Twitch out of his back pocket and the tanto blade deployed. It was pure reaction, a move he'd trained on, but what he saw in front of him made him pause. His attacker was lying on his back in the grass, his headlight blazing down crookedly on his distorted face. His eyes were as wide as they were physically able to open. His mouth was the same, trying to suck in air for another scream. From the side of his head, from his ear, stuck a clear light stick tube. Blood oozed around the light stick, seeping from the man's head.

Jim recognized it. It was a six-inch infrared chemical light stick. He'd given one to both Randi and Gary back at Lloyd's house when he'd packed his gear for this segment of the trip. When cracked and shaken, it emitted a glow that was only visible with a night vision device. They had many tactical purposes, included marking the good guys so that you could tell them from the bad when you were wearing night vision. He'd given each of those guys one in case they got separated in a situation exactly like this. He told them to hide in the darkness, hang the IR light stick in a visible location near them, and he'd find them using his night vision monocular.

Jim knew that it was six inches long, though less than an inch was visible. The five inches inside this man's skull must have wrecked his inner ear and caused devastating pain, but not a fatal injury. Jim took care of that. He lashed out with his knife, slitting the man's throat and finishing the job. He leaned forward and tore the man's headlamp off his head, shading the lens with his cupped hand, leaving only a pale glow that wouldn't carry for any distance. He turned around and found Randi just where he expected her to be.

"Help me find water. I need to rinse my eyes."

Randi dug around in his pack and found a bottle. She poured it across his open eyes and it washed the remaining ashes and grit free. He now realized how lucky he'd been. Someone out there in the dark had taken a head shot at him but missed, hitting the embers.

When she was done, Jim's eyes still burned, but he could see a lot better. They searched their attacker's body, finding some 9mm ammunition and a pistol to go with it. There was a hunting knife, a lighter, and that was it.

"He must have stashed the rest of his gear somewhere else," Jim said.

"We need to find Gary," Randi said.

"We will. I'm hoping he remembered his light stick, like you did."

"Sorry about that. I think I broke mine."

"I'll forgive you this once."

Jim dug into his pack, feeling a rush of panic that the night vision monocular might have been hit by the bullet that struck his pack. Thankfully, it was safe and secure in the nylon pouch that he stored it in. He held the device to his head, pushed the On button, then the second button that powered the IR spotlight attached to the device. The IR spotlight increased the range greatly.

"Holy shit," Jim whispered.

"What?"

He handed Randi the night vision device. "Look at the body."

In stabbing the chemical light stick into the man's ear, Randi had successfully broken the small glass vial inside it and activated the IR chemical reaction. The light stick had been jammed so violently into his ear that the plastic capsule inside had ruptured, leaking the chemical all over the side of the man's head and allowing it to run into the gaping wound of his slit throat. In the green glow of the night vision device, all of this glowed brilliantly and ghastly.

"Holy shit is right. I could have gone all damn day without seeing that. Thanks a lot."

Jim took the device back and scanned the surrounding woods with it, seeing nothing. "Logic tells me that we should hide out, but I think we need to try to find Gary tonight. If I can spot the glow of his light stick, it will make finding him a lot easier. If we have to search for him in these woods in the daylight we may never hook back up. What do you think of hanging out here and letting me look for him?"

"What do you think of kissing my ass?" Randi countered. "I am not being left here with a glowing corpse."

"Without the night vision you can't see that he's glowing."

"I'll still *know* he's glowing, even if I can't see it. I'm not staying here alone."

Accepting that he couldn't win this argument, Jim walked down the trail with Randi in tow. He had the night vision monocular glued to his eye and the heavy Gregory pack strapped on his back. Randi had been forced to abandon her gear at the campsite, but there was nothing critical in there. If they found Gary, his pack, along with Jim's, would have enough food and supplies for the three of them.

After a couple of hundred feet, they crept out of the woods and the valley opened up before them. They could see the corral below, their fire still blazing as several men heaped their firewood upon it. Jim lowered his monocular and watched the men go through the gear they'd left behind. Some of it was gear they'd planned to abandon. The rest of it was gear they'd planned on taking with them on the back of the ATVs – the coolers, their boxed food, extra ammunition. Jim counted three men and assumed there could be others out there looking for them. There was no gear down there worth dying for. Not even the ATVs. Those men could have it.

He raised the monocular back to his eye and began scanning the darkness. To their left, at a distance of around fifty yards or so, he saw an IR light stick hanging from a tree. He felt a wave of relief that Gary had remembered to use it.

"I see the light."

They made their way to Gary as quietly as possible, announcing themselves as they approached to avoid being shot. They were pleased to find Gary intact and uninjured. He had his bug out bag and his weapons, although he'd not been able to get any of his extra food or gear from his ATV.

"I say we leave it," he said. "Let's start walking and walk through the night. This place could be crawling with people tomorrow. We don't even know how many there are. If we keep going we can hole up in the morning and get some sleep."

Randi and Jim agreed.

"You know that was stupid of us, Gary," Jim said. "We thought we had the world to ourselves up here. We should have known better. We can't assume any place is safe anymore. We need to remember that and make sure we don't get caught off-guard again or we're not going to make it home."

CHAPTER 8

The Cave
Russell County, Virginia

Ellen was making an after dinner cup of tea when Pete approached her with an unusually serious demeanor. "I want to talk to you about something."

"Then talk," she said, smiling. "I'm listening."

"Not like this," he said. "I want us to go outside and sit down and talk. Just us, with no interruptions, and I want you to listen."

Impressed by his seriousness and mature approach, Ellen agreed. "Let me finish making this tea and I'll join you at the picnic table outside." She looked around. Ariel was playing a game with Pops. Nana was laying down on her cot. She'd been feeling under the weather today and had spent most of the day in her sleeping bag.

Pete was waiting for her when she went outside a few minutes later. "I want to help protect the camp."

About halfway through the sentence she knew where he was going with this and was already turning off her ears, preparing her rebuttal.

"Listen to me, Mom," he pleaded, sensing it. "Don't say no yet."

She folded her hands in her lap, forcing herself to bite her tongue and listen. "Okay."

"I've been helping out a lot, haven't I?"

She nodded. "You have."

"I've been building the fire in the woodstove each morning."

"You have."

"I've been bringing in a supply of wood, splitting kindling, and I've even got more firewood piled up outside in case we can't go get any for a few days."

She took a controlled sip of her tea. It was still too hot. "Yes, that's all true."

"I'm trying to help out with Dad gone," Pete said. "I'm trying to think about the things he would want us doing."

"That's what we're all trying to do. He left us that manual and I've been trying to follow it."

"Yes, but he told me things," Pete said. "I'm remembering more and more stuff all the time that he taught me but didn't write down in that book. I didn't always pay attention because it seemed farfetched. You know how Dad was about all this stuff."

Ellen felt a pang. She did remember how he was and it hurt. "Like what? What do you remember that we're not doing?"

"Like we need to be keeping a better eye on things. We're holed up in this cave and we're safe, but everything else is unprotected."

She shook her head. "I don't care about the house, I care about you and Ariel, and Nana and Pops."

Pete's look made her uncomfortable. He was pleading. "I care about them too, and that's part of why I need you to let me start keeping an eye on things."

She gave him a wary look, certain that she would not be ready to hear whatever he was proposing. She had to admit, though, that he'd been demonstrating more and more maturity. She owed it to him to hear him out. "Okay. Continue."

"We need an observation post," Pete explained. "We cannot see our house. We can't see our driveway. We can't even see the main road to see what's going by. That's not safe. People could be moving in on us right now and we wouldn't know they were coming."

"I will not have you walking the property looking for trouble," Ellen said. "I told you, there's nothing out there that's worth your life."

Pete sighed. "I'm not talking about walking around. That would be a *patrol*, anyway, not an *observation post*. I'm telling you that we need an *observation post*, a concealed location where we can see around us and I can keep an eye on things. If trouble is coming, we need to know about it. The only way we can make sure this cave stays secret is by not letting people close to it. We don't know if people are on our property or not. What if they are and they see the tire tracks coming down here? What if they follow the tracks and they pen us up in here for a long time? Or what if they just watch for us and pick us off one-by-one?"

Ellen looked Pete in the eye. "I'm not sure I could handle you doing that. I'd worry constantly."

"We can use the radios. We can check in together as often as you want to."

She thought about it, turning it over in her head. "Did you have a spot in mind?"

He nodded. "There's an old fallen tree on the hill above us. It's surrounded by tall grass and those wild rose bushes that Dad hates. I could get in there with a small spotting scope and see what's going on all around us. I could pile up more grass and branches and build a nest up there that would keep me hidden. No one would know I was there."

"Did you come up with that idea all on your own?" Ellen asked, genuinely curious if he was thinking that strategically now.

"No. Dad talked about it once. He wanted to build something permanent up there but hadn't got around to it yet."

She had to admit it did sound like a good idea. "There would be rules. You would only be up there to *look*, not start shooting at anyone, not without my permission."

"I know that, Mom," Pete said. "I want to have guns in case I need them. I've already thought that I want to carry that Smith & Wesson M&P 22 pistol because I've shot it a million times and I know how to work it. I want to take my deer rifle because I'm good with it. It's got a scope so I can see a good distance with it."

Ellen was impressed that his choices were so practical. She had expected him to want a .45 caliber pistol and either the AR-15 or Mini-14. His choices displayed forethought and planning, displaying the same maturity that he seemed to be showing every day now. Still, he was her child and sending him outside the cave on such a mission scared the hell out of her. She acknowledged, however, that it was something that had to be done. They'd been lucky so far, and that streak might not continue.

"Okay," she said. "We'll try it."

*

The next morning, Pete finished his chores around the cave, restocking the firewood they'd used the previous night. He emptied the ashes from the woodstove, took them outside, and scattered them. When his mother agreed that he'd done all he needed to do, he announced his intention to go start setting up his observation post. Ellen assisted him with preparing his gear. She pulled the .22 pistol from its case, placed a loaded magazine in the weapon, and chambered a round. She made sure the safety was on, then placed the weapon in the holster on his – *Jim's* – tactical vest. She dug extra magazines, loaded the previous night, from the pistol case and gave them to him, letting him stow them as he preferred. She knew he'd organized the vest meticulously and would not want her tampering with his system.

Next, she got his .270 hunting rifle. It was a Ruger American rifle. She pulled a box of ammunition from a storage tote. "Go ahead and load it," she told him. "Don't chamber a round until you're outside the cave."

Together, they loaded a backpack with a short tripod, a spotting scope, a fleece camping blanket for him to lie on, and a cheap set of binoculars. He picked up his radio and hung it in a chest pouch beside the pistol. Even though the radio was rechargeable, it worked on AA batteries, and Pete pocketed a spare set for when the rechargeables ran down. When he was geared up, Ellen hugged him long and hard.

"I love you, Pete."

"Love you too. You don't have to say it like I'm marching off to war."

She hoped that was true – that he was *not* marching off to war.

She followed Pete outside and watched him stride off. He seemed excited, anxious to assume the role he was carving for himself. From the back, without the face of her child visible, he looked like a man determinedly setting about a task. He walked across the field, coming and going from view as he followed the contours of the land. When he reached the hillside below his destination, Ellen thought of when she dropped him off at school when he was little, waiting to see that he reached the door safely. When he reached the top, he dropped from view and began laying out his gear. She could see this from where she sat, but as he settled in and built the walls of his nest she gradually lost sight of him. He was disappearing in plain sight.

Ellen turned to go inside. Nana had been coughing a lot and Pops was concerned that the damp air of the cave was causing her to develop some type of respiratory infection. They'd kept the stove going nearly all the time, trying to make sure their chamber stayed warm. The stove did dry things out slightly, but a cave with an open water source running through it could only get so dry.

"Mom?"

She frantically pulled her radio from her back pocket.

There was a note of *something* in his voice but she wasn't sure what it was.

"What's the matter, baby?"

"There's something at the gate."

There was definitely something in his voice. Something ominous. "What is it?"

Silence.

"I'm not sure," he finally said. "It might be something we need to go look at."

"Let me get Pops. He and I will drive down there and look at it. You stay up there to provide cover in case anything weird happens."

In case it's a trap, she thought.

*

Descending the driveway in Ellen's Suburban, she and Pops could see shapes at the gate but could not tell what they were. It almost looked like two people were hunched down in front of the gate, peering through it. This angered Ellen. She thought she'd made herself clear to the folks that had been bothering them, but apparently they weren't getting the message. She was becoming exasperated with them. Though she was not a cruel, heartless person, Jim had made her read several books where people in disasters shared their food with someone or disclosed that they had made some level of preparation for disasters. It always turned out the same way. Those people ended up on your doorstep wanting your supplies and ready to take them by force. If that didn't work, they kept coming back with more and more people until things ended badly. She could not soften her resolve. She could not weaken.

She wove through the maze of steel beams that Pops and Pete had left in the road as obstacles. The idea wasn't to completely block their driveway, but instead to slow down anyone trying to rush toward their house. It worked, because it took her several minutes to make her way close to the gate. She neared it and stopped the vehicle about thirty feet away. She stared out the windshield at the sight before her, words temporarily failing her. She started to get out but Pops put his hand on her arm. It was a light touch, reflexive on his part, but she knew that the intention was to prevent her from getting out. He apparently had no words either.

ASHES OF THE UNSPEAKABLE

In front of her, their dear friend and neighbors, Henry and Kathy Sullivan, hung dead from the gate. The bodies were inside the gate and facing her. They were about five feet apart, their arms extended as if they'd been crucified, their fingers touching almost poignantly. Barbed wire bound their arms to a cross-member of the gate, tracing Kathy's, wrapping her neck, following the opposite arm, then jumping between the bodies and binding Henry's arms to the rusty red gate in the same manner. The gate was not tall enough for them to be truly suspended in crucifixion, and their legs were bent at the knee, their feet extending back through the gate. Either to prevent the feet from dragging or to hold the heads up, a strand of barbed wire was wrapped around their ankles and then stretched to their heads, wrapping around the forehead of each corpse. The heads gazed upward as if staring at the sun. The pose left them with a ghastly bearing, their faces void of familiar characteristics due to swelling and injury, the tangle of wire making their bodies appear to be the bloated fruit of some encroaching thorny vine.

It was not clear how they'd died, but each wore a mask of clotted encrustation that bespoke violence and horror. If Ellen had to guess, she would say that the pair had been shot in the face or beaten to death. Her heart broke for the sweet, thoughtful neighbors who had been so kind to her family. She wondered if their son had been killed. She would have to try and raise him on the radio. If he were alive he would need to know about this. "Who would do something like this?" Pops asked.

Ellen considered the question for a long time. "It's a what," Ellen said, her voice sounding too loud in the insular environment of the car. "Not a *who*, but a *what*."

"Surely you don't think an animal…?"

"A human animal," Ellen finished.

Pops turned this over in his head. "Why?"

"They want us out of here," she said. "If they wanted to kill us, they would probably be trying harder to do so. I think they want us to leave so they can have our stuff."

Pops shook his head, unable to take his eyes from the bodies before them. He'd once been a high school principal, and Henry Sullivan had been one of his students. "How can we ever survive in a world like this, Ellen? How can the kids survive this? If people can do something like this just to send a message, then how do you deal with it? How can you possibly interact with people who have gone so far beyond the boundaries of what's acceptable in civilized society?"

"You can't interact with them, Pops. That's what I've been trying to tell you all along. It's what Jim tried to drill into my head. In every disaster, morality behaves like floodwater seeking a new level. It establishes a new normal – a new morality. Like with Hurricane Katrina, the new morality for a nurse may be that she feels she needs to euthanize her critical care patients so that they don't die a miserable death from lack of oxygen. A cop in the same disaster may decide that the new acceptable punishment for theft is immediate execution because there is no longer a functioning system for arrest, detention, and trial. Every person has to determine their own new morality and sometimes it revolves on hairpin, split-second decisions. What is acceptable to me now is a whole lot different than what was acceptable a few weeks ago."

"Like burying two men under the mud of a cattle field?" Pops asked. He wasn't accusing, merely trying to understand.

"Exactly. And clearly what we are looking at here is, in the eyes of some madman, an acceptable way to scare us into running away and leaving our supplies behind."

Pops was completely lost in incomprehension. "So what is the acceptable way of making sure that none of us end up hanging from a gate like this?"

Ellen turned and looked Pops in the eye. "After all you've seen, you really have to ask that?"

Pops was silent for a moment. He released a deep breath, his words quietly mingling with the last of it. "You kill them." There was a resolve in his voice, a final indicator of acceptance. He had surrendered.

She nodded, then turned the vehicle in a tight arc and began driving slowly back up the drive.

"Mom?"

Ellen thumbed the transmit button on her walkie. "Yes, Pete?"

"What was that?"

She wondered if she should continue sheltering him and lie about what she found at the gate. Should she tell him the truth so he could be better prepared for whatever animal stalked their community? After a moment, she made up her mind.

"It was Mr. and Mrs. Sullivan, honey. They're dead. Someone killed them."

Pete didn't reply for a long time. "There's something else, Mom… There's a big fire. I can see a lot of black smoke. I think it might be a house."

*

Ellen and Pops sat in her vehicle near the house, watching the road. She used the radio that morning and put out a call on the channel that Henry had mentioned to her previously, the one he used on his farm. Going on a hunch, she assumed that his son David would monitor the same channel so that he could keep a check on his parents. She called for David every fifteen minutes for nearly two hours before he caught the transmission and answered her. She told him who she was. Then she told him that his parents were dead. There was no way to sugarcoat such a piece of information. Regardless of how she described it to him, nothing would be able to prepare the young man for the state that he was about to find his parents in. She had thought about taking them down and maybe wrapping the bodies in a tarp but she could not make herself touch them. It was too much.

The smell of smoke was reaching them now. The wind must have changed and brought it in their direction. Within the smell itself, she could detect burning plastic. It definitely smelled like a house fire. She wondered whose home it was and how the fire started. Certainly with more people cooking over fires there was the potential for one to get out of control. She hoped that's what had caused it anyway.

After a short wait in the Suburban, Ellen saw David driving along the main road toward their gate. She started the engine and drove down the long gravel driveway, weaving around the steel beams. David was leaning against a gatepost, sobbing uncontrollably by the time they got there.

"You keep an eye out," Ellen warned Pops. "They may be watching us. Scan everywhere. If you see anyone, shoot at them."

Ellen got out of the vehicle and approached David. She put her arm over the gate and patted his shoulder. "I'm sorry." It was all she knew to say.

"What kind of monster would do this?" he sobbed.

"I don't know. Some kind of sick bastard, I guess."

David looked up at her, his face red, eyes welling. "You know they turned the jails out, don't you?"

Ellen shook her head. "What do you mean?"

He wiped his face with his sleeve and pushed back from the post. He stood upright then, fighting to regain control of his emotions, fighting to speak. "They couldn't feed the prisoners, so they let most of them go."

"How could they do that?" Ellen asked in shock.

"They didn't know what else to do with them. They didn't think it was humane to let them starve to death in their cells."

"So a monster from our jail or someone else's has possibly passed through here," Ellen surmised.

David looked around the hillside. "Or has moved into the neighborhood."

Ellen didn't know how to respond to this piece of information. She couldn't imagine simply letting prisoners go. "And besides whoever did this, there's now murderers, rapists, pedophiles, and thieves roaming the countryside too?"

David nodded.

"And they all know they won't be locked up now no matter what they do?"

"Probably."

Ellen was aghast. "You know, when criminals realize that there's no consequences, decent people won't have a chance."

David's eyes locked on her, red and wounded. "We don't have a chance in hell anyway. If you don't have food, you'll be dead in a few months. If you do have food, you'll be killed for it and dead in a few months just the same. This might as well be the end of the world."

Ellen had been scared before, but had always maintained the illusion that there was a framework of law and order behind her, imagining that social order would return in no time. With that illusion gone, leaving only images of anarchy and chaos, she was suddenly and completely terrified.

"Let's get these bodies loaded. I don't think we're safe standing in the open."

After they'd completed the grim work of removing the fragrant corpses, wrapping them, and loading the bodies into David's truck, Ellen stood and eyed the hillside, scanning for threats. "Where are you going from here?"

"I'm going to bury my mom and dad," he replied, the words obviously sour in his mouth.

"Where?"

"At their home. They always said they wanted to be buried there."

Ellen put her hand on his arm. "I don't think that's a good idea. Whoever did this may be at your parents' house. That may be why this happened."

David brushed by Ellen and climbed into the cab of his truck. "I hope to hell they are."

CHAPTER 9

FEMA Camp: Near Natural Bridge, Virginia

Although Alice had no standard by which to judge, her position as a volunteer at the FEMA camp had given her the opportunity to hear more news and information than most people in America had access to under current conditions. For most of the country, their direct experience of government was at seventeenth century levels. Washington, D.C. had become a remote place that no longer spoke directly to them, did nothing for them, and whose actions seemed wholly to have little effect upon them. This lack of information was probably for the best anyway. If there had been widespread access to television and the internet, average folks would be glued to it, dutifully absorbing the empty promises of rescue and a speedy recovery. Without those assurances, folks were probably quicker to realize the truth – that they were on their own and that their survival was in their own hands.

The National Guardsmen who provided security at the camp were receiving messages through their command structure. They had working radios and were receiving orders from somebody somewhere. Although the officers at the camp did not question it, the orders they received were generally vague and purposeless. It was as if the military structure knew that if they didn't issue orders and keep their men busy they would pack up and go home. Much of the busy work they were ordered to do was to gather intelligence.

As part of this order to gather both electronic and local intelligence, the soldiers working in the radio tent were constantly listening to HAM radio, CB radio, and any other frequencies from which they could garner some level of information. While any intelligence picked up through this avenue was classified and maintained on a strict need-to-know basis, the camp was small enough, and the circumstances unusual enough, that information was making its way out to the campers.

In a wartime scenario, there was no doubt that the men working the radios would try harder to make sure information was not leaked, especially to civilians. In this case, however, the current circumstance was something more akin to a disaster response than a military operation. Soldiers with information felt that they were doing the right thing by sharing this information. People wanted to know about the level of risk outside of this camp. How was the food supply? Were roads open? Was there a lot of violence? Some soldiers felt that part of disaster relief was calming the population and that this was best achieved by sharing what you knew.

Even though some information was held closer and never reached the level of the individual campers, very little got by the volunteers. They talked as most coworkers do when working side-by-side all day. Additionally, they had the benefit of being seen by the FEMA folks, and even the National Guard troops, as part of their team. Both the FEMA and the military folks talked a little more freely than they perhaps should have in front of the volunteers and, for that reason, those willing to contribute their time as volunteers received the benefit of some of the most accurate information on current events available.

Through these sources, Alice was shocked to find that the prognosis for the repair of the national electrical system was rather poor. It was not that it wasn't repairable, but that it could take one to two years to return power to the county. For starters, many of the electrical components that had been destroyed were not available in the United States. Some were made in South Korea, others in Germany. The components would have to be made to order, then shipped to the U.S., then installed. This was nowhere near as easy as it sounded. There were thousands of logistical nightmares along the way.

With a few exceptions, the networks for cellular and satellite communications were not damaged in any fashion that made repairs impossible. In general, it appeared that the terrorists had not targeted the cellular network directly. However, towers and antennas required power. Many had backup generator systems for power outages but those most commonly relied on propane. As the propane tanks ran out, the generators went silent and the towers died. Until those towers had their power restored, they would not come back to life and cell phones would be little more than paperweights.

It was from conversations with the FEMA folks that Alice learned even more about the poor prognosis for how society would fare without power. She learned that the government and the military had done extensive studies on this. Such reports were the realm of people like Jim – doom mongers, paranoids, and survival nuts. Even as she thought about her co-worker, she realized that now she was the one who looked like a fool. She was the unprepared one, stuck about two hundred miles from home with no idea how she would get back to her son and husband.

The FEMA folks she had spoken with over the course of the last few days had told her that there had been some limited research by the government into management of grid down scenarios. Much of the research was done in order to explore how the U.S. might weather an EMP, or Electro Magnetic Pulse. An EMP could occur as the result of a nuclear detonation high in the atmosphere, which would then fry most modern electronics with sensitive micro-circuitry. Though there were methods of hardening electronics to resist an EMP, the electrical grid was not hardened and would be unable to withstand such an attack. There was also the possibility that an EMP would occur as the result of a coronal mass ejection from the sun. The government had even formed a commission to explore this EMP risk and produce a report. Everyone felt certain that a damaging EMP would occur at some time from a solar flare, but nothing had been done to harden the grid against it.

While this was not an EMP attack as far as Alice knew, much of the research was still relevant. Particularly interesting was the projection that an eighteen month long grid-down scenario, which this could very likely turn into, had a minimum projected death rate of somewhere around sixty percent. If one accepted the projections of the Naval War College, then you were instead looking at a death rate of somewhere around ninety percent, primarily from starvation, disease, and social unrest. Alice tried to image nine out of every ten people she knew dying. By those numbers, the six hundred employees she managed in her job would be reduced to a work force of merely sixty people. The idea was staggering.

This was clearly not an extinction-level event. She knew from the rumor mill that there were still pockets of civilization in the country that had power. Hydroelectric dams were still producing power. The problem was that the weak points of interconnectivity, where the various smaller power grids of the country tied together to make a larger, unified grid were damaged. Those were the components that could not be replaced very easily. How long would those remaining hydro plants keep working as the fuel shortage kept stores from restocking their shelves and people began

ASHES OF THE UNSPEAKABLE

to starve? How much of a priority would electricity be then? Very little, Alice imagined. People would simply quit going to work, including those power company employees.

Troubling, too, was the rumor that there were nuclear disasters occurring in the western part of the U.S. The power had gone down so quickly that there was very little news available about what they experiencing out there. With their functioning communication network, the military folks had some knowledge of this. It was one of the pieces of information that they did not voluntarily share, but, as they often had conversations in the presence of volunteers, this information had been overheard. Other relevant bits slipped through and the volunteers were able to piece these bits together to form a vague but alarming picture.

Apparently the terrorists had conducted mortar attacks on several nuclear power plants in the west. Some of these plants were able to do controlled shutdowns, giving folks living in the danger zone around them time to evacuate. Others experienced unmanageable meltdowns that resulted in discharges of radioactive material into the atmosphere. With no communication, officials were not able to get out proper warnings. There were folks in the path of nuclear fallout who had no idea it was coming. While this was alarming to folks in the know at the eastern FEMA camps, they hoped they were far enough away that the risk of significant radiation exposure was minimal.

The by-product of this expanding picture of the scale of the post-attack disaster was that it was now clear that there were not enough resources to rescue everyone. FEMA officials in Washington were probably scrambled into bunkers by now with their families to wait this out. Alice began to understand more about how this disaster response was playing out, and she could even imagine a scenario where the folks in Washington might decide that they should no longer waste food and medicine on folks who would likely be part of the ninety percent who died anyway. They could easily say that the best use of those resources would be to preserve them for the post-disaster recovery after this whole event had run its course.

With such a grim scenario before her, Alice became even more intent on finding out when and if she would be able to make her way home. She quickly discovered that this information was as scarce as the intelligence that the military communication folks were bringing in. Could it be that military men would so easily share the allegedly confidential information about threats, disease, and the dire state of a country but somehow manage to more closely guard the relatively benign information about when they would begin shipping out campers? She didn't think so. That left only one possibility in her mind.

There *was* no plan for getting anyone home.

Someone had come up with this idea of engaging the military in rescuing stranded travelers on the pretense of getting them home. It was inescapably obvious to her now that the entire ruse was to keep the military occupied so the troops wouldn't desert and at the same time give folks hope that they had a future. Perhaps the troops did have a future. Perhaps they would be called into action on some other mission, abandoning the campers here to their own resources. She didn't know and apparently no one else did either. She didn't think it was any grand conspiracy on the part of the government, and instead concluded that they would be left here to die out of sheer ineptitude, selfishness, and disinterest on the part of those in power.

If she wanted to live, she would have to get out of there as quickly as possible.

*

While Alice had volunteered for camp duties to keep her mind occupied, Rebecca had only found peace in keeping her body physically exhausted. She ran laps obsessively around the camp, exerting herself until she collapsed into her cot at night. Alice thought she seemed like a caged dog pacing the perimeter of her fencing. When Alice got off her volunteer shift for the evening, she went in search of Rebecca. As usual, she found Rebecca running her laps. Alice flagged her down.

"We have to get out of here."

Rebecca was breathing hard. "Walk with me. I've got to warm down gradually. Don't want to cramp."

Alice fell in stride beside her and they walked, keeping a good distance from any other campers. "God forbid that you get a leg cramp while people around the country are dropping like flies."

"What do you mean we have to get out of here? I thought the general idea *was* to get out of here. We're waiting on our turn, right? Waiting for our bus ticket?"

Alice took a look behind her to make sure no one was close by. "I don't think our turn is coming. Matter of fact, I don't think anyone's turn is coming. The word is that no one has been delivered home from *any* FEMA camps."

Rebecca continued walking at a fast pace, swinging her arms in a goofy, exaggerated speed-walking movement. "I thought they were in the collection phase now and would move on to the delivery phase next. That's what you said before, right? They're going to pick everyone up first and then map out delivery routes based on where people need to go. It makes complete sense."

"That's what I was told initially," Alice said. "Now I'm concerned that there isn't going to be any delivery phase."

Rebecca stopped, bent over, and stretched the back of her legs. When she straightened back up, she started walking quickly again. "Surely you don't think we're going to be prisoners here? You're sounding like Jim. You think they're going to eat us too? You starting to buy into all this FEMA conspiracy bullshit?"

Alice was beginning to get short of breath. She was not used to walking at this pace. She reached out and grabbed Rebecca's arm to slow her down. "I don't think it's anything that sinister. I don't think that anyone cares what happens here. The government has bigger problems. I'm afraid we're going to wake up one day and the army is going to pull out of here for another assignment and we're going to be left behind. What happens then?"

Rebecca turned this over in her head. Even though she thought Alice might be overreacting, that thought was concerning. She was beginning to realize for herself, though, that everyone she'd recently accused of overreacting had turned out to be right in the end. She thought about being abandoned to this camp and didn't like what she saw: rioting, people killing each other over food, rape. It was not a pretty picture.

"I can't believe I'm saying this, Rebecca. I always thought Jim was crazy, but I realize now that I couldn't let myself think like him. I couldn't accept that he might have been right. I still don't know that he's right, but I'm now more afraid of staying at this place than of leaving."

Rebecca stood there, sweat rolling down her face, staring at Alice. She raised her shirttail and wiped her face. "Any idea how we get out of here without drawing any attention?"

"Maybe," Alice said. "I don't have it all worked out yet. If I wake you up tonight be ready to go. You can't take your suitcase, but stuff some extra clothes and anything else you can't live without in your purse. We'll have to travel light. Grab any food or snacks you can get ahold of and maybe a few water bottles. I have a plan to maybe get some more."

"Are we going to walk?" Rebecca said, a note of concern in her voice.

"For someone who has been running every damn day since you've been here, you seem awfully concerned about having to walk home," Alice said in frustration. "If you can run for eight hours a day, then surely you can walk for that many."

Rebecca looked at Alice very seriously. "It's not the walking that worries me. I'm worried what we might walk into. I've felt safe since we've been at this camp. Once we leave that gate, that sense of safety is gone."

*

Over the past few days working the front desk, Alice had learned that there was a method to the collection trips. The soldiers assigned to communications spoke with law enforcement officers throughout the region to get intelligence on problem areas where a lot of travelers were congregated. On their way to these destinations, soldiers would stop at common gathering points along the way such as rest areas, travel plazas, truck stops, and roadside attractions. These bus trips were not considered to be secret and were a common topic of conversations. Soldiers would joke with FEMA staff about which part of scenic Virginia were they going to get to see today. Would it be the Blue Ridge Parkway, the Crooked Road, or the Wine Country?

After speaking with Rebecca, Alice knew that she had to find out tomorrow's bus destination. The only way she could find that out without being obvious was to spend some time with her coworkers that night and hope that someone said something. If no one mentioned it, she would have to find some other way to draw that information out. Although it was not known to the campers, there was a nightly staff meeting held in one of the smaller buildings on the facility. In fact, it was not really a staff meeting at all, but a social gathering for FEMA staff, the military personnel, and the volunteers. It served the same function that the Officer's Club might serve in a war zone, a place to decompress and blow off some steam. Because the supply of alcohol and snacks was limited, this nightly event couldn't be opened up to the general population of the camp. To maintain the impression that it was an official function, it was dubbed the Nightly Staff Meeting.

Alice had not attended any of the so-called staff meetings up to this point, although she knew of their existence. She'd been invited but felt bad about the thought of socializing and drinking under the current circumstances. Some people used alcohol to quell their pain. Others, like her, found that it only accentuated her depression if she was already feeling down. She knew that the slightest bit of alcohol would probably make her cry herself to sleep. Tonight would not be about socializing; it was a mission. The first step in her new mission home.

Under that guise, Alice attended the staff meeting, drawing the line at two ice-cold Rolling Rock beers. While enjoying those beers, she turned on her social charms and inserted herself into conversation after conversation until she found the one she needed to be part of. Two soldiers and two male FEMA staff were having an in-depth conversation in one corner of the room. Because there was no laughing, she correctly assumed it to be a conversation of a more serious nature. She loosened her gait, prepared to act a little more intoxicated than she was, and strolled into the group. This was a group of men that would not turn away the company of a woman. They all smiled at her, one man even winked, and they continued their conversation.

She soaked it up.

In less than ten minutes she knew that the morning run was going to be traveling down Route 460. While she had hoped that there might be a chance that the buses were running south on Interstate 81, ideally in the direction of Abingdon, that was not the case. From the men's conversation, she leaned that the camp at Wytheville, established at the juncture of I-81 and I-77, was taking care of anything on the interstate further south. There would be no hope of going that far on a bus from her camp. However, Route 460 passed within a mere five miles of her office and twenty-five miles of her home.

Tomorrow's buses were headed for the stretch of Route 460 between Pembroke and Pearisburg, Virginia to pick up stranded campers who were staying along the New River. It was a popular travel destination for fishermen, kayakers, and bicyclists riding the New River Trail. Now all those folks were stuck and causing trouble for local residents as they tried to steal to survive. In a car, Pearisburg was maybe two hours from her home. She had no idea how long it would take on foot, nor how best to tackle the trip. Was it better to travel the smooth, level surface of the road, or was Jim correct in his theory that travelling public roads on foot was a death sentence?

When Alice returned to her cot that night, she shook Rebecca awake. "We need to get on the morning buses. They're going to Route 460. That could get us home."

"I found someone wanting to go with us," Rebecca blurted out.

Alice was taken aback. She stared at Rebecca for a moment. "I told you not to tell anyone."

Rebecca shrugged. "It just kind of came up. This guy and I were talking about where we were from and I told him that you and I were thinking about heading out."

Alice rested her forehead in her hand. She shook her head in disbelief. "What if he told someone? Do you know what could happen to us for trying to break the rules?"

Rebecca smiled. "He wouldn't do that. I think he likes me. I'm pretty sure of it. Besides, I thought we'd be safer with a guy around."

This angered Alice, the thought that they needed a man to take care of them. "I am tougher than you think. I may work in an office, but I can take care of myself. I grew up on a farm and I'm pretty damn tough."

Rebecca quickly dismissed this. "You're not a big, scary dude. Either way, I've invited him already. Can he go or not? I think we should take him."

"Then he's your responsibility," Alice said. "You pick up the stray puppy and he's your problem, not mine. You got it?"

Rebecca frowned, obviously angry at being talked to like a child. Alice didn't care. As far as she was concerned, she'd not seen any adult behavior out of Rebecca since this whole crisis had occurred. To be such an educated, accomplished professional, it appeared to Alice that she really didn't have that much common sense.

*

The caravan of three diesel buses departed camp in the morning darkness, with Alice, Rebecca, and a man named Boyd stowed away in the luggage compartment. Alice knew nothing about Boyd other than his name. He was slightly stocky, and was powerfully built. He carried a small backpack with him and looked like a student in his jeans and black t-shirt. Alice had thought on the matter overnight and conceded that maybe having a strong, physically intimidating guy along with them might not be such a bad thing after all, even if she was mad at Rebecca for not keeping her mouth shut. To her, it was simply further evidence that Rebecca was not someone who could be depended on.

The luggage compartment was on the underbelly of the bus and was accessed from doors along each side. These compartments were never checked when leaving the camp because it was assumed that no one would want to flee the safety and provisions provided by FEMA at the camp. At the same time, any official request on Alice's part to be allowed to ride on the bus would have most certainly been denied. She'd seen others attempt this. Though they weren't prisoners, FEMA would not assist them in leaving. You could walk out the gate if she chose, but would not be given a ride out. Her only way out on a bus was as a stowaway.

She was not sure if the compartment was safe from the carbon monoxide in the bus exhaust, which worried her a little bit. Her plan, if they began feeling sleepy, was to crack the compartment door slightly and allow fresh air to flow in. She also wasn't sure how they were going to escape the buses undetected when they arrived at their destination. They couldn't just pop out while the bus was parked in a crowd of people, could they? People would notice. She would have figure that detail out on the fly.

The doors swung upward on hydraulic lifts when opened, and Alice thought there might be emergency latches on the inside of the door that would allow them to open them if they shut completely, but they were afraid to take chances on this so they held each door slightly open as the bus drove away. Each woman was wedged in tight along the sides of the compartment. There was not much headroom. The taller of the two, Rebecca hit her head several times as they jostled out of the facility parking lot.

Boyd was in the middle and Alice had to lean around him to talk to Rebecca. They'd not had much time to discuss their plan. She could feel

Boyd breathing on her in the dark, not making any effort to give her room. It felt intentional and intrusive.

"From the map, it looks like it may be two hours or so to Pembroke, depending on what they run into on the drive. We'll need to get out of this compartment wherever they stop first. We can't afford for them to find us as they're loading people's luggage. Things probably wouldn't go well for us back at the camp if we got sent back."

"How do we know when to get out?" Rebecca asked.

"We'll have to be prepared. When they start slowing down, we'll get ready. Most of these campgrounds are on gravel roads. If they slow down and get off the highway, we can listen for gravel. When we hear it, then we need to be ready to go."

"How exactly?"

"We might have to jump."

Rebecca didn't immediately respond. Alice could almost hear her thoughts – her doubt. "Jump?" she said after a long moment.

"Yes, jump. How did you think we'd get out of here?"

"Okay, Alice. I guess we jump."

Alice became angry at the sarcasm. She was trying to save Rebecca's life, wasn't she? "You might not have to jump. I may just push you out."

Rebecca didn't say anything else for a long time.

CHAPTER 10

Mount Rogers National Recreation Area
Virginia

Jim and his crew made slow progress walking through the night. There was not enough moonlight to be useful and with only one night vision device between them, they couldn't move very fast. After about an hour, they stopped to rest. Except for the usual forest sounds, the woods around them were quiet.

"Maybe we can use flashlights now?" Randi asked hopefully.

"I think we might be able to, as long as we hold them at our side and shield the lenses," Jim said. "I've already been targeted once tonight. I don't want to repeat that mistake."

Once they got back on the trail, the lights helped tremendously. They made better time, taking long strides and stepping more confidently. They walked in their individual cones of light for the next two hours. Around the time that the sky began to lighten, they started looking for places to hole up for the day. While much of their earlier walking had been in deep forest, the trail now cut its way through the high meadows and balds atop Mount Rogers. These areas were kept eaten down by longhorn cattle that grazed here. They had passed a lot of those cattle in the last half mile and as the sun began to rise, they could see hundreds scattered through the dewy meadows.

Gary stopped in his tracks and stuck his arm out to halt them. "I see a tent."

Jim could see it too. It was a large white outfitter tent, not the kind used by campers and backpackers, but the roomier and sturdier type of tent that a hunting guide may set up at an elk camp out west. It was the kind of tent you set up when you planned to stay a while.

"You think it belongs to the guys that attacked us?" Randi asked.

"I don't know," Jim said. "Do you see a sentry?"

Randi frowned at Jim. "Like a *guard*?"

"Yes, a guard," he confirmed. "A lookout."

"Fucking tactical bullshit," she said irritably. "If it's a damned guard,

105

call it a guard."

"I can't see anything," Gary said. "How about you guys wait here and let me take a look?"

Gary slipped his pack straps off his shoulders and lowered the pack to the ground. He drew his Glock, held it in a ready position, and crept toward the camp. Randi and Jim stood in silence, weapons in hand, eyes glued to Gary's movement.

After a moment, Gary paused to look at something, then spun quickly back in their direction. Jim's throat tightened in panic, thinking Gary had been discovered and that a gunfight was about to ensue. Jim crouched and raised his weapon, waiting for a target to present itself, though instead of running, Gary leaned over and sprayed vomit into the weeds. He started to raise back up, glancing behind him to check the scene again, only to turn and spew once more.

"Let's go," Jim said. "Carefully. Keep your eyes moving."

Weapons at the ready, Randi and Jim advanced toward Gary. He was about seventy-five feet away and as they closed the distance they could smell the possible source of his distress. Something was dead. Jim prayed it was only a cow.

Please let it be a cow!

It wasn't.

They could see four bodies lying together in front of the tent, a man and what looked like three children. Three sons, judging by the clothing. They all had gunshot wounds to the face and head that had obviously been inflicted some days ago judging by the smell, the bloating, and the masses of flies.

Acid rose in the back of Jim's throat. He turned from the scene and took a deep breath, trying to choke down his sickness, only managing to suck in more of the smell. When he tasted the smell of death on his tongue he could not stop the convulsion that rose in his stomach. They were vulnerable in this situation, with he and Gary both in distress. Puking men couldn't shoot. "Randi, keep an eye…" he croaked.

He threw up at his feet, trying to speak between the streams that poured from him. After a long moment, the waves of powerful nausea passed and he was able to straighten his body. His eyes were watering and he wiped his mouth on his sleeve. He scanned the scene again, looking for clues as to who might have done this. He intentionally did not look at the bodies again. He could not.

Randi came from behind the tent. "There's a woman back there."

"A woman?" Jim said, still struggling.

"A woman's body, I should have said. Naked. Beaten to death. Raped by the look of things. A wedding ring on her finger," Randi said flatly. "Probably the mother of these dead children. Whichever way this played out would have been horrible. Did she see them die or did they watch her die?"

For the first time since this experience began, Jim was utterly devoid of hope. Three of the bodies were children around the age of his own children. He could imagine the way these kids talked, what they liked to watch on TV, and the kind of things they liked to eat. These kids had died *with* their father here to protect them. He, on the other hand was not home to protect his own kids. Would he walk all the way home just to find a scene like *this* in his own yard? He could not bear the thought.

Gary had finally regained control of his stomach and joined the others. They looked around, finding it clear that the camp had been raided, everything of value taken.

"They probably died for food," Randi said. "That breaks my heart to pieces."

"If I was not so worried about my own family," Gary said, "I would track down the people who did this just on principle. I would make them hurt in a way that would make God turn his back."

What did one say to something like that? They stood for a few minutes in silence.

"Can we cover them?" Randi asked, breaking the silence.

Whatever the family had been using for sleeping – blankets or sleeping bags – had been stolen. In the end, Gary and Jim took down their tent and covered the bodies with it. It was difficult on all levels, but they moved the woman's body alongside her children. They weighted the tent down with some rocks to keep it from blowing away.

Randi stood and stared at the tent, the outline of the dead family. "I wish we could have buried them right."

"We didn't have the tools," Jim replied. "Not sure we could have dug a hole in this rocky ground either."

"I know. I can still wish."

Jim looked at her. "You doing okay?"

She nodded.

"You handled this better than we did."

"I said at your friend Lloyd's place that I'd not shed another tear over anything we see on this trip."

Jim could see in her eyes that she meant every word of it. No one seemed ready to take the first step away from the scene. "Look, I know we're all tired, but if we can turn this rage into fuel we might be able to burn up a few more miles," Jim finally said.

"Let's do it," Gary said.

"Randi? You up for it?"

She nodded. "Yeah. I couldn't sleep."

In a grim, silent procession they rejoined the Appalachian Trail and descended from the high country into the Fairwood Valley. People assume that going downhill is easier than going uphill, but it's usually the opposite. With a heavy pack on your back, the wear and tear that your joints suffer while descending a trail is brutal. The front and back of your legs become sore and your feet ache. The stabilizing muscles of the knee and ankle, muscles you ignore most of the time, began to weaken and fail. Your legs become wobbly and less dependable. In the uneven terrain of Mount Rogers, this descent after a sleepless night, after the scene they'd just witnessed, was one of the low-points of the trip so far. No one talked. They staggered, stumbled, and stewed in their own sour thoughts.

Despite their current state, they covered a good bit of ground that morning. The fact that they were getting in better walking shape combined with their frustration made for a gain of seven additional miles after they left the murder scene that morning. By noon, however, they couldn't go any further. One of the benefits of traveling at night and sleeping during the day was that they didn't have to bother with shelter for sleeping since the weather was decent. When they all agreed that they could take no more walking without a break, they left the trail and found a sheltered spot that could not easily be seen by anyone else that might be using the trail.

Everyone was too tired to eat but Jim convinced them to eat something quick and easy. He assured them that they would sleep better with full stomachs. The food could digest and fuel them more efficiently if they ate it at rest rather than on the run. Although they did eat, Jim took no pleasure in it. All he could taste was the rotten death smell he'd inhaled earlier. He knew that his clothes would most likely smell that way for a few days. He decided that he would burn them when he reached home. He would strike a match to them and hope that these memories would burn away, as well.

There was thick moss on the ground and they spread their dingy hotel blankets over it. Jim propped his pack up and laid his head on it. He closed his eyes and the warmth of the sun on his face washed all his thoughts away. He started to say something to Gary about whether they should have a watch in place, but he was asleep before the words came.

*

Jim awoke later to a feeling of panic and exposure. He hated waking up like that, and it happened more often than not anymore. He sat up quickly, his hand falling to his Beretta, but saw nothing around him to be concerned about. He tried to calm his rapid breathing. He knew that waking up in such a panic was the result of his mind trying to process all of the crazy experiences they'd had. It was a generalized anxiety that could not be escaped, even in sleep. Randi and Gary were still out cold. He checked his watch and saw that it was nearly 5 p.m. He was ravenous and decided he'd rather fuel up with a good meal than sleep longer. He was still tired, but had accepted that he would probably be tired for a very long time.

Digging into his pack, he thought fondly of Lloyd's camping groceries that they'd eaten on their way through. A rage rekindled itself at the thought of the men who'd attacked them at the corral and how they had probably enjoyed all of the food still remaining in the boxes and coolers. The fresh meat, the buns, and even the greasy potato chips. What he found in his pack was dehydrated beans, rice, a few expired flavoring packets, some ramen noodles, and some beef jerky. Not much to work with.

He fired up his canister stove and started some water heating. Jim had only brought two canisters of fuel, as had Gary. They were each down to a single canister now. He expected that any day they'd run out of fuel and be forced to cook over a fire. Jim worried about that. Not only did it increase the time required to prepare a meal, but the smell of a burning fire carried for long distances. It was like sending out a beacon that informed people of your presence.

When the water started boiling, he dumped in the jerky, an expired packet of beef-flavored broth powder, and the noodles. In about fifteen minutes, it actually began to smell like something a person might eat. In fact, the smell brought Randi and Gary around from their sleep. When the meal cooled enough to eat, Jim put some of it in Gary's cooking pot, some for Randi in a spare cup, and ate his portion directly from his own cooking pot.

"Not bad," Randi said.

"Being half-starved helps," Jim said.

"I appreciate you making this," Gary said. "I was in such a stupor of hunger and exhaustion that I couldn't even think anymore. I could have laid there and died."

"I know," Jim said. "It took a lot of effort to move."

"Are we there yet?" Randi asked.

Jim smiled at her halfhearted attempt at a joke. "I'll have to take a closer look at the map to be sure," he said. "The good news is that, going by memory, I'd say that we're about a day or two from crossing the interstate, then about another day to Burke's Garden."

"I said I was done crying," Randi said, "though I might cry when we cross the Tazewell County line. I know it's not quite home, but I was afraid we'd never get this close."

Gary scraped the last noodle from his pot and dropped the spork in with a rattle. "I'm ready to take on the world now," he said. "How far did you say to Interstate 81?"

"Maybe twenty-two miles," Jim said. "Not one hundred percent sure without looking at the map. I'll fire up the GPS when we start walking and get a better estimate."

"Let's get out of here. We can wash these pots when we stop to fill water bottles. Until then, let's burn some miles."

"Now you're starting to talk like a backpacker," Jim said.

He stuffed his blanket and cooking gear into his pack, noticing the outline of his iPhone in the outside pocket. He took it out and powered it on. When it completed the long boot sequence, he saw that there was still no service. He didn't know what he was expecting, and still it was a blow every time he saw the lack of signal. It merely served as a reminder to keep going. To get himself home.

CHAPTER 11

The Cave
Russell County, Virginia

From Pete's lookout post above the cave, Ellen tried repeatedly to raise David Sullivan on the radio. Every fifteen minutes she would walk up where she had better reception and repeat her message, like she had when she tried to reach him the first time. She tried all day and never received a response.

"This worries me, Pete," she said.

He was lying prone beside her, scanning the countryside with a spotting scope. He was dressed in camouflage and was wearing a head net that broke up his profile. He'd been putting some effort into making his observation post less noticeable. It now blended so easily into the landscape that it took her a moment to spot when she was looking for it from a distance. Had she not known that it was there, she'd never have located it. When she was making her daily trip to check on their house, she would turn and try to find it. She knew Pete was there with his eyes glued to her, watching for any signs of danger.

He raised up and looked at her. "Maybe we should go to Henry's farm and see if we can see anything."

Ellen shook her head. "That would not be safe. We know that whoever killed Henry is obviously crazy. I do *not* want to be running into them."

"It's not really safe staying here. We don't know what's going on out there in our community," Pete said. "If we knew how many people we were dealing with, then we might have a better idea of what kind of defenses we need."

Ellen mulled this over. When he spoke, she noticed that his voice was changing too. He was growing up. She couldn't even think about that.

"Any idea how we could do it?" she asked. "I don't like the idea of just driving up there. It would be too easy for them to ambush and then kill us. If we were dead, what would happen to Ariel, Nana, and Pops? You always have to remember that when making a decision. You have to think of what happens to everyone else if you don't come home. I'm thinking that maybe David forgot that."

111

"We don't have to use the road. You can walk the fields and get there."

"Would we be exposed?"

"Not too badly," Pete said. "We could stay in the higher fields so that we have a better vantage point. We have to stay off the peak of the hill so we aren't silhouetted against the sky."

He does know what he's talking about, Ellen realized. "When do you think we should go?"

"Now," he replied. "It's the best time. It's late enough that we could walk there and get a good view in daylight, but the sun will be going down when we come back. The long shadows will hide us better."

Ellen stared at her son, surprised that he had such an understanding of this activity they were about to undertake. "Have you been reading those military field manuals that your dad buys?"

Pete shook his head. "No, Mom. I used to watch a lot of hunting and outdoor shows. Staying hidden from game is not much different than trying to stay hidden from people. The principles are the same."

*

In slightly less than two hours, they were approaching Henry's farm. It had taken a bit of time for them to go to the cave and gear up. Each of them had a day pack with a little food and water, a first aid kit, their spotting scope, a couple of headlamps, and some spare ammunition for their weapons. Ellen had tucked the night vision monocular in her pack in case they somehow failed to make it back before complete darkness, but she certainly hoped it didn't come to that.

Pete had convinced Ellen to wear his old camouflage hunting coveralls. Although they were a summer weight material, they were too big on her and she had to roll the cuffs up. She'd allowed Pete to bring the Ruger Mini-14 and he had six spare magazines for the weapon. She was carrying Jim's customized Remington 870 tactical shotgun, and had several boxes of spare shells for her weapon. They each carried a handgun in secure holsters and packed several spare mags for those.

Although there were a couple of other farms and homes between their home and Henry's, the pair kept their distance from any other homes. They wove through fields and over hills, avoiding everything that might bring them into contact with people. Most farm families had cattle dogs and the last thing she wanted was dogs giving away their position. They saw no one, smelled no cooking fires, heard no human sounds, and found no indication that anyone else was even living on their road at all.

She knew that couldn't be true. She and Pete were keeping quiet so that they could better hear anything they needed to be concerned about, leaving her to turn things over in her head. To worry. Maybe her neighbors were hiding out, like she and her family were. Others may have chosen to leave and go stay with family, finding strength in numbers and sharing their resources. It still concerned her. She assumed that Pete must be feeling that way as well. Where were the neighbors?

At the fence that marked the boundary of Henry's farm, Pete paused. "Hear that ticking sound?"

Ellen nodded. It was a faint, insectoid clicking.

"That top strand is electric fence and it's still hot."

"Without power?"

"Solar."

Ellen should have known that, but she'd never paid any attention to electric fences. "How can we get over?"

Pete pulled a multitool from a pocket on his vest and opened it to expose the wire cutters. He pulled a bandana from his pocket and wrapped it several times around his hand, then snipped the wire. The wire sang as it retracted violently under tension.

Pete stowed his pliers and shoved the bandana into a pants pocket. "It's not powerful enough to hurt you, but it's not fun getting shocked by it. You first."

Pete took her weapon, leaned it against the fence, and helped her climb. When she started climbing in the middle, centered between two posts, he redirected her to climb nearer to the post. "The fence moves less if you climb near a post. It's more stable."

The wire creaked some as she climbed, the tension adjusting as she added weight to it. When she was over the top, Pete handed the two long guns to her and climbed over the fence with smooth efficiency. She was impressed. She'd thought at any moment that she was going to lose her grip and fall off. She couldn't remember the last time she'd had to climb a fence.

"I can't tell where we are, Pete."

He pointed. "That little hill probably looks down on his house."

They climbed the hill, stepping firmly through the waist-deep broom sedge. Pete climbed faster than Ellen and was dropping to his knees in the weeds before she caught up with him. Gesturing at her to get down and crawl toward him, he continued moving forward until he had the vantage point that he wanted. When Ellen reached his side, he was already setting up the spotting scope on its miniature tripod and focusing on the scene below.

He adjusted knobs and panned the scope across the scene. "There's Henry's truck."

About that time a screen door flew open and several small children came streaming from the house, yelling and chasing each other around the yard.

"Who are those children?" Ellen whispered. She didn't expect Pete to know, but she couldn't stop herself from asking it aloud. "David doesn't have that many children."

Pete continued scanning. "There's the truck that David had at the house the other day. It's parked in the door of the hay shed."

Ellen scooted over. "Let me see."

Pete rolled to his side and let Ellen move into position. She moved the scope slightly. "Can it zoom more?"

"Twist the lens."

She did as he told her, zooming in on the bed of the truck. From their elevated position, she could see down into it, and spotted what looked like the bloated corpses of Henry and his wife still lying in the bed of the truck, just as she and David had placed them. It appeared that their blankets had blown free. She was panning from the truck bed back to the house when she noticed that there appeared to be too many limbs in the back of the truck for the two bodies she saw. She traced limbs through the tangle of blankets and bloated flesh and finally noticed the shirt David had been wearing when he came to retrieve his parents. She could not see any of his head, which was covered by a flap of blanket. She could see no movement, and it was apparent from the volume of blood soaking the back of the shirt that it was not likely he was alive.

"I found David," she said. "He's dead."

With a sigh, she panned back toward the house to try and see who these children might belong to. There was another clatter of the screen door and she moved her scope to focus on it. A wave of anxiety gripped her. It was a woman and a younger man. She recognized them.

It was the folks whom she had confronted at her gate. They were the people from the trailer park, the people who had come to her house looking for their missing men – the men that she and Pete had killed. She had exchanged heated words with this very woman. She had leveled a gun at this young man as he'd threatened to climb her gate and search her property for his father without her permission.

There was another bang of the screen door and a man exited the house. She had not seen this man before. He was scruffy, in a checked shirt that hung unbuttoned over dirty jeans. He was thin, with missing teeth and tattooed forearms. He was eating an apple and watching the children play. He looked like a meth addict.

The man went over and stood with the woman and her son. He placed his free arm around her and let it hang casually over her shoulder. She stiffened and stared at his unwelcome hand, though she made no effort to move free of it, nor did she say anything. Her son did not appear pleased with the gesture. He stared openly at the man, disapproval on his face. The man ignored him for a moment, then turned and coldly met the boy's challenging gaze. The boy stalked off through the yard.

This apparently angered the man. He stepped away from the woman, squared up as if he were on the mound, and then pitched his half-eaten apple as hard as he could. With surprising aim, the apple struck the young man in the back of the head. The boy spun, rubbed the back of his head, and stared at the man.

In the dead calm of a summer evening, the air still, the sun setting, the man's words carried through the yard and to the hilltop where Pete and Ellen lay watching.

"Grab a damn shovel and bury those bodies. I done told you once."

*

Now familiar with their path, Pete and Ellen walked with more certainty than they had when traveling to Henry's farm. Pete had assumed that their goal was to return back to the cave as quickly as possible.

Ellen stopped in her tracks. "You up for a detour?"

Pete shrugged. "I guess."

"Do you think we're close to the fire you saw?"

"Probably. If we climb this hill we might even be able to see it. Why?"

"I want to know whose house it was. We don't have to actually go look at it."

Pete slipped out of his pack and handed his rifle to Ellen. "Let me get up this hill and take a look. Then I'll know for sure."

He scurried up the hill, through hay that was overdue for a cutting. When he reached the top, he dropped to his knees and scanned the horizon. To the south, he could see a dwindling column of smoke, though a wooded hill stood between them and a clear line of sight. He headed back to his mom, reporting what he saw.

"Do you know an easy way there?" she asked.

"Probably. If we top this hill and go down the other side, there's a farm road. It goes by a pond, then weaves up around that hill. We could probably stay on that farm road and see whose house it is. We could find out for sure in about thirty minutes."

She handed him his pack and gun. "Let's do it."

Pete led his mother over the top of the hill and they quickly descended the steep slope into a small, isolated valley. The valley held a pond for watering cattle but otherwise contained nothing other than grassy pastures. A farm road bisected the valley and they followed it across the pasture to where it began to angle sharply upward. The road was used for hauling hay in and out of the pasture and was poorly maintained. It was more than adequate for a tractor or for foot traffic.

After fifteen minutes of steep climbing, they were both sweating and tired. The sun had already set and a general grayness was dropping over their valley. The road began to level out, taking a sharp turn to the left, then the valley opened up before them. The paved road was clearly visible, winding its way between homes and barns for as far as they could see in both directions. They could also see the home of one of their neighbors, the Kaisers, was now a heap of smoldering rubble.

Pete pulled his spotting scope out and quickly set it up. He lay prone and scanned carefully. "I don't see anyone. No people at all."

"If they'd been home when the fire started, they probably would have tried to get their belongings out," Ellen said. "Do you see any sign of personal items in the yard or anything like that?"

Pete looked. "No. The yard is clear. It looks like all their cars are still there."

"What about their barn? Any signs of life up there?"

Pete redirected the scope, adjusting the focus for the new distance. "No. Nothing."

Ellen couldn't put it all together. Or maybe she could, and didn't like where it was leading her. "It's getting dark. Let's get out of here."

CHAPTER 12

The Appalachian Trail
Smyth and Tazewell Counties

When Jim came to a sign on the trail indicating that they were near the Mount Rogers National Recreation Area Headquarters, he could not resist taking a quick look.

"You guys can stay here in the woods if you want, but they may have fresh water and bathrooms," he said. "We need to clean our dishes and refill our bottles anyway. It might be a good place to do that."

"Hurray for bathrooms," Randi said.

"Fine with me," Gary said. "Let's take a look."

They took the branch trail and entered the field between the forest and the headquarters building. Across the field, they could see that there were no cars at the headquarters. Under current conditions, Jim didn't really expect the place to be open but he hadn't expected it to be abandoned. There were no other backpackers that he could see. There were no staff being paid to stick around and guard the place. There were no stranded car campers. There was nobody.

They approached the place cautiously, walking down the trail, listening for any sounds, watching for any movement. As the amount of violence around them increased, so did their wariness. The next attacker could come from anywhere and could be anyone. Anyone, no matter how innocent they looked, could be waiting to kill them.

When they reached the building, Jim tried the front door to the welcome station, which was locked. He was not surprised that it was locked as much as he was surprised that no one had yet broken in. It was only a glass door and there were a lot of rocks laying around the place.

He walked around to the side of the building, where he knew from previous visits that the restrooms were located. He pulled the handle on the men's restroom door. It was unlocked and came open with a squeal. In this new world, opening a closed door did not always spell opportunity. It could spell death. Jim removed a light from his pack and shined it into the room.

Nothing.

He moved to the women's restroom and tried that door. It was unlocked. He held the door open with his body and shined his light around inside. There were no people, but the floor contained some empty food wrappers, empty water bottles, and some discarded clothing.

Randi and Gary were standing by another door. "They left the vending area unlocked," Randi said. "They obviously didn't know you were in the area."

Jim gave her a look. "Next time I'll keep my stolen candy bars and jerky to myself. You can eat shoe leather and grubs."

She laughed.

"As long as you're standing there, is there food in the machines?" Jim asked.

Randi winked at Gary. "I told you he wouldn't be able to stay out of here."

Gary shined his own flashlight into the room. The vending area was surrounded by glass walls and a full-glass door but not enough light penetrated the shaded interior to allow them to see into the vending machines without flashlights. "I see Oreos."

Jim walked inside, stood in front of the machine, and sized up his opponent. He drew his Gerber LMF knife and shattered the machine's Plexiglas window with the sharp steel pommel of the knife. He grabbed two packs of Oreos and left the room.

"You shouldn't have mentioned the Oreos."

*

They gorged themselves on vending machine loot, trying to throw calories at the insatiable voids their stomachs had become.

"It's getting late," Jim said. "We should probably find a place here to bed down for the night."

Randi had removed her socks and was rubbing her bare feet. "Fine with me. Everything from the neck down aches."

Jim placed his headlamp on his head and disappeared into the nearby men's bathroom. Gary fed Mike & Ike candy into his mouth at a steady pace, like he was stoking a coal furnace.

A crash from the bathroom got their attention. It sounded like a fight.

Gary stood, drew his Glock and approached the bathroom door. "Randi, pull this door open and stand back out of the way."

There was another series of crashes that shook the building. Randi got to the bathroom door, pulled it open wide, and held it while standing with her back against the wall of the building.

Gary played his light over the room. "Jim!" He stepped into the room, checked each corner, then ducked and ran the light beneath the stalls. No legs.

He went to each stall, kicked open the unlocked doors, and looked into each as the door clattered within the tight confines of the stall. "He's not in here!"

Randi poked her head around the corner. "He went in there. We both saw him."

"I know what we saw but he's not in here."

A hand from nowhere grabbing Randi's shoulder made her scream. This startled Gary, who appeared suddenly in the doorframe, gun at the ready. He found Jim laughing at Randi as she clutched her chest.

"You scared the fucking shit out of me," she said.

"How did you get out of there?" Gary asked, holstering his weapon. "There's no sign of anything and I didn't see another door."

"I went in through the ceiling, kicked through the firewall, and came down in the staff bathroom inside the building."

"*Inside* the locked part of the building?" Randi clarified.

Jim walked to where they had all been sitting and grabbed his pack. "Let's get in there and lock the door behind us. I think a night of sleeping behind a locked door would do us all a lot of good."

Once they were all in the building Jim locked the front door behind them. "We need to get out of sight of these windows in case other people show up."

They moved deeper into the building and found an employee lunchroom that had no windows. While Jim was sliding the folding plastic lunch table to the side, Randi began opening wall cabinets. "Oh. My. God."

"What's wrong?" Jim asked in alarm.

She turned slowly. The first thing he noticed was that she was grinning ear-to-ear. The second thing he noticed was that she held a jar of peanut butter in one hand and a can of Folger's coffee in the other. "The gods have smiled on us."

He gave a low whistle. "Shit. That's a good find."

She swung open another door. "There's more. All kinds of stuff." It was the same kind of stuff you find in a lot of office breakrooms —cans of soup, cans of tuna, crackers, hot chocolate, and all the other things people bring for lunch and don't eat for one reason or another.

"How about we make some coffee," Gary suggested. "Then we can do a thorough search of the building and see what else we can find."

Gary quickly whipped out his stove and filled a pot from their water bottles. He added a couple of scoops of coffee to the water and brought it to a boil. He then took a coffee filter from a pack in the cabinet and folded it into a funnel shape. When the coffee was boiling, he placed the cone filter in a Styrofoam cup and poured the coffee through it. Since the filter quickly lost shape when used in this manner, he had to make a new one for each of their cups, but within a few moments all three of them had a steaming coffee before them.

"There's even creamer and sugar," Randi said, her voice reverent. "I am so happy right now."

Gary picked up his full cup and took a sip, then closed his eyes. "I think I'll go ahead and start a second cup for each of us. The more we drink now, the less we'll have to carry."

"There's more water bottles in the bottom cabinet," Jim said. "That'll be plenty of water for what we need tonight."

Gary adjusted the flame on his stove. "I'm hitting on all cylinders now. I didn't even realize how much I missed coffee."

"I realized it. Every time I've missed a cigarette I also missed the cup of coffee I would have been having with it." Randi placed her empty cup beside Gary, ready for it to be refilled.

"Randi, if you're desperate enough, there's some of those big ashtrays outside of the bathrooms," Jim remarked. "There are probably some nice fragrant butts in there with a hit or two left on them."

Rather than frown, Randi considered the idea, then said, "I'm not that desperate…yet. But don't tempt me."

*

Although the building was primarily an informational center, there were a few offices and a storeroom in the building. They started at one end of the building and worked their way through. It was clear that the building had been locked since the very early stages of the disaster. There was no disarray, no indications of chaos or that anyone had closed up in a rush. Everything was in its place. It looked like people had closed down one evening with the full intention of re-opening the next day.

The offices yielded nothing of value or interest. They looked to be the kind of offices that different people used, depending on the day of the week. There were no personal photos, no half-empty cups of old coffee, and no food in the drawers. The storeroom was a different story. There were two backpacks hanging on hooks with Search & Rescue patches on the back. On a shelf beside them were a dozen handheld radios sitting in charging cradles.

Jim picked one up and turned a knob. "Dead."

Gary held out his hand. "Let me see one of those."

Jim tossed him one.

Gary opened the battery compartment. "We pull out this battery pack and it will operate off two AA batteries," he said. "Let's take one of these for each of us. Maybe one more as a spare."

"I didn't know you could switch out the batteries," Jim said.

"I told you several times over the years that you should learn more about radios, didn't I?"

Jim nodded, rolling his eyes at Randi as he did. There was a shelf of flashlights with spare batteries. There were some headlamps in the stack and Jim took one.

"Switch this out with the one you have, Randi. It's better."

He got some spare batteries and shoved them into the backpacks. He didn't bother exploring the backpacks yet. He would do that when they returned to the break room. There were some spare blankets and sleeping bags on another shelf, but they ignored those. There was a case of eight-ounce bottles of drinking water. Randi picked one up and carried it to the break room to refill their water bottles, probably envisioning a morning cup of coffee.

Jim unfolded the lid of a cardboard box. "Jackpot." The box was full of freeze-dried Mountain House meals.

"Ziti and Spinach in Alfredo Sauce," Gary remarked. "These must have been for search and rescue missions."

Nearly everything remaining in the room was clothing of some type. They found some raingear to replace what Randi had lost when they were attacked at the corral. There was a box labeled 'Lost and Found' that had some spare socks, a couple of shirts, and a cap with *North Face* written across the front. Jim tossed the box to Randi, who had just returned to the room, and she started going through it.

"You can have one of these packs for carrying your gear once we go through them," Jim said. "They're decent packs and will hold a lot."

"So you're going to go through *my* pack and steal all the good stuff first?"

Jim looked at her, unsure if she was joking or not. "No. I'm going to see what's in here and we'll share anything good. There's probably a lot of crap in there that you don't need to carry and we can get rid of it so you don't have to haul the extra weight around."

"So you're going to go through *my* pack and share *my* stuff? You're a communist aren't you?"

Jim gave up and drew back to toss the full pack at her.

She held her hands up. "I was only joking with you. It's fine. Really."

The only other item of interest was the display of maps they found in the information center. Jim already had a *Virginia Gazetteer* which was very detailed, but the map kiosk had a National Geographic map of the entire park. There were other maps of the local sections of the Appalachian Trail, the Jefferson National Forest, and the George Washington National Forest. Jim took these.

"I want both of you to stick these in your pack. If we get separated for any reason, these maps will save your life. I know we're close, but things can happen. You know where we are at and you know where you need to go. Sunrise and sunset will orient you if all else fails."

Jim made one more pass through the storage room while Randi and Gary sorted the gear in the packs. The two went to the break room and started sorting through the gear.

"Jim told me what you did back there with the light stick," Gary said. "He said you saved his life."

"I did what I had to," Randi said, not looking up from what she was doing. "It was the only weapon I had handy."

"It was still pretty hardcore," he said. "Are you doing okay with it?"

She looked up at him. "Remember, that's not the first person I've killed on this trip. Technically, I didn't even kill him, I only wounded him. Jim finished him off."

"Even so, it was still pretty brutal. I wanted to make sure you were okay with the whole thing."

"Thanks, Dad," Randi said sarcastically. "You worried about me?"

Gary shrugged. "Just want to make sure you're doing okay. I have daughters and I can't help but think of them being in that same situation."

"I'm fine, thanks for asking. I'm definitely too old to be one of your daughters. Anyway, I pretended that guy was my ex-husband. It was easy."

Gary laughed, but Randi didn't crack a smile. "I'm serious. That's exactly what I did."

"So, obviously marriage wasn't for you?"

"Definitely not."

Gary wasn't sure what else to say. He shifted uncomfortably.

Randi picked up a compass from the pile of gear that they had dumped from the Search and Rescue packs. She balanced it on her leg and watched to see which direction was north. "It wasn't the marriage particularly that didn't work out for me. It was the choice of husbands."

Gary picked up on her tone. "Sorry I mentioned it. Awkward topic. We can change the subject."

"No, it's okay. He was an asshole. A serious asshole. And we're not together anymore. He's yesterday's news."

"I feel like a jerk now," Gary said.

"*He* was a jerk. You're not so bad. You don't have to feel bad about it," Randi said. "I'm tough because I made it out of that marriage. There were times I thought it would turn out different. I was young and dumb and he was older, louder, and liked to drink. We fought a lot."

"Yelling fights or physical fights?"

Randi spun the dial on the compass. "Definitely physical fights. He was always threatening to kill me. The final straw was when my kids were seven and ten. I'd taken them to church one Sunday because I hoped that by taking them to church they wouldn't turn out like their daddy. When we got home, he was laid up on the porch completely shit-faced drunk and looking for a fight. I told the kids to go inside and change clothes before I started dinner. He asked my oldest daughter to come give him a hug. She wouldn't do it because she was scared. They knew by then that, if he was drunk, they didn't know who they were getting. He could be sweet or he could be a jerk."

"Did that piss him off?" Gary asked. "That she wouldn't come to him?"

"Oh yeah. He got up and slapped the fire out of her. Then he started telling me that I was wasting my time taking the kids to church because there wasn't any God. He started hollering and acting like an idiot, telling my daughter that he could beat her to death and God wouldn't come help. Then he decided he was going to slap her again and I completely lost it. I grabbed a stick of firewood from the stack on the porch and I started beating him in the head with it."

"Really?"

"I beat him until he was unconscious and I kept beating him. There was blood all over the porch, blood all over him, and blood all over me. Then I went in the house, lit a cigarette, and called 911. I told them I had killed my husband and they needed to send somebody out. I told the girls to go upstairs and get changed. I didn't want them seeing me go to jail."

"Did you go to jail?" Gary asked.

"Well, two deputies finally showed up about forty-five minutes later. They'd been out there before. They knew how he was, so they told me to go wait at their car while they checked out the murder scene. Then one of them came over to the car and I went ahead and stuck my hands out for the cuffs, and he told me that he was sorry but my husband wasn't dead. Then, to beat all, he asked if I wanted them to leave and come back in ten minutes."

Gary laughed. "They were giving you the opportunity to finish the job?"

"Exactly."

"Did you?"

"No. I gave it some serious thought though. I looked at him lying there and thought about all the things I could do to hurt or embarrass him. I thought about burning the house down with him inside it. I thought about cutting his private parts off. Instead I asked the deputies to wait while I packed our stuff and then we left for good."

"Did they charge you with anything?" Gary asked.

"No, the deputies left him lying on the porch. They never took a report. Never even called an ambulance. "

"Did he come after you?"

She smiled. "My dad and brothers 'talked' to him before he even had a chance to think about it. He was in the hospital for a couple of weeks and they went to visit him there. They made their intentions clear."

"Which were?"

"That they intended to finish what I started if he ever came near me again."

Gary smiled. "I think I'm going to like your dad if I ever meet him. He sounds like a good dad."

*

Jim slept better that night than he had in the last several. It was not the comfort of being under a roof, but the comfort that came from being behind a locked door. He'd always loved camping. While many of his friends refused to camp because of fear of bears and snakes, Jim had never lost sleep over those things. What he lost sleep over was the human predators that they were encountering now. He worried about people that might come across them and kill them in their sleep so that they might steal their supplies. He had thought they would be safe enough in the vast wilderness of Mount Rogers that a watch would be unnecessary, and he'd clearly been wrong. When they left this place tomorrow, they would have to start posting a watch every night.

They all had slept better. Everyone was moving about the next morning in a good mood, without the usual grumbling and sluggishness. They took time to pack their new acquisitions carefully. Randi was just glad to have a decent pack again.

"Try to hold onto this one," Gary said, lifting it so that Randi could slide the shoulder straps on. "You lose them as fast as we get them."

"I'll try." She bounced a few times, settling the weight. Gary helped her adjust the various straps so that the load would ride easier.

In what had become a daily habit, Jim took out his iPhone and pressed the power button. Every day, before heading out, he looked at pictures of his family. It reminded him of why he was pushing himself. It reminded him to be careful and not risk his life. It reminded him of why he had to get home at all costs.

The boot process was always slow. He set the phone down and finished packing his few remaining items into his pack. Today's plan was to cross the interstate into Bland County. This would be a significant accomplishment in that they would finally feel close to home. From Bland, they would trek to Burke's Garden on the trail.

By the time Jim closed the lid of his pack and tightened the last straps, his phone had completed the boot cycle. He continued with his pack since everyone else was done, deciding he could look at his pictures when they started walking out of there. Then he heard the text alert.

He froze. It took a moment to register.

When he looked up, everyone else had stopped what they were doing and were staring at him. He let his pack tip over and turned to his phone. There was indeed a text alert on the screen.

"I'll be damned. There's one bar of signal."

Packs dropped around the room. Buckles and zippers flew. Hands scrambled. They all wanted their phones.

Jim stared at his phone. "Randi, you still have your phone? Wasn't it in your pack?"

"Are you kidding? I'm a woman – I keep my phone in my back pocket."

"Good damn thing." Jim unlocked his screen and clicked on the message.

It was from his son:

Dad. I hope u are ok. Hurry home. Neighbors scaring mom.

Jim completely lost his shit. "Hold this so I don't fucking break it." He tossed the phone to Randi.

Jim went to the wall cabinets and wrenched a door off the hinges. He began beating the countertop. He swung the door again and took off the sink faucet, but it was unsatisfying since nothing came spraying out. He took the same door and began beating the walls, punching the door through labor law posters, job advertisements, and retirement seminar notices. He roared and cursed. Then he threw the door down and began kicking. He kicked holes in the drywall. When the drywall was gone, he kicked metal studs until they buckled and came loose from the tracks that held them.

"Jim."

He kept kicking.

"Jim!"

He stopped, his chest heaving.

"Are you going to keep kicking until the roof falls in?" Randi asked.

He didn't answer. He was blind with a rage that he'd never felt before.

He'd never been unable to protect his family before.

Never.

"I read your text."

Jim turned around.

"I wasn't snooping," she said. "It was on the screen when you threw it to me."

Gary's eyes were wide, as if Jim was a maniac that needed to be humored. Perhaps he was.

Randi extended his phone toward him. "This is not helping. The best thing we can do is get our asses off this mountain and get home."

She was right. Jim knew it. His reaction was not helping. He was a parent – an angry parent – but he needed to instead be a responsible parent and, just as Randi said, get his ass off the mountain.

Jim held out his hand and Randi placed his phone in it. He slipped it into the cargo pocket of his 5.11s, shouldered his pack, slipped his holster in place, and faced his friends.

"I'm sorry. Let's get the fuck out of here."

CHAPTER 13

Banks of the New River
Pembroke, Virginia

The bus turned a corner and rocked on its suspension, making Alice nauseous. She had no doubt that exhaust fumes were contributing to her nausea since she was becoming sleepy despite the adrenaline coursing through her. She was getting close to taking control of her own journey in the way that Jim and Gary had talked about. She had beat herself up enough already for not going with them.

"Boyd, look out each door and tell me what you see," Alice said.

The man stretched himself out at their feet in the tight compartment and placed his head against the hatch door, peering out the crack for a moment, repeating the action from the other door.

"There are people on the driver's side of the bus," Boyd said. "On the right side there's nothing. Just a bank off the shoulder of the road that drops down to the river. It's hard to see but it looks steep."

Alice felt a surge excitement. "That's the New River. We're there."

"What do we do?" Rebecca asked.

On the driver's side of the compartment, Alice pulled on her hatch door until it latched. "We need to get out on your side. We wait until the bus stops, then we wait for all the soldiers to get off and go around to the crowds on the other side of the bus. If we get out too early, while they're still exiting the bus, they'll see us. Once the coast is clear, we climb out, throw our gear over the hill and climb down after it. We don't move a muscle until the buses pull out and anyone that's left behind is gone."

"Got it." Rebecca's voice sounded strained.

"Boyd?"

"Got it. I'll keep watch out the hatch."

Footsteps reverberated through the bus and echoed in their metallic compartment. When there were no more footsteps, Boyd opened the hatch a little wider and peered out. "That's it. They're gone."

Rebecca pushed her hatch open and unfolded herself. Boyd followed.

Alice slid three of the stolen 72-Hour Go Bags out the door. She'd stolen the bags last night after they'd made their plan and had hidden them in the weeds close to where the buses were parked. Rebecca grabbed one of the bags, Boyd grabbed two, and they began picking their way down the steep riverbank.

Alice slid quietly across the length of the compartment and got out. She closed the hatch, then gently pushed it hard enough for the latch to lock. *Click.* No sooner had her door locked than she heard the compartment doors on the other side of the bus begin opening. Alice could hear luggage being shoved into the underside of the bus.

That was too close.

She held her breath and stepped through the tall weeds of the bank. It was so steep that she sat down and scooted on her butt, holding weeds and tree roots to slow her down. She joined Boyd and Rebecca near the bottom. They were huddled in the shadow of a thick log that had washed down the river at flood stage and became stuck on the bank.

"That was scary," Rebecca said.

Alice held her finger to her lips.

The crunching of gravel at the top of the bank warned them that someone was now on their side of the bus. They pushed themselves tighter against the weeds and mossy rocks of the bank, tighter into the shadow of the log. They heard the splatter of liquid and surmised that someone had taken advantage of the private side of the bus to relieve their bladder.

They did not even breathe.

The faces of the three escapees were mere inches apart in the cavity they huddled in. They could do nothing but stare at each other and wait for the person at the top of the bank to go away. It seemed as if they'd never finish. Alice felt a tickle on her hand and looked down. A fat water snake was moving across the back of her hand. She yanked her hand away in fear and revulsion. She *hated* snakes. The movement of her hand startled the snake and it surged toward Rebecca, weaving through her legs and across her kicking ankles.

Alice was biting her lip to halt her scream. Rebecca sucked in a lungful of air, fuel for the scream that she was preparing to unleash. Alice's eyes widened. There was no way a scream would go unheard. They were done for.

Boyd's hand shot out and wrapped around Rebecca's face, his fingers tight together, trying to seal the scream inside her. This only scared

Rebecca more and she twisted her body. Muffled cries escaped around Boyd's fingers.

They tightened.

Rebecca was sitting in front of him, her back to him, and he wrapped his free arm around her torso, his legs around her waist. He squeezed and clenched his arms, the muscles of his forearms bulging from the effort. The hand that covered her mouth was now covering her nose, too, preventing any air from reaching her lungs.

Alice raised her eyes to Boyd's face. She expected fear and panic, but was disturbed to instead see what she thought was pleasure and excitement. He was smiling and biting his lip. Alice could see that he no longer even knew she was there.

She did not know what to do. She was scared both for the scream that Rebecca was trying to let loose and for the sudden explosion of violence from this man. Rebecca's muffled cries now became attempts to breathe. Her face reddened and her eyes watered. Rebecca tugged at this hands but did not have the strength to pull them loose. She was dying. Alice could see the light inside her fading.

Alice then heard the bus start its engine. She patted Boyd hard on the arm. "Let her go. They can't hear us now. Let her go. It's okay. Let her go!"

Boyd hesitated long enough for Alice to wonder if he was actually going to comply or if he was going to choke Rebecca unconscious. If he were to choose the latter, she had no idea what she would do. She had nothing in the way of a weapon. Not a pocketknife, not a nail file, not even pepper spray.

He did let her go. He loosened his legs first, then his arms, but kept his hand across Rebecca's mouth until he was sure that she was subdued, that she was not going to scream. When he no longer had his hands on her, Rebecca surged toward Alice, throwing her arms around her in a terrified embrace. She sobbed quietly, muffling her cries against Alice's shoulder.

Over Rebecca's back, Alice watched Boyd as his breathing slowed. His reptilian eyes met hers. His gaze did not falter. She watched the monster recede, slithering back in its cave. Alice had never felt so alone in all her life. Above her was a highway that would lead her home. She had no plan for getting there beyond climbing the bank and starting her walk.

Alice was no stranger to walking. When she felt like she needed to burn off steam, she would sometimes walk the high school track back home; however, she found walking down this road to be an alien experience. Accustomed to driving on roads, the act of walking on a highway didn't feel right. She expected someone to jump out at her any moment and scream at her to get off the road. Anyone who had ever participated in a 5k run or charity walk had probably felt this. Roads were for driving.

Alice felt very exposed. There were houses within sight and those homes probably had people in them. How would they react to strangers walking by their house? What if they had dogs that chased them? She had not thought out all of these aspects of this journey. Even though they were closer to home, there was still a lot of exposed road between her and home. There was also a lot of danger.

She took the lead in their formation, walking purposefully and taking the longest steps, even though she was the shortest of the three. Boyd and Rebecca lagged a little behind, speaking between themselves in a conversation that was not meant for her ears. She had assumed that whatever bond those two had might have been broken by the incident on the riverbank; however, that appeared not to be the case. Boyd had no doubt spun some justification that Rebecca accepted. He'd probably made himself out to be the hero, saving them all from the soldiers, saving Rebecca from herself.

Over the first hour, they went from walking ten feet apart, to three feet apart, to holding hands. Alice could only shake her head. As a Human Resources person, she had long ago accepted that people as a whole were an inconsistent and disappointing lot. Their capacity to make poor decisions was nearly infinite. She could not forget that Rebecca had been facing her and not Boyd when he was restraining her. Rebecca had not seen his face, had not seen his enjoyment at her helplessness. She wondered if they had saddled themselves with a psychopath. She had seen something there, and it was something dark and deeply troubling.

As the day progressed, the heat quickly became a factor. The surface of the road reflected it back into their faces. Alice could already feel herself getting sunburned. The lack of sunscreen served to remind her of all the other items she didn't have that they might need. She remembered bitterly that Jim had carried sunscreen in that damned Get Home Bag of his because he'd offered it to her once. That did her no good now, except to reinforce that *if* she made it home alive she would have her own Get Home Bag next time. She would never be reduced to this level of impotence again.

Each of the stolen Go Bags that they carried had eight water bottles in it. Rebecca had finished one of hers. Boyd had finished two of his already, showing absolutely no restraint. Alice was trying to ration herself to sips and not gulps. She had only used half a bottle and worried about even that. When she'd cracked open her first bottle, she realized that finding fresh water to replace what they drank might not be so easy. She was very aware that she was consuming something she had no means to replace. She didn't know what natural water was drinkable and what wasn't. If you spend your whole life drinking from a faucet, you assume that any water coming from it is safe and any water that doesn't come from it is not safe. She had not planned for the resources they would require to get home beyond the 72 hour bags. This was going to be harder than she imagined.

Alice stopped and sat down on the guardrail. She remained determined, but was overwhelmed at the moment by the way her mind was bombarding her with reminders of her lack of preparedness. She removed her water bottle from her pack, took a sip, and replaced it. Rebecca and Boyd joined her, taking seats on the guardrail as well.

Rebecca wiped her forehead with the tail of her shirt. "How far do you think we've walked?"

"Maybe three miles," Boyd replied.

"How far is it from here?"

"I checked the map at camp yesterday," Alice said. "It's around eighty miles to the office."

Rebecca's eyes grew large. "Eighty? And we've travelled three? How long is this going to take us?"

Alice sighed. "You have the data, I think you can figure that out. I'd like to get twelve miles behind us today. That would get us to Narrows."

Rebecca took her pack off and tossed it down angrily. "This is going to take forever. At twelve miles a day, it will still take us two weeks to even get to the office. Then we're still not home."

Alice was becoming less tolerant of Rebecca. Even as exhausted as she was, walking on her tired feet in the relentless sun was preferable to sitting with her. "We can probably work our way up to twenty miles a day after we get used to it. Jim said that fifteen was easy, but that we could quickly work our way up to more than twenty miles a day."

Boyd stood and placed his foot on the guardrail to tie his shoe. "If this Jim character was so great why did you guys not go with him? Sounds like he was the man with the plan."

"Because he was full of shit," Rebecca spat. "He was paranoid, always planning for the worst case scenario."

Boyd dropped his foot to the ground, stood up straight and considered Rebecca. "Still sounds like we'd be a hell of a lot better off if we were travelling with Jim."

Rebecca stood, snatched up her pack, and brushed by Boyd, taking long, angry strides up the center of the road. She stopped once to see if Boyd and Alice were following her. She frowned at them, then turned and kept walking.

"Jim tried to get us to go with him," Alice said. "We blew him off."

Boyd nodded, then turned and followed Rebecca. Alice stood, adjusted her pack, and fell in line.

*

Most people had pulled off the road and abandoned their vehicles on the shoulder, but occasionally they ran across cars stopped dead in the center of a traffic lane. Alice guessed that some people must have given it their all, driving until their vehicles burned the last fumes of gas and stalled. They had passed cars all morning before Boyd pulled open an unlocked car door and began searching the vehicle.

Rebecca stopped walking and stared at Boyd. "That's someone's car."

He didn't even look up at her. "No shit."

"So you're just breaking into people's cars now, like some kind of criminal?"

"Yep."

Alice had been lagging behind. Her Nikes were too thin for this and her feet were beginning to throb. She leaned on the car as Boyd popped the trunk latch and began going through that.

Rebecca sat on the warm hood and let her pack slide off her shoulders. "He's as bad as Jim. He thinks there might be stuff in there we can use."

"He's probably right," Alice said. "We're going to need more than what we have now. If stuff we can use has been left behind in these cars, then we need to take advantage of that."

"Yahtzee!" came a cry from the car.

Rebecca looked back toward the trunk, an eyebrow raised. "What did you find?"

"Vehicle emergency kit."

"How do you know?" Alice asked.

"Says so right on the box." Boyd held up what looked like a plastic toolbox with white letters on the lid. He dumped the contents of the box in the trunk and rifled through them, finding a couple of bags of water that looked like children's juice boxes labelled *Emergency Water,* survival energy bars the size of candy bars, some Hot Hands hand warmers, two highway flares, a lighter, a roll of paracord, an orange triangle for showing that your vehicle was in distress, and two Mylar emergency blankets.

Rebecca reached in and picked up an energy bar. Boyd snatched it from her. "That's mine."

Rebecca stared at him. "Uh, *we* brought *you* along. Alice stole one of those Go Bags for you, and now you're not going to share?"

Boyd's expression hardened. "Then fucking take it."

"I don't want your stupid survival bar." She crossed her arms and stared a hole through him.

"Take it," he repeated.

"No."

Boyd stalked to the front of the vehicle and grabbed Rebecca's pack off the hood of the car. He carried it back to the trunk and slammed it down, then began cramming the contents of the emergency kit into her pack.

"What do you think you're doing? I don't want to carry all that."

"You wanted it, *you* fucking carry it." He continued angrily pushing gear into her pack. Not just the stuff they needed but everything he could find in the trunk – an ice scraper, de-icing spray, a tub of car cleaning wipes. When he was done, he closed the pack and held it out to her.

She continued glaring at him, making no effort to take the pack.

He reached out, took Rebecca's shoulder and spun her body violently, until she faced away from him. He put the pack on her forcefully. She went limp and allowed it, then turned back to him, and put a finger in his face.

"You don't fucking touch me ever again, you bastard."

They were still staring at each other when Alice walked off. She was tired and hungry. There were rations in her Go Bag, but she could not stomach eating with those two. They deserved each other.

*

They did not stop as a group again that day. They rotated their order as they walked, not through any planning, but simply because that was how it worked out. They ate their rations on the go, so there were times that each of them felt more energetic and refreshed than the others. Boyd continued to search each abandoned vehicle they passed. It had become an obsession. He started that morning with the unlocked ones. Now if they were locked, he broke out the window with a tire iron he'd found and continued his search.

Having made his feelings clear as to who owned the plunder, Rebecca and Alice no longer paid any attention to what he found. They did not ask, did not look, did not engage him. They continued walking. Alice noticed that Boyd's pack was getting much heavier than it had been earlier in the day. She didn't know what he'd found, but he now leaned forward against the weight when he walked.

When Alice paused to rest for a moment on the guardrail, Boyd passed her on the road. She let him go without a word, not even acknowledging him. When she continued walking, she came upon him going through an abandoned pickup truck. His pack was open and he was still shoving items inside. When he heard her coming, he positioned his body so that she could not see what he was doing. She kept going, but she thought she'd seen him shoving a handgun into the side pocket of his pack. That could be a concern.

They passed many houses and no one greeted them. Somehow, Alice had assumed there might be people who would take pity on stranded travelers and be standing by the road to offer drinking water and PB&J sandwiches, like relief stations at a marathon. She had really thought that and was incredibly disappointed to find that there were no crowds waiting to commiserate. Instead, all they saw was fleeting glimpses of distant forms taking shelter upon their approach. They saw shadows melting into windows. There were signs of life, but they were not friendly.

Outside of Narrows, Virginia, the houses became more frequent, but no more welcoming. Possibly due to the proximity to town, the frequency of abandoned cars dropped off. Boyd rejoined them and silently fell into stride beside Rebecca. The two of them did not speak, but she didn't discourage him.

When they came upon a country church beside a creek, Boyd halted in the road. "It's getting late. Maybe we should consider staying here for the night."

Rebecca looked around. "Where?"

"I saw a picnic shelter behind that church. We could stay there."

Rebecca looked at Alice. Alice shrugged. She hadn't thought about where they were going to stay, only about getting out of the camp.

Boyd took their silence as assent. "Alright, then we'll take a look."

They walked from the shoulder of Route 460 down a gravel driveway to the church. It bore white wooden clapboards and had a bell tower that was missing a bell. Instead, there was a speaker, probably connected to an old record player that rang out the Sunday call to worship. The picnic shelter behind the church was large and had a stone fireplace at one end.

Boyd looked around. "This place is kind of hidden back here. We might be able to have a fire in the fireplace tonight and not draw too much attention. A fire would help drive the bugs off."

Alice dropped her pack onto a picnic table. "Fine with me." She carried her pack to the far end of the shelter and sat down at a table where she could look at the creek. After a moment's consideration, she removed her shoes and walked down to the creek. She sat on a rock and dipped her swollen feet into the chilly stream. It was cold enough to make her flinch but her feet instantly began to feel better.

After fifteen minutes, her feet were numb and she could tell that some of the swelling had gone down. She walked back to the shelter and dried her feet with a spare shirt. She hung her socks, damp from her sweaty feet, over an electrical wire that ran between two nearby posts.

She noticed that Boyd had his pack open and he was eating with Rebecca. They were smiling and laughing. She could not tell what they were eating, but it did not appear to be one of the Go Bag's ration packs. Alice felt that she was clearly on the outside of this triangle. Though they were not particularly a group that she wanted to be part of, the rejection still bothered her. She was human, after all. It hurt that they did not acknowledge that it was her plan that had gotten them out of the FEMA camp in the first place. She had come up with the plan, she had collected the intelligence, and she had taken the Go Bags. Where was the appreciation? She should throw on her pack and take off down the road without them. If her feet hadn't hurt so badly, she probably would have.

She dug into her own pack and retrieved a ration packet, not caring that they were standard military MREs. Anything would help fill the void in her stomach. She could not let herself care about being singled out from the group. Even if her feelings got hurt, she would have to remember that these people were not her friends, they were merely travelling companions.

With this acceptance, she realized that this was how Jim must have felt when she and Rebecca had ganged up on him early in this disaster. He was only trying to help and no one was giving him any credit for his efforts. She hoped that his group was doing better than hers and that they had made it home. If she ever saw Jim again, she would tell him that she was sorry.

Then she'd ask him how to build a Get Home Bag.

*

Alice reluctantly joined Boyd and Rebecca around a fire that night. They made small talk with her but maintained a distance that clearly distinguished where she stood in this pack. She was okay with that, she had accepted it. She was a strong, independent woman and she had invited these people because she wanted to help them, not because she needed them.

Alice could not recall the last time that she'd been at a campfire in such blackness. She'd been to bonfires at social events and sat around fire pits with friends, but this was different. The fire was the only light. It was remarkable to her how much light a fire could put out. She wasn't sure she'd ever paid attention to that.

Suddenly, the way that the fire brightened the area around the shelter concerned Alice. She wondered if the local people noticed it. She wondered if people were watching them from the dark. Were they good people or bad people? Were they waiting for them to go to sleep?

Before long, Alice told Boyd and Rebecca that she was going to bed. They still sat around the fire, lost in talking quietly to each other and they paid her no attention. Boyd may have raised a finger in acknowledgement from where it lay on his leg, but it may just as easily have been to stir an insect from his finger. She walked the aisle between the picnic tables until she was at the same table where she had eaten her solitary dinner, beyond all but the occasional stray flicker of the firelight. She reclined on the top of a picnic table for a while, her stolen FEMA blanket folded in her arms, not quite ready to wrap herself in it and commit to sleep, thinking that sleeping on the table would keep her out of the reach of snakes and spiders. She could not get comfortable, though. It had nothing to do with the table, which was probably as comfortable an accommodation as she'd find out here. It was the conversation taking place by the fire that bothered her.

She could not hear what was being said, only the tone of the words. In her exhausted delirium, the conversation reminded her of classical music. There was cooing and giggling, reminding her of flutes and woodwind instruments. Then the music would change to reprimands and strong words that made her think of cymbal crashes and atonal chords. Then there was the male voice, softened by desire, promising. Then there was the female voice, accommodating, then rejecting. It was a cycle of romance to anger to romance. Alice wondered if Rebecca wasn't just playing some game with Boyd, where the prize was his assistance in surviving this ordeal. Alice worried that this would not turn out well for Rebecca if that was her game. Boyd did not seem like the kind who would enjoy being played. Either way, she could not listen to this all night.

She gathered her gear quietly. She did not want them to see her leaving and did not want them to see where she was going. She had no idea where she was going either. She slipped on her shoes and pulled the socks free of the wire where they dried, cramming them into her back pocket. She walked into the dark, her eyes adjusted enough by now that she could see slightly in the sliver of moonlight. She hoped that she did not step on a snake because she could not see well enough to notice one if it lay across a warm rock in her path. She would scream if that happened and she did not want to scream.

She tried several spots along the creek and in the woods before she ended up at the back door of the church. Even in the darkness, the tall white walls of the church caught light and loomed over her. She tried the door and found it unlocked. She thought that must certainly be a sign. A welcome. She went in and closed the door behind her, taking out the small flashlight that she'd stolen from the camp. It was the only one between the three of them. She turned it on and flashed it discreetly around the room. The old oak pews were padded. She slid some of the pads into the floor and made herself a thick bed in the middle of the center aisle.

Before she lay down for the night, she went to each door of the church. Each had an old-fashioned surface-mounted deadbolt. She locked them and made certain that they engaged. She asked herself what was out there that she was afraid of.

The answer was *everything*.

CHAPTER 14

The Valley
Russel County, Virginia

Charlie Rakes got in the Dodge that he'd stolen from Henry when he'd killed him and taken his house for himself. He no longer saw it as a stolen truck. It was *his* truck now, just as the house they'd taken was now *his* house. Of course Henry's son had thought he had a right to it and had come to claim it back. That had been a problem for about all of thirty seconds until Charlie fixed it. The boy had been full of big talk. Charlie had never cared much for talk. As he often said, most people didn't have the ass to back up their talk. That boy was still talking up to the second that Charlie killed him dead. Some people just didn't know when to shut the hell up.

He drove down the road a short piece and stopped at a little ranch house just off the road. The whole house looked to be about five rooms. It always made him wonder why some of these folks had these big sprawling farms with hundreds of acres and tiny brick houses that weren't any size at all. He didn't get it.

He walked straight in through the front door because he knew he could. There had been an elderly couple here when he stopped by yesterday. They'd still been eating fairly well from their root cellar, but they were old and weak and no match for Charlie. He'd not even had to use a weapon. He'd taken the old man's cane and beat him like a bony piñata. The old woman howled the whole time. It pissed him off. He'd kicked her to death. The pair didn't weigh any more than a bag of dog food when he carried their bodies out to the barn. There was an old horse stall, so long in disuse that the tack hung in decay from rusting nails in the wall. He tossed their bodies into it, one atop the other, and slammed the stall door shut.

He could have demanded that Angie and her kids come help him but he wasn't running a commune. He cared for them because they were family but his main interest in life was still taking care of himself. He would share some things, but other things were only for him. Before he shared anything from this house, he wanted to find and separate out those things that were just for him.

In a habit that had been established long ago, he started his exploration in the medicine cabinet and kitchen cabinets. That was where he usually found the drugs. He'd never considered himself an addict, but nothing took the edge off the day like a good pain pill. He lucked out that the old man had apparently had several surgeries in the recent past and there were hundreds of pills to choose from. He loaded them into a pillow case. He felt like the Grinch looting Whoville.

There were several framed commemorative coin sets hanging on the paneled living room walls. A few months back he'd have taken those too, but he could think of no use for them in this current world. After finding the pills, he searched for booze, finding nothing in that category. He then went on a weapons search. There were several guns in a walnut cabinet in the spare bedroom. The cabinet was locked, so he knocked the glass out with a porcelain rabbit and removed several long guns and some old boxes of shells. The only pistol he found was a .22 caliber Colt Woodsman. He carried the guns out and put them in the back of his truck. The sack of pills went behind the seat.

The last item on his search list was food. He scoured the cabinets and found quite a bit. These people apparently kept themselves well-stocked so they didn't have to go out to the store much. He found more pillowcases and filled them with the contents of the kitchen and pantry. In the basement were shelves of home-canned goods. He filled every milk crate and cardboard box in the house with the items he found down there. He noticed that among the Mason jars was stewed venison chunks. He unscrewed the ring on the jar and used his keychain to pry the lid off. There was a satisfying pop, indicated a good seal on the jar.

He shoved his dirty fingers into the neck of the jar, fished out a cube of venison, and shoved it into his mouth.

"Damn, that's good." He licked every bit of juice from his fingers.

He continued about his business, hauling out jars until nothing was left. In the process, he finished the jar of venison that he'd opened. He hoped there were more cans of that. If there were, he was hiding that shit for himself. In a slouching smokehouse of grayed poplar logs, Charlie found a dozen country hams curing on steel hooks. This was better than the venison. He backed his truck up to the smokehouse and emptied it. While he loaded hams, an aging coonhound crept from the barn and slunk toward him, tail wagging, ribs showing. Charlie cut off a chunk of ham and fed the dog, then shot it in the head while it ate.

When he was sure that this farm had nothing more to offer him, Charlie pulled his truck away from the house and left it running. He found a can of charcoal lighter fluid on the back porch, squirted it across the shag carpet of the living room, then stuck his cigarette lighter to it. The fire spread quickly. Charlie backed out the door and watched the fire flicker through the windows. He did the same in the barn, striking his lighter to a pile of straw bales.

His work complete, he popped two hydrocodone pills and sat on the tailgate of his truck, admiring his handiwork. The smell and the smoke would carry for miles. He hoped it did. Maybe it would motivate those remaining in the area to pack up and leave. If they didn't, this might be them next time. This was his valley now, whether folks knew it or not. Farm by farm, he would take everything and burn what he couldn't use, leaving nothing for people to return to.

CHAPTER 15

Route 460

Narrows, Virginia

When Alice woke in the church, she was struck by the stillness. Not since this whole mess began had she been so immersed in silence. Even the hotel where they'd originally stayed in Richmond was so noisy at night with the air conditioning running, vending machines being used, and people closing doors. From that point forward, things got worse every night. The FEMA camp had been the worst of all with most people sharing a single open room. Every night was creaking cots, coughing, people stumbling over stuff, and stifled crying in the darkness. They couldn't even turn the lights down low because it caused more people to trip and fall. It had been safer than anywhere they'd been up to that point, but it had not been a comforting safety. An underlying feeling of unease had settled on her shortly after her arrival at the camp and had never left.

She rose awkwardly from her improvised bed on the church floor. In full light, she felt almost guilty for having slept here, now surrounded by all of the religious items that she'd not been able to see in the night. She replaced the pew cushions she'd slept on, as if attempting to erase what felt like a desecration. She rubbed her eyes, stretched, and sat down on a pew to put her shoes on.

She soon realized she needed to go to the bathroom before she did anything else. She hadn't gone to the bathroom much yesterday – a sure sign of dehydration. She saw a side door at the front of the church, grabbed her gear, and headed for it. The hallway was white, with pictures of past ministers framed on the plaster walls. Around a corner, she found the bathroom she was looking for. She opened the door apprehensively, aware that the lack of water had created some sanitation nightmares in other bathrooms she'd seen recently. This was not the case here, fortunately. It looked no one had been there at all.

When she finished, she looked at herself in the mirror. Yesterday's sweating had left her hair a mess. She would have to find something to tie it back with since there was little else she could do with it. Her face was dingy from the dust. She'd never even noticed the dust as she walked but there had apparently been plenty of it. She was wearing it like a coating of gritty flour over her body. She tried turning on the faucet, hoping there was water for rinsing her face but nothing came out. She would have to use the creek. Still, she felt blessed that there was even a creek to use.

At the outside door, she unlocked the deadbolt and opened it. The morning light hit her fully in the face and she shielded her eyes. It was hot already and held promise of being a miserably humid day. She looked toward the picnic shelter but could see no one moving around. She went straight to the creek and crouched on the bank. She cupped her hands, caught water in them, and dipped her face into it. It felt fantastic and she continued doing it until her skin felt mildly numb. When she was done, she dried her face and hands on a spare shirt from her bag.

She stood and considered leaving. Simply walking away from Boyd and Rebecca. She knew that continuing with those two would lead to nothing but frustration, fighting, and hurt feelings. It was already clear who the odd man out in this trio was, so why didn't she just go? Was it fear? A sense of responsibility toward her coworker?

Unsure of what else to do, she walked to the shelter. She decided that Boyd and Rebecca's treatment of her this morning would help clarify the decision. She would go to them and see how the mood was today. At the first rude or condescending remark, she would leave without a word. No confrontation, no threats, just leave.

She stepped onto the concrete floor of the picnic shelter at the end farthest from the stone fireplace. At the other end, where the pair had slept, she could see no movement. She saw a sleeping bag curled up on the floor and a few items scattered around. She didn't think that she saw but one sleeping bag. She walked closer, mildly confused.

"Rebecca?"

She walked closer. She looked around, toward the road and the creek, and did not see anyone else. She was certain now that she was only seeing one sleeping bag.

"Rebecca?"

When she was within a dozen feet of Rebecca, she was beyond concerned. Rebecca should have heard her. Alice could not see her face. She appeared to be lying on her side, facing away from Alice. Panic rose in her throat.

"Rebecca?" It was a little louder this time. A note of desperation. A plea.

Then she was standing above Rebecca and all she could focus on was the blood. It saturated the sleeping bag beneath Rebecca. It was crusted to the concrete below her head. Her misshapen and damaged head.

Alice could not scream. She could not even breathe. She looked around her. Had Boyd done this or had someone killed him?

No, she knew that Boyd had done this.

Then she saw the rock. It was about the size of a softball. Dark red and brown blood encrusted it. He had used that rock to bash Rebecca's head in. He had killed her.

It was then that she noticed Boyd had also stolen Rebecca's Go Bag. Had this been his plan all along? Had he used them to escape the camp? She wondered if he'd looked for her last night, wanting to finish both of them and erase his tracks completely. Had he raged at not finding her?

She didn't know what to do. If she got help, they might accuse her of murdering her friend. There might not even *be* anyone to help. She was a stranger here and the law seemed to be getting very put out with the trouble that strangers were causing. What about Boyd? Would he track her down and do the same to her tonight? Which way had he gone? What was she going to do?

"I'm so sorry, Rebecca," she whispered.

She teared up and started walking. It was all she knew to do.

*

Yet again, Alice found herself thinking of Jim as she walked. She had to admit she'd been pissed off that he was carrying a gun. Not even one gun, but *two*. He was management – he knew better. She took it personally that he would violate a policy so flagrantly. At least this was how she'd felt a few days ago. Now, she had to admit that things were completely different. She wished she were with Jim, Randi, and Gary. She also wished she had a gun of her own.

Leaving behind Rebecca's body, she felt like she was on the run. They had camped on the outskirts of town last night, saving the passage through town for this morning. Unlike some towns, this one did not have a roadblock. Travelers were free to walk through town, but it did not mean that they were welcome. Homes and businesses began to appear, and she tried to keep her eyes forward, appearing as if she had a place to go. Most business were closed, though she did notice a parking lot where people had tables set up, like a flea market or a farmers market. There were only a few vendors and not many customers. Folks turned and watched her as she passed by. Their stares made her uncomfortable. No one waved. They were not welcoming. She expected at any moment that they might begin walking toward her, then running, pursuing her through the town and chasing her out the other side.

None of the homes she passed had children playing outside. Most doors were closed, but she saw shadows in the recesses of windows that she knew were from people. They appeared to be watching her. This town had either had a bad experience with people passing through or they just had a general distrust of strangers. If that was the case, such distrust was warranted. Either way, she kept walking.

This town that she could drive through in less than five minutes took her an hour to walk through. That was concerning to her. It was over twenty miles to her next destination. Near Princeton, West Virginia, she could get on Route 19, a road that would take her home. She would like to make those twenty miles today if she could. She wondered about Boyd. Which direction had he taken? Was he waiting for her out there or had he moved on with no regard whatsoever for her?

Leaving Narrows, the road passed beneath a railroad bridge. She paid no attention to it as she passed beneath, walking with her eyes straight ahead, focused on the miles she needed to cover. As she came out the other side, there was a tremendous clattering noise that startled her. She flinched, but tried not to look back. Then there was sharp pain on the top of her head, followed by more clattering. It was then that she noticed empty food cans were raining down on her. She tried to run but it was awkward with the backpack and she could not distance herself fast enough. More cans bounced off her as she ran. She heard laughter behind her and knew then that it was boys, probably teenagers like her own son. She could not hold it in and started crying. She kept running until the town was nothing but a bad memory, the latest of many, but far from the last.

CHAPTER 16

The Cave
Russell County, Virginia

The days dragged on in the cave. That was true for most of them, but not Pete. He seemed to be almost enjoying himself as he had become completely obsessed with his observation post. Although he returned to the cave to sleep, he insisted on taking all his meals up there where he could keep an eye on things. Ellen's routine consisted of visiting their house each day to make sure things were okay there, and shuttling a few items back with her.

Her goal was to get as many of the things that were important to them into a safe place in case something happened to the house. She hoped that would not be the case but she had to assume the worst. Each day, there was the lingering smell of smoke in the air. They did not seek out all the fires, fearing that the whole thing could be a trap, but the inevitable conclusion was that someone was methodically burning down houses throughout their valley. While they had a safe place to stay in the cave, Ellen could hardly sleep at night for fear that she would find her own home reduced to ashes and rubble one morning. She knew it was the safety of her family that was of utmost importance, but she wondered if she'd be able to handle the loss of her home. It would be a devastating blow.

Pops helped out by keeping the fire going since Pete was in his lookout post all day. Sometimes he would have to drive a vehicle around to one of the woodpiles scattered about the farm and bring back firewood. He kept it stacked neatly outside the cave and covered with a tarp.

Ariel had recruited her Nana as her full-time play partner. Nana did not mind this a bit. They did crafts and made many things that decorated the walls of their cave. Nana continued with Ariel's piano lessons using a battery-powered keyboard that they brought down from the house. Ariel found the acoustics in the cave to be very cool, with natural reverb. She liked to play spooky sounds and practice her evil laugh.

In order to get fresh air and exercise, Nana and Ariel would play outside some each day. This was usually done down the hill from the cave at a small creek that passed through the property. Ariel liked to catch crawdads and minnows and put them in plastic cups. She would name each of them. Once she tired of this, she'd let them all go for the day and do it again the next.

Cave life had been hardest on Nana. Already prone to respiratory disorders, the damp cave air was not beneficial to her. Even with the fire going and Jim's improvements, the cave was still a damp place to live. Within a few days of living there, Nana was starting to have fits of asthma, which she treated with an inhaler. They had all noticed, that her coughing was getting worse. It was deeper and now a wet cough. Ellen was afraid she might be developing pneumonia or a respiratory infection.

One morning, Nana did not feel like getting out of bed. This was unusual for her. She always got up before dawn and was moving around before anyone else. Despite her age, she was always active and energetic. This was a bad sign.

"Do you have a thermometer?" Nana asked between coughs.

Ellen sent Ariel to get it. When Ariel returned, she insisted on taking her Nana's temperature and placed the thermometer in her ear. When it beeped, she removed it. "101.7," she announced.

"Maybe we should start you on an antibiotic," Ellen suggested to her mother-in-law.

Nana offered no protest. "Do you have any?"

Ellen went to the tote where they stored their medical supplies. She searched through bottles before removing one and opening it. She took it to Nana, along with a bottle of water. After Nana placed the pills in her mouth, Ellen passed her the opened bottle of water. Glued to Ellen's hip, Ariel looked at the medicine bottle in Ellen's lap.

"Mommy, you gave Nana fish medicine! What are you doing?"

Ellen cringed. Nana's eyes widened. She should have taken greater measures to conceal the bottle.

"Are you trying to kill me, Ellen? Putting me out of my misery because I'm old and sick?" It appeared that she really thought Ellen may actually be trying to poison her.

Ellen shook her head. "No. These are fish antibiotics."

Nana started gagging. She put her hand to her mouth and started to put a finger down her throat. Ellen placed her hand on Nana's shoulder to stop her.

"No, really, it's okay, Nana. Sit back down. Fish antibiotics and human antibiotics are practically the same. You can get the fish versions without a prescription and for a lot cheaper. We buy them in bulk. Jim and I have used them for years with no ill effects."

Nana did not look convinced. "I noticed you swam really well when we went to the water park last time."

"I hope that's a joke. You know I wouldn't give you anything that would hurt you."

Nana lay back and put her hand across her forehead. "I know you wouldn't. It's just a little startling to think about taking fish medicine."

"Sorry. I guess I should have warned you. If it makes you feel any better, don't look at it as if you're taking fish medicine – look at it as if people give the fish human medicine."

"Will it help me hold my breath longer if I take it, Mommy?" Ariel asked.

"No sweetie, it won't. But it may make your scales nice and shiny."

*

To allow Nana to get some rest, Ellen tried to keep Ariel busy outside the cave. She sat at the picnic table and drew pictures, and Ariel made her Nana five different get well cards. She did another craft with pine cones and paint. Then she made a bracelet that she wanted to give to Nana, but Ellen told her she'd have to wait until Nana woke up from her nap.

When it was time for Ellen to make her daily trip to check on the house, she told Pops to stay with Ariel. She would go alone today. Pete could watch her from his observation post and alert them if she had trouble. Ariel wanted to go, but Ellen told her that she could go catch some crawdads if she was bored with crafts.

"I wish Pete would play with me," Ariel said.

"Pete has a job do to," Ellen said. "He's keeping watch over us until Daddy comes back."

"Have I told you that I hate the apocalypse?"

"Yes, baby, you have."

Ellen got in her Suburban and drove off toward the house.

"Pops, I want some rocks to paint," Ariel told her grandfather, who was splitting wood.

"There's plenty here to paint."

"I want *creek* rocks."

"You'll have to wait until I finish cleaning up this wood," he said. "If I leave it here, someone may come out of there tonight and fall over it. Do you want to help stack it?"

Ariel took a seat at the picnic table. "No thanks, I'll watch."

Not surprised, Pops continued splitting. He had four more logs to go, then he would stack all the wood he'd split. He was already a couple of days ahead but there weren't many activities to keep him occupied. Splitting wood was about his favorite of the options he had.

While Pops continued eating away at the edges of his logs with his splitting maul, Ariel looked down the hill toward the creek. It wasn't that far away. She knew that she could walk down there and grab a handful of rocks and Pops would never know she was gone. She liked to think of herself as *sneakretive,* a word she'd made up herself, which was a combination of sneaky and secretive.

When Pops was mopping his forehead with a bandana, Ariel slipped away from the picnic table and walked down the short path to the creek. The creek could be seen from where Pops was splitting wood, but Ariel didn't want to be seen. Once she arrived at the creek, she slipped off upstream and out of sight. She began picking up paintable rocks and sliding them into her pink purse.

Further upstream, from a thicket of blackberry, eyes peered at Ariel. The boy from the trailer park, Robert, had to get away from his family for a while. Back at Henry's house, his Uncle Charlie had taken up with his mom in a way that left him feeling very uncomfortable. With his dad gone, his mother told him that she had no choice. He thought she had a choice but was too weak to make it. She didn't seem to realize that he was old enough to take care of them. He was a man now. He could take care of the whole family. Charlie was nothing but a washed-up old jailbird that had never amounted to anything and never would. Robert didn't like him and didn't trust him as far as he could throw him. He knew the feeling was mutual. He expected any day that Charlie would tell him he had to leave the house and not come back. When that day came, Robert hoped to kill Charlie.

Charlie would leave every day and not tell them where he was going or what he was doing. When he came back, they would smell the smoke.

They knew he'd burned another house, but they didn't know which one. No one ever asked. All that mattered to them was that he brought back food each time. After they ate, Charlie and his mom disappeared into the house, locking the kids out in the yard. Robert was supposed to be watching over them, but today he couldn't stay there. He couldn't take it anymore. He told one of the older girls to watch the kids. He was going to take a walk.

He set out walking along the creek that flowed behind Henry's house. It was a small stream that fed a larger creek a few miles off. He'd never followed it and didn't know where it went. A couple of weeks ago, he couldn't have followed it for fear of getting charged with trespassing. Now, according to Charlie, there wasn't any law. So he set out along the creek without a thought in the world.

He walked for some time, not paying any attention to time or distance. After a while, he started hearing a *thunk*, like someone was using an axe. Not sure who was still living back here, he was drawn to follow the sound and find out. After a while, he could tell for certain that it was indeed the sound of wood being split with an axe or splitting maul. He couldn't tell where he was, but suspected he might be near the farm where his daddy disappeared.

He began to stalk the creek, taking careful steps, pausing and listening. He had not yet reached the person splitting wood when he heard the clatter of rocks. He froze. Was someone coming toward him? He hoped not. He did not have any weapon at all with him.

Ahead of him, there was a flash of color and he saw a little girl gathering rocks from the creek. She picked them up, then discarded most of them, tossing them back into the creek. He was sure this was the little girl that belonged to the family that had killed his dad. Even if the woman hadn't admitted it, that's what he suspected they had done. That was also what Charlie thought.

What would happen if he were to take the little girl and deliver her to Charlie? What if he maneuvered his way to her and sprang, silencing her scream with his hand and dragging her off into the woods? He wondered if it might win him some points with Charlie and help get the man off his back. What would his mother think? She might not care much for him kidnapping a little girl, but if they had her, they could use her to make her mother tell them the truth about his dad. He also knew that if he took her back to their house, Charlie would use her to make these people go away and leave them all their supplies.

While he wanted a steady supply of food to eat, he worried that Charlie would never leave if he succeeded in running everyone else off. If there were no supplies, maybe he would eventually go away and leave them. Then Robert could start taking care of his family himself. The smartest move to him was not to help Charlie succeed in taking over this whole valley.

"Ariel?"

Robert flinched, drawing back into the thicket. It was a man's voice.

"Ariel?"

The girl panicked and ran from the stream bank. "I'm here, Pops. I was getting rocks."

"You can't run off like that," the man said. "You know your mother will kill me if she finds out you went down there alone."

"Then we'll be sneakretive and not tell her," Ariel said.

The older man came into view and took the little girl's hand. They walked back up the hill.

Robert wondered what they were doing this far from the house. Surely they didn't come down here to cut wood. He slipped from his hide and moved toward them, hoping for a better vantage point. He found it. From his new spot he could see what looked like a house built into the mountain, like a cave-house.

"I'll be damned," he whispered, watching the man and child disappear through a door into the rocky hillside.

CHAPTER 17

Appalachian Trail
Bland County, Virginia

Jim hiked like he had never hiked before. His legs worked like pistons, climbing hills and eating up miles. Had he not built some degree of respect and friendship toward Randi and Gary by this point, he probably would have stripped his pack down to the bare essentials and moved on at a jogging pace. He knew that they needed to stick together and he thought he'd lose them if he pushed any harder than he was pushing now. As it was, it was all that Randi could do to keep up with them now.

The pinch point for this whole section of the trip was the crossing at Interstate 81. Although the section where the AT crossed the interstate was rural, the interstate was paralleled by U.S. Highway 11, which had a lot of homes and businesses along it. True to his expectation, they crossed Highway 11 and were on their way to the underpass that the AT used to cross the interstate when a man called to them from a porch next to the trail. He was sitting in a lawn chair, drinking from a pint bottle.

"Yo, that's my yard now, man. You all got to pay a fucking toll to go through there. People can't be walking through a man's yard without giving him a little something for it." The man was skinny with a mullet and baggy denim shorts. His hair was close cropped and he looked to be in his late 20s. He smiled, but it was not a friendly gesture. Jim could recognize the type – drugs, probation, living with his parents.

"Keep walking," Jim told his companions. "I'm not slowing down for this shitbag."

The man got up from his chair, hopped off the porch, and started closing the thirty feet between them at a trot. Jim noticed that the man's front pants pocket was heavily weighted. He probably had a gun.

Jim drew his Beretta and faced the man. He pointed the gun toward his head and started walking aggressively toward him.

The man paused, held up both hands. "Easy man. We're cool"

Jim walked faster. "We're far from cool."

The man turned and ran, calling back over his shoulder. "Go on, man.

155

Go on. I was just fucking with you. Crazy bastard."

It was all Jim could do not to fire a warning shot and send the man running even faster, but a warning shot would draw more attention. He stopped, kept his gun raised, and backed steadily toward the underpass. He did not take his eyes from the lowlife. In a moment, he caught up with Randi and Gary. They all double-timed it under the interstate and in a few moments were back in the deep forest of the Appalachian Trail. Jim kept an ear turned to the sound of pursuers but none came.

Jim had tried to be considerate throughout the trip toward his companions and make sure they were comfortable with the pace. He wanted to get everyone home in one piece. He still wanted to get everyone home, but he was less concerned about their comfort now. When they were hungry, they ate on the run from whatever provisions they had that required no cooking. They stopped when a blister required attention, for muscle cramps, and to use the bathroom. Other than that, they walked relentlessly.

They did not talk much. No one was feeling all that conversational anymore. Gary and Randi spoke some between themselves and Jim assumed it was about him. He was back to feeling like the obsessed outsider now, the same way he'd felt when they started home from Richmond. All he could hope was that Gary and Randi understood why he was doing what he was doing. They both had families of their own. He was sure they knew.

By around 3 p.m., they were so exhausted that they were starting to stumble. After Randi took two hard falls over logs, Gary began to get a little frustrated.

"We need to take a good break, Jim. I know you're in a hurry, but getting someone hurt is not going to help us. If one of us gets hurt, what the hell are we going to do? We need to take a good break, rest, cook some real food, and then we can start walking again."

Jim looked at his friends. Randi was still sitting where she had fallen, rubbing a bloody shin. She looked ready to cry. He knew it was frustration on her part. She would not cry from the pain. She would gnaw her own leg off first. But she would cry if she thought she was slowing them down. He unbuckled the chest strap on his pack, slid the shoulder straps off, and let it drop.

"I'm sorry," Randi said. "I—"

Jim held up his hand. "Don't apologize to me, Randi. You have nothing to be sorry for. I appreciate you all being understanding with me today. I know I'm hard to be around sometimes."

Randi laughed quietly. "That would be all the fucking time, but I can't say I would be acting any different if I'd got the text you got. I know you're worried."

"Either way, I'm sorry if I'm being a jerk."

Gary dug in his pack and held up three pouches of freeze dried food. "I've got three lasagnas. Each serves two people. We can carbo-load on these. That should be good for some quick energy."

Jim started digging in his own pack and removed a gallon-sized plastic bag. He'd dumped all the coffee into it this morning while they were packing. "You cook the dinners and I'll start boiling coffee. We can drink some now and I'll fill a liter bottle for each of us to drink on the trail. That may help prop us up a little bit when we start to sag."

"Did you bring creamer?" Randi asked.

"Damn right I brought creamer."

Randi gave him a tired thumbs up, then flopped over backwards onto her pack and closed her eyes.

*

They stopped for about two hours. Even Jim had to admit that it was a good move. He could drive himself to collapse but that would not help anyone. He still had to help his friends get home. They ate all of the freeze-dried lasagna, then cut the pouches open and licked them clean. It was actually pretty good. Jim boiled some very stout coffee, aiming for a brew so dense that no light penetrated it. When he could not see the bottom of his pot, it was ready. He poured the mixture through his bandana, with apologies to Gary and Randi, straining it into liter Nalgene bottles.

Randi did not fall asleep but rested after they ate. Gary immediately fell into a deep sleep, laid back against his pack. Jim alternated between watching the water boil and staring into the woods. He was obviously preoccupied.

"Worried about home?"

He looked at Randi, preparing a smart comment, but none came. He didn't even have the energy to be a smartass anymore. "Yes. It's all I can think about."

"What worries you in particular? I mean, what kind of neighbors do you have that your family might be having trouble with?"

The pot of water came to a boil and Jim spooned ground coffee into it. "There's a trailer park about a mile or so away. Rough folks."

"Now wait a fucking minute," Randi said. "I live in a trailer. Not all people who live in trailers are *rough folks*."

"I know. It's not that they live in trailers, it's that there is this particular trailer park near my house that houses a pretty indigent population of people. I know there are good trailer parks full of families and grandparents, but this is not one of them. This is an old trailer park full of cheap trailers that attract lowlifes. Some of them aren't much more than old campers with porches built around them. The people who live there are not the kind of people who would be prepared for a disaster like this."

"*Most* people aren't prepared for a disaster like this."

Jim looked into the pot, gauged the darkness of the coffee and sat back. It needed more time. "I know they aren't. But we live in a farming community where most people around us have some degree of ability to weather a short-term problem. We have ice storms, power outages, and blizzards nearly every year that require some degree of preparation. The people who aren't even able to weather short-term bumps in the road are going to be a problem. They will start stealing off their neighbors when times get hard."

"They probably didn't choose to be poor, Jim. Most people don't choose it."

"I don't have any problem with being poor. But when I was a kid poor people had gardens and grew their own food. They took day work on farms cutting hay and tobacco. They didn't live off handouts from the government. I respect anyone who tries to better themselves and improve their conditions, but I have no respect for a bunch of deadbeats sitting around addicted to pain pills and not working. Especially when I'm the one footing the bill for it."

"I understand that, Jim. I have to work to support myself. I don't like my money going to take care of people who are too damn sorry to work. I get a little riled when you start talking about *trailer* people."

Jim turned the burner off and let the coffee sit to cool a little before he poured it. "What would you prefer I call them?"

"I don't know," she said. "If they're deadbeats, then that's probably a good word for them. Call them deadbeats." She sat up and stretched. "Let's wake Gary up now and get this show on the road. I feel like a new woman."

*

By dark, they'd eaten again and drank their bottles of coffee. As they'd gone a few days without caffeine, it didn't take much to energize them now. They could all tell the improvement in their stamina and agility that caffeine had made.

"I love coffee," Gary said. Jim couldn't tell whether he was speaking to himself or the universe.

"That was clearly a major oversight in my Get Home Bag provisioning," Jim said. "Caffeine is the safest performance enhancer available. I should have included it in several forms in my bag."

"Like caffeine pills?" Randi asked.

"Not just caffeine pills. There are energy gels you can buy for endurance sports that pack carbs and caffeine into a little packet that you squeeze into your mouth. They come in every flavor you can imagine. Then there's caffeinated jelly beans."

"I had no idea," Randi said. "What a wonderful idea."

"If I ever leave home again – which is doubtful – I will have my pack stocked with them," Jim said. "This is the best I've felt on the trail in days."

Gary looked at his watch. "Since we all agree we're feeling good, how far do you think we can go tonight?"

Jim powered on his GPS, waiting while it acquired satellites and located his position. When it had finally locked on and he plugged in his destination, it provided him with a distance. "Ten miles or so to the shelter at the edge of Burke's Garden."

"We all have fresh headlights and batteries so I guess we should keep going. That sound okay?"

"Gary, if we can make it to Burke's Garden tonight, you might be home tomorrow night. It will probably take Randi and I a day longer because we're one county further. Can you believe that?"

Gary didn't say anything. Jim saw him wipe his eyes.

"We're almost there, buddy. We're almost there."

"As prepared as we thought we were, Jim, there were times when I had my doubts about whether we'd make it home or not. I can't even really comprehend that I might see my family tomorrow."

"That's okay, Gary. I understand. I can't go there in my head, yet. When I am walking up my driveway, I'll relax. Until then, I just can't do it."

CHAPTER 18

Russell County, Virginia

Charlie Rakes drove the empty road down the valley on one of Henry's ATVs. He saw no lights at the looming old farmhouse that the mailbox indicated belonged to Lonzo Wimmer and his wife. The gate at his driveway had no lock. Charlie opened it and drove through, but left the gate open behind him in case he had to beat it out of there. In the flash of his headlights, Charlie saw black cows wandering the fields around the house. He stopped the ATV about halfway up the gravel driveway and sat astride it in the dark, the engine ticking. There was a large moon that night that allowed him to see shadows. The night had a smell to it that Charlie found pleasant, but he could not tell what it came from; a combination of clover, grass, and crushed mint.

When his presence in a stranger's driveway prompted no immediate reaction, Charlie started the ATV again and drove the rest of the way to the house, parking directly in front of the porch steps. Again, he turned the engine off and listened. In an old wooden house like this, surely if there was movement inside he would have heard it. Charlie removed a headlamp from where it dangled on a handlebar, turned it on, and placed it on his head. He dismounted, removed a small pry bar from the crate strapped to the luggage rack and climbed the porch steps, taking each step slowly to measure the noise it would produce. The porch was made of old tongue-and-groove boards thickly painted, but now peeling.

Charlie was not native to this town nor valley, but Angie said that the folks who lived here were old. Old folks meant medication and no resistance. Although he enjoyed using pain pills, he could only take so many himself, but as far as he was concerned they were like money in the bank. Regardless of how fucked the world was, junkies still had to get high. When he reconnected with the people he knew, they would trade food, gas, or whatever they had to get pills from him. Sure, it would all be stuff they'd stolen, but that didn't matter to Charlie. Stuff was stuff. Didn't matter if it was your stuff or his stuff, as long as it all eventually ended up becoming his stuff.

They might have guns in the house, too. Old people didn't have the kind of guns that brought good money these days. They didn't have semi-automatic pistols and tactical weapons. They usually had old worn out hunting guns, but he'd take them anyway. If he couldn't use them, someone else could and they'd pay for them. Guns had always been better than cash in his world.

He reached an oak door stained so dark that it almost appeared black. He could see that the door hardware was old, probably original to the house.

He fingered his pry bar, looking for a weak spot in which to insert it. He realized that he should probably try the door first. He twisted the door handle slowly. It was not even locked. He smiled, and pushed on the door.

Had Charlie been directly in front of the door, the first shot would have killed him. As it was, he heard the blast at the same time that oak splinters showered his face, embedding themselves in his flesh. He ducked backward, stumbling and falling off the porch. His face burned from the splinters buried in it. He knew pellets had hit his hand. He rolled onto his hands and knees, adrenaline masking the pain.

He scrambled toward the ATV. When he reached it, the front door flew open and in the glare of Charlie's light he could see a man about his own age step onto the porch with a shotgun leveled and ready to fire. The man saw Charlie's light and aimed for it. Charlie ducked, grabbing his headlamp and trying to turn the beam off. Unable to find the switch in his panic, he flung it into the darkness.

The shotgun boomed again and Charlie was showered with bits of plastic fairing and fragments of aluminum. There was more burning in his chest and neck as either the shotgun pellets or bits of shattered engine metal sprayed him. Charlie heard another shell being pumped into the chamber of the shotgun.

I'm fucking dead, he thought. He remembered the pistol holstered at his belt. He knew there was no way he could hop on the ATV and have time to start it before he was gunned down. He was going to have to shoot it out. About the time he edged his hand toward his pistol, a rifle round punctured one of the ATVs front tires. Charlie panicked and looked around, seeing another flash of gunfire from the corner of the house.

Shit, there's two of them. These people are going to fucking kill me if I don't get out of here.

Charlie took off running blindly through the dark as fast he could. He was wearing cowboy boots he'd found at Henry's house and they were about the worst running shoes imaginable. Without a light to go by, he hoped the moonlight would give him enough light to escape, without making him too obvious a target for the people shooting at him. About a dozen steps into his escape, he ran full tilt into a wheelbarrow full of firewood that had been split that day.

Charlie fell ass over teakettle, hurting nearly every part of himself that hadn't been hurt already as he, the wheelbarrow, and the wood rolled together in a heap. There was another shotgun blast, obviously aimed at the clatter in the darkness. Pellets struck the metal hopper of the wheelbarrow and startled Charlie back into motion. He ran in the general direction of the road, then realized that was not a good idea since the road would afford him no cover if they pursued him there. He changed direction a little too fast, slid in the dew-moistened grass, and stumbled. He ran now for the woods to the left of the house. More shots were fired, but they were not as close now. They'd lost track of him.

A veteran of thousands of packs of cigarettes and nearly as many joints of marijuana, Charlie did not have the cardio capacity for prolonged evasive maneuvers. As soon as he noted that the shots were not following his movements, he slowed to a trot, gasping and choking to the point that he vomited on his boots. He was certain that the sounds of his retching must be loud enough that the murderous family would soon find him, but they didn't. When he could, he wiped his mouth on his forearm and slogged onward.

When he reached the woods he stood there behind a clump of brush and watched the house. Flashlights moved about in the darkness, examining his ATV and searching the yard. In a fit of anger, the still gasping man thought of firing upon the house. He reached for his pistol as he considered this and found it to be missing. He assumed that it lay somewhere in the firewood he had unsuccessfully hurdled in his escape.

Damn!

The gun was replaceable, but he was now totally pissed off that his whole mission had gone south. He had been confident in his assessment that there was no one at the house. He'd become relatively confident that he would meet no resistance at all in this valley of elderly farmers and middle-class families. He had fully intended to enter this house and kill the old folks who lived there. He would then steal all things worth stealing and burn the house to ashes.

Apparently Lonzo Wimmer had children who decided that dad's place was more suited than their own for weathering this rough spell. They were pretty damn sneaky, too, not having any lights on, making him think no one was home. He wasn't done with them yet. He'd find a way to get even. No one ever made a fool out of Charlie Rakes.

When Charlie could tell that the men intended to continue searching for him, he decided to move on. The woods were full of noisy twigs and leaves so he stepped carefully. His plan was to cut through the woods until he had a hill between him and his searchers. That hill would buffer any noise that he made. He would then cut back down to the road where he could make better time.

When he eventually rejoined the paved road through the valley, he found himself to be near the gate where he'd hung the bodies of Henry and his wife. Even without a headlight, the road glowed like a pale river winding through the valley. He stood in front of that gate and smiled to himself, wondering what that woman must have thought when she found their bodies in the state he'd left them.

Angie and that boy of hers thought this woman didn't have her man home with her right now. Just a couple of kids and her. Charlie wasn't so sure. He'd noticed a couple of vehicles up there and they were being moved around from time to time. Of course, it could be that she was trying to make them *think* she had other people with her. Most people weren't that smart, though. Most people didn't go to that much trouble just to throw people off their trail.

He wanted to know what they had at that house. Angie didn't know anything about guns, but Robert said they had good ones. Military-style assault rifles. Tactical shotguns like the police had. He thought he'd heard a generator there once before. Maybe they were survivalists? Maybe they were just hippies on some back-to-nature kick.

But not with the guns. Everybody said hippies hated guns.

In the moonlight, he could see the profile of the house. There were no lights there, and he knew now that this didn't mean anything. He had the cuts, bruises, and wounds to prove it.

Whatever these people had, he wanted. Even if they had nothing, he wanted to find out. The question was how to get them out of there. He thought about walking up there and burning the house down right now. Supposedly, trying to get to that house was what got his brother and the other man killed. He didn't want to burn their house down until he knew what they had in there. He could continue to threaten them, but that hadn't gotten any reaction so far. He could take something that meant something to them and threaten to destroy it if they didn't leave.

He could take one of them.

He liked that idea. Aside from the fact that they pissed him off by their very refusal to move out of his valley, there was the fact of his brother's death. Like himself, his brother had been handed nothing in this world. They'd earned what they had through sheer stealth and wiliness. Stealing was against the law, but what was a man to do if he had nothing and his children were hungry? He stole and he fed them. It was Charlie who'd introduced his brother to stealing when they were children. It was a bond they shared going way back. Maybe he wouldn't run these people off until he took revenge for his brother. Maybe one of them had to die.

Maybe they all had to die.

CHAPTER 19

The Cave
Russell County, Virginia

Inside the cave, twelve-volt hanging lights struggled to cast a warm glow over the living space. As always, there was a fire in the stove that kept the temperature warmer than the normal fifty-eight degrees of the cave and helped make the space a little less damp. Despite's Jim's work, this still was not a healthy environment for his mother. She had declined throughout the day. Ellen had done what she could. Jim had an entire binder of prescribing and treatment guidelines for various ailments and they'd followed all the recommendations. Nothing was working.

They kept fluids in Nana, pumped her full of fish antibiotics, and gave her ibuprophen to lower her temperature. In one of the medical totes, Ellen had found a prescription cough medicine that Jim had received when he had the flu. They'd given Nana a dose of it but it produced little effect. She continued to run a fever and cough a deep, chest-wracking cough that had them all on edge.

Ellen attempted to distract the kids with a game of Scrabble. Games were not a good choice for her kids because playing them always turned into an argument. One or the other of the kids would accuse someone of cheating, feelings would be hurt, someone would quit, someone would pout, and everyone would end up angry, including Ellen. She had somehow forgotten that when she suggested the game.

Pops sat with Nana, reading a magazine, and occasionally tending the fire. Nana lay still on her cot, her breath a deep rattle that they all pretended not to notice. Pops suddenly closed the magazine and tossed it onto the camp table beside him. "I think I'm going to have to get her out of here for a while."

Ellen looked at Pops. She completely understood why he wanted to do that. She may even have attempted to do the same thing herself if she were in his situation, but she was completely aware that it was a risky decision. "It could be dangerous. When you drove out here, people weren't as desperate as they are now. You don't know what you're returning to."

"I don't intend to leave permanently. I won't turn my back on you and the kids, but I'm not going to sit here and watch my wife die either. I'm afraid she will if I don't get her out of this damp air. I need to get back home and into her own bed until this passes."

"We could all leave the cave and move back into our house," Ellen offered.

Pops shook his head firmly at that. "With that crazy man out there? I think you all should stay in here, like you're doing now. The kids are fine here. This air doesn't seem to be bothering anyone but Nana."

"You don't know that your house is safe. What if someone broke in? What if you get back there and somebody is living in there."

"Like *Goldilocks and The Three Bears*," Ariel said.

"We're right beside the Emergency Services Command Center. It's probably the safest spot in town."

"If there's even a Command Center there anymore. With no resources, what if they all just went home to their families?"

Pops looked at Nana, listened to the rattle of her breathing. "I still have to try. What would you do?"

Ellen knew the answer. "I'd do the same thing."

"I know you would," he said. "I just can't stay here and do nothing."

"We'll pack up gear for you tomorrow. I can set you up with antibiotics and everything you should need to take care of her. We'll set you up with a couple of weapons, plenty of ammo, and food for a week or two. We'll plan that by the time the food runs out, you'll either be back with us or we'll come looking for you. Deal?"

"Thanks for understanding, Ellen. It wasn't an easy decision to make."

Ellen stood and went over and hugged Pops. "I know it's not, but you're right. There's no other choice to make."

"Will your radios reach out as far as my house?"

"I think so. At least from the top of the hill up there. You should be able to reach Pete when he's *on-duty."*

Pops looked affectionately at his grandson. "He's turned into a man before my eyes, Ellen. It's the only reason that I can go off and leave you all here. I know he can help protect you until Jim gets back."

That was something they'd not really discussed much. For all of them, the topic of Jim's absence, especially when they were here benefitting from all his preparations, was painful. They all missed him too much for words. She knew he had to be coming home because she could not imagine the alterative. She was too busy these days to spend much time thinking about it, but at the same time it was never far from her. The only relief she could imagine at this point was that with Pops leaving, she'd have that much more to do. She would have no time at all to think about her missing husband and whether he would make it home to them.

CHAPTER 20

Burke's Garden
Tazewell County, Virginia

The night spent at the A.T. shelter above Burke's Garden was not a comfortable night. The group was so exhausted and their muscles so spent from their push for distance that no sleep position was comfortable. Each tossed fitfully, only taken into sleep by pure exhaustion for short periods. They slept with a watch that night. Their plan was for six hours of sleep, with each of them taking two hours of guard duty. They built no fire, both from a desire to keep their position concealed and due to the fact that sheer exhaustion made them not want to expend the effort when they could instead be sleeping.

For each, the two hours of guard duty was a lonely and tortuous time. With no distraction, the mind was constantly drawn to the places one did not want it to go. Combined with the emotional frailty brought about by sheer exhaustion, they had no defense against the merciless stream of painful speculation and worry. They thought of family, of friends, and of co-workers. They wondered whom they knew who might have died already in this event. They wondered if their children would ever know a normal world again. Was this all it would be from now on? Starvation? Unrest? Fear? Violence?

In the morning, they again anticipated a day spent in a desperate push for miles. For Gary, twenty-five miles would take him home, if he could do it. For Randi and Jim, twenty-five miles would put them back at the office, where they hoped to spend the night in one of the buildings, then hike the remaining fifteen miles to Jim's house the next day. Randi's house would be an additional ten miles beyond that and he intended to deliver her there personally after a night's rest at his house. If conditions were right and the roads safe enough, he may even have a vehicle and fuel to drive her home. It would be fuel that he may never be able to replace, but he would do it. They were a tight group now. They'd kept each other alive this far.

They took the time to cook a good breakfast and fortify themselves for the journey. As hard as it was to sit still this close to home, they knew that food was fuel and they'd get farther with a full tank. They drank all the coffee they could drink and boiled more to fill the spare water bottle they each carried. They knew that water sources would be more common from now on as they moved to lower elevations and that was one less worry they'd have. For that reason, they could cut back slightly on how much water each of them carried, drinking their fill when water was available and carrying only a single bottle to get them between refills. At eight pounds per gallon carried, any reduction in what they had to carry translated to less weight on the feet and less pain.

They left the Appalachian Trail behind for the last time at that shelter and descended a hunting trail into the odd round valley of Burke's Garden. The valley was four miles wide and almost nine miles long. It resembled a volcanic caldera, but was actually created by the collapse of an ancient cave system, causing the mountain above it to collapse into a bowl. The valley sat at three thousand feet in elevation and was the highest valley in Virginia. In the 1800s, the Vanderbilts tried to buy the entire valley for the creation of a massive estate. Unable to convince enough people to sell, they instead moved to Asheville, North Carolina, for their Biltmore House project.

After an hour, the trail plateaued out on the flat valley floor. When the forest opened to farmland, the first thing they saw was a man working a field with a piece of horse-drawn farm machinery. He wore old fashioned clothes and a black hat with a wide, flat brim.

"What the hell?" Randi said, stopping in her tracks. "Things must be worse here than we thought. People have taken up the old ways already."

Jim laughed. "I forgot about this. There's a small Amish community here."

"You think they even know what's happened out in the world?" Gary asked.

"I'm sure someone has told them. I guess the question is whether they even care."

They approached the man, who waited calmly and without judgement. He reached for no weapon, made no attempt to flee, and generally accepted their presence as he might the appearance of a buzzard, a cloud, or rain. Jim raised a hand to him, waving.

The man nodded a reserved greeting.

When he was within thirty feet or so, Jim called to him. "We're only passing through. We've come a long way and we're walking home."

The man nodded again.

"Do you know what's happened in the world?" Gary asked. Apparently he'd been unable to resist the impulse to ask.

"What's happened in the world is the same thing that always happens in the world," the man replied. "It's a stage for the drama of man. I'm aware of what's happened, but we do not bother ourselves with it."

None of the group replied to this, because what the hell do you say to a thing like that?

The man broke a faint smile after a moment of staring at them. "If you follow me to the house, there's fresh bread and butter if you'd like some."

"That just made me weak in the knees," Randi said.

"That would be wonderful," Gary said.

The man dismounted his machine and started walking. They followed him to his house and sat on a bench in the yard while he went inside. In a moment, the man returned with his wife and daughter. The wife had a dish of butter and a loaf of bread on a plate. The daughter carried a pitcher of water and three cups.

Randi did not hesitate. She was immediately at the woman's side to receive a slice of the fresh bread. She stuck it to her nose and inhaled. "It's still warm."

Jim and Gary weren't far behind. The bread was amazing —one of the most amazing food experiences Jim had ever had. He realized that his palate had been abused as badly as his feet over the past week or so. He looked to his host. "Thank you for this. This means a lot to us."

The man smiled but said nothing. They stayed long enough to finish the loaf and have a cup of cold spring water. When they prepared to leave, Jim thanked the man again and left him with a warning. "Keep an eye out. We've seen ugly things out there on the stage of man, as you called it. The world is becoming a rough place."

The man smiled and shook his head as if he were privy to some joke that Jim didn't get.

*

The walk to Tazewell, Virginia, mercifully took them less time than they'd planned. They encountered a man going the same way, riding a horse-drawn hay wagon. The back was full of various goods that the man said he was going to sell at the local flea market. There was some produce, a box of blankets, and a box of odd tools that Jim assumed must be spares.

"The flea market at the livestock market?" Jim asked.

The man nodded. "The same."

Jim shook his head. "Everything that's happened in the world and that flea market is still going strong?"

"It's gotten even bigger. Used to be just junk, as you probably know – cheap tools, antiques, pocket knives. Now you can buy anything you need there. It's replaced most stores as the place to get goods. You can buy anything from honey to homemade butter and cheeses to car parts."

The man allowed them to ride with him as far as the flea market, which was not only to the town of Tazewell but several miles beyond it.

"Thanks," Gary said. "That probably took ten miles off our trip."

"Every bit of it," the man agreed.

The others thanked the man and started to walk off, back toward the road.

"You shouldn't leave yet," the man called after them. "There's probably someone here that can give you a ride in that direction. People come from all over. Even if you had to wait a while for them to leave it would still be easier than walking."

They all agreed that he was right.

"I trade here a lot," he said. "You guys look around some. I'll be set up there selling my wares. Let me know if you can't find a ride and I'll see if I can help you out."

*

The group found it difficult to patiently walk around looking. They were all anxious to continue their journey. They could practically smell home. It felt odd to be here among so many people. The people actually did not look that much different than the normal crowd that would be here for the flea market, except that there were a lot more of them and many were armed. Jim assumed that there were probably more guns than he could see, with some opting to keep their weapons concealed or stowed in whatever transportation they'd used to get here.

Despite the lack of power and modern amenities, most people dressed the same. Their clothes were a little more wrinkled and people were wearing clothes a little more stained than they used to. Apparently, with it requiring significantly more effort to wash clothes now, the threshold of what constituted *dirty* had been raised. People lacked the polish and veneer you would have previously found in a social setting such as this. Most women were not wearing the amount of makeup they would have worn previously, if they were even wearing any at all. There was still a proliferation of perfume and after-shave and it was easy to assume that it was being worn for the purpose it was originally designed for centuries ago – to mask the smell of the unwashed.

Hair styles were another area where tastes had relaxed. Jim could tell that people were going further between shampooing than they typically would have in the recent past. This would change even further as most people ran out of shampoo. When soap was gone, he assumed that those with the knowledge of making lye soap would be here at this very event selling and trading bars of it. It was simple to make and he had the instructions at home for making it. If this event dragged out past his soap supply, he'd be using lye soap, too.

Even among what was a less refined society than the one they had left, Jim and his group stuck out. With their backpacks, it was obvious they were travelers. While many had walked here and carried packs and bags for their wares and purchases, the packs that Jim, Gary, and Randi had were larger, dirtier, and crammed with gear. They lived out of them and that was hard to hide.

They were professional people, unused to appearing in public in the state in which they found themselves. This became more apparent as they noticed the stares of those they passed. Even in a world turned rough and hard, they distinguished themselves. Their clothes were dirty and showing signs of very hard wear. Their bodies were dirty. Their nails held black crescents of filth. Their faces were masked with dust. Their knees and palms showed signs of frequent contact with the ground. Even though they had nearly become immune to it, they knew they reeked of body odor.

Jim halfway expected to run into people he knew, having worked in this community for most of his adult life. He dreaded it, uncomfortable in the state that he found himself in, but he was spared and ran into no familiar faces. Of course, if that familiar face had a vehicle going in his direction, he'd have been more than glad to see them. When they began to look for the man that had transported them this far, they noticed a cluster of people leaving. Jim saw the man headed for the field that used to be the parking lot rather than walking out the entrance gate on foot like most were. His heart started racing when he realized that the man was heading toward a tractor with a hay wagon.

Jim set off walking quickly in that direction. "Come on. Let's see where this guy is going."

He approached the man carefully, not wanting to give the impression that he was any sort of threat. The man was with a woman who appeared to be his wife, several children, and another couple who also had a child with them.

Jim called to them and held up a hand in greeting. "My friends and I are looking for a ride in the Richlands direction. You all going that way?"

The man turned and regarded Jim and his group. He wore clothes that had never been in style even when they were new, but he was neat and had his hair slicked back with some type of oil. His wife and daughters all wore dresses that came to their ankles. They were obviously Pentecostal folks from one of the many churches of that faith that dotted the area. Religious or not, the man was all business.

"Fuel is hard to get," the man said. "I hear they ain't making any more right now. I ain't against taking on passengers but there ain't a free ride to be found in this county no more."

Jim knew that this statement was not entirely true. The Amish man had not charged them for the bread he shared, and the man who'd hauled them down there had not charged them for a ride. In fact, if they were already going in that direction anyway, why would they even feel a need to charge passengers for riding along with them? He was aware, however, that debating the man on this would not help him in obtaining a ride. It would make him look petty and he might become defensive.

"I realize that a ride is a precious thing these days. We've walked hundreds of miles to get this far. Nearly all the way from Richmond, Virginia. If we have to pay to get a little farther, we'll pay."

The man looked a little sheepish after hearing how far they'd come. His wife gave him a stern look. Jim thought that it was intended as a prompt to the husband that he might consider being a little more charitable to a couple of folks who obviously needed the break. "I wouldn't be looking for a whole lot, but if you had anything to trade it might help me barter to refill the tank next time. We'd be helping each other out."

Well aware that the currency of hard times was beans or bullets, Jim cut straight to the chase. "Can you get us all the way to Claypool Hill?" It was a major intersection a few miles from their office. It would be the point where Gary cut away to head toward his own home.

"I can," the man replied. "I'm heading toward Cedar Bluff myself."

Jim glanced at Gary, who seemed thrilled by this possibility. Cedar Bluff would knock off half of Gary's walk from Claypool Hill. It would only be a four mile walk from there to Gary's house.

"I'll give you twenty-five rounds of 9mm ammo if you take us to Claypool Hill and then drop him off in Cedar Bluff."

The man rubbed his chin and considered. He looked up at Jim. "A full box would make it a little easier to accept your offer."

Jim squared his body and crossed his arms. His voice was firm. "You're going that way anyway. With only the three of us, you'll be burning about the same amount of fuel, you'll just have twenty-rounds of 9mm that you didn't have before. It sounds like a reasonable offer to me."

The man caught his wife out of the corner of his eye. She was looking at Jim's group sympathetically and attempting to remind her husband that he should definitely be considering a little Christian charity in this case. The man knew he better accept the offer or his wife would find some way to make him do it for free. He accepted the offer.

"In advance now," he added quickly. "Not that I don't trust you. I just don't want to forget about it when we get down the road. It would be easier for all of us to get that whole payment business out of the way right now."

Rather than dig into his pack and display how much ammo he was carrying, Jim instead dug a Beretta clip from the pocket of his 5.11s and began flipping rounds out into his palm.

"I feel bad you're the one paying for the ride," Gary said. "I don't have any 9mm."

Jim didn't look up from his counting. "It'll give me an excuse to come visit you in a few weeks. I can come collect the twelve and a half rounds you owe me."

When Jim had thumbed twenty-five rounds out of his two spare mags, he reached out and dumped them into the man's sweaty palm. The man counted them, then dropped them into his pants pocket. He raised his arm and gestured toward the wagon. "All aboard. Ladies first."

The man's wife smiled at them. Jim nodded at her and smiled back, his expression acknowledging that her contribution was not to be underestimated. Gary, Randi, and Jim tossed their packs onto the hay wagon and joined the man's family there. Two of his children chose to sit on the fenders of his blue Ford tractor alongside him. Once seated on the wagon, Jim could not wipe the stupid grin off his face. Home felt closer than ever.

CHAPTER 21

The Cave
Russell County, Virginia

After a large but somber breakfast, Pete assumed his normal spot in his observation post. He was always up there by 8 a.m. these days, watching for anything but seeing very little. Ellen was glad that it kept him occupied, and at the same time did not discount the potential benefit of having him up there keeping an eye on things. Ariel had quickly complained of being bored after the meal was finished, which Ellen solved by having her do the breakfast dishes. That was not the resolution that Ariel was hoping for, but after a stern look from her mother she conceded defeat. She was still a little girl and the disruption in her routine was making things hard on her.

This was the day Pops and Nana were leaving and it hung like a cloud over the family. Despite this being the only real option at this point, the idea made Ellen sick with worry. She felt she was disappointing Jim by not keeping an eye on his parents, and she felt responsible for Nana's illness because it had been her idea to drag them out to her house in the first place, and then on to the cave. Pops felt like he was disappointing Jim by not keeping an eye on Ellen and the kids. Basically, no one felt at ease with the whole matter, but no one had another solution. With Pops occupied packing their personal items, Ellen took responsibility for outfitting the older couple's trip back to their home in town.

Ellen assumed Pops would be taking the 9mm Ruger pistol he'd been carrying since he got here, so she made sure that he had spare magazines and two boxes of ammunition for the weapon. It was more than he should ever need but *extra* was preferable to *empty*. She dug out the shotgun that he'd brought with him and packed an ammo can of shells for that. Surely those weapons should be sufficient for anything he'd encounter on his brief trip. They were weapons he was familiar with, which was of utmost importance in a panic situation. In emergencies, you needed muscle memory that would react without you having to think out basic actions, such as the location of the safety switch, how to cycle the action, and how to reload.

Unsure of what remained at the house in town, Ellen found a battery-powered lantern and spare batteries. Pops had a headlamp and flashlight already, so she packed some spare batteries for them in the oversized Cabela's duffel bag that she was using for their gear. She also packed a large baggie of medical supplies and placed those in the duffel bag with the rest of the gear. Pops said they had fever reducers as home, but she packed him some anyway, along with a bottle of the fish antibiotics and some cough medicine.

Since Pops and Nana had brought much of their food supply with them, Ellen wanted to make sure they had plenty to eat. The meals needed to be simple to fix since Pops wasn't known for his cooking abilities. She packed a box with canned food, coffee, a few just-add-water noodle and rice meals, and even a few MREs. She had an old green Coleman camp stove that ran off white gas and she put that in his vehicle along with a can of Coleman fuel. Pops had lent them this very stove years ago so she knew that he could operate it.

From the cans he'd brought with him, Pops topped his truck's fuel tank off and put a spare five-gallon can in the back. When he was done, he turned and faced Ellen. "I feel bad about this," he said.

"You don't have anything to feel bad about. You're right that Nana needs to be in a dryer environment until she kicks whatever it is that's making her sick. In a few days, we'll all catch back up and maybe Jim will be back here by then. Maybe things will even be back to normal."

She caught his eye. She hadn't believed that bit about things being normal when she said it, and it was clear he wasn't believing it either. "I always thought Jim went overboard on this stuff, Ellen. I admit it. I see now that he knew what he was talking about. Now I agree with what you said when you convinced us to come out here. You said things might never be normal again and I think you're probably right."

"I'm not sure I ever believed that something like this could happen either," Ellen said. "I certainly never figured things would go downhill as fast as they did, but Jim always said they would. I'm just hoping that his understanding these kind of events has helped him travel safely through this one. He said he had a plan for getting home but I never asked him much about it because I assumed he wouldn't ever need to do it. I hope his plan was a good one. I have faith in him."

When the truck was completely loaded, Ellen helped Pops load Nana into the passenger seat. She was still running a fever and coughing. She didn't look good at all. She was extremely pale and there was no way she'd been getting enough fluids. Under normal circumstances, Ellen would have recommended they go straight to the nearest Emergency Room, but with no power and no food she couldn't imagine that any hospital had remained open. Most of them had generator power for short term, but would those generators still be operational? It might be worth checking. Pops had to pass by there anyway on his way through town.

Ellen stopped Pops as he started to get in the truck. "The ER is on your way. Why don't you stop and see if they're open? If not, you're no worse off. If they are, you might be able to get some help."

"You know, I used to be on that hospital's board of directors."

"I know," she said. "Maybe that will give you some pull with them."

"I'll try it," he said, giving her a hug, then climbing into the driver's seat.

"Me too!" Ariel said, running up and hugging Pops.

He hugged her back, then waved at Pete up at his post. They all hugged Nana, but she was pretty incoherent and unresponsive. With all the goodbyes over with, Pops started his truck and followed the farm road out of sight of the cave.

As Pops crested the hill that led him from the cave, Pete was able to follow him with the spotting scope. He watched Pops drive out past their house. Pops hesitated there for a second, as if he was going to cut through the neighbor's field, the way that Pete had brought him in. Instead, he opted to leave by the driveway, weaving back and forth between the steel beams that had been laid out in the driveway as barricades. When he reached the gate, the very gate where Henry and his wife had hung dead a few days ago, he unlocked it and drove out through it. As he got out of his vehicle to relock the gate behind him, Pete zoomed the spotting scope in on his grandfather and followed his every move. He wanted to make sure that no one tried to sneak up on him. Only when Pops returned to his vehicle and drove away did Pete breathe easier.

With Pops leaving the area now, Pete pulled back his focus on the spotting scope and began to search the fields. He didn't know what he was looking for, but figured he'd know when saw it.

CHAPTER 22

The Valley
Russell County, Virginia

When Charlie had arrived home last night, he burst through the door like a train wreck. He woke everyone in the house up with his cursing and yelling. They were horrified by the blood-covered apparition that paced the living room.

"Bring me a bottle of liquor, woman!" he'd screamed at Angie.

She hadn't moved, unable to figure out what had happened to him. This didn't sit well with Charlie. He wasn't in the mood for waiting.

"Liquor!" he bellowed.

She was still frozen, unable to pull herself from the gore-encrusted tornado that spun and cursed around the living room.

"Robert," Charlie said, stopping in front of the boy. The young man stepped forward, not meeting Charlie's eyes. "You go to my truck, boy. Get me that pillowcase that's behind the driver's seat and you bring it to me. I'm going to be watching you. You open the damn thing and look in it, I'll break every fucking bone in your body."

"Charlie!" Angie said. "Don't—"

He whirled on her, raising a hand. "Robert, I mean it. Now go." He turned back to Angie. "And where's my bottle of liquor, woman? I've done asked you once."

Robert took off out the door. Angie stepped to the kitchen and returned with a bottle of Jim Beam and handed it to Charlie.

"Is there a first aid kit in this place?" Charlie asked.

Angie sped off toward the bathroom looking for one.

Charlie collapsed into the recliner, nearly toppling it backward. The army of children stood in front of him, mesmerized by the bleeding and raving maniac before them.

Robert returned with the pillowcase and tossed it into Charlie's lap. Charlie stared at the boy. "Don't go throwing shit at me unless you're wanting your ass beat. You hear me? I ain't in the mood to be disrespected by the likes of you."

183

Robert didn't respond. They all watched as Charlie removed a pill bottle from the sack, read the label, and opened it. He shook three white pills into his hand and swallowed them, washing them down with Jim Beam.

Charlie wasn't addicted to pain pills, but he sure liked one occasionally. This time it wasn't about getting a buzz. This time it was about trying to wash himself free of the burning in his face, the pain and stinging that was nearly driving him mad. He remembered once, when he was in his thirties, wanting pain pills so bad that he took a Phillips screwdriver, shoved it between his ribs, and collapsed his own lung. When he collapsed to the parking lot and felt the pain of what he'd done, it was the worst he'd ever experienced. This was not nearly that bad, but it hurt like fucking hell.

Angie returned with a handful of Band-Aids, alcohol, gauze, tape, and other supplies. "What happened to you?"

"I got shot," he moaned.

Robert could not hold back a smile. "You got caught," he said, the words out of his mouth before he even knew what he was doing.

Pain or no pain, Charlie was out of the chair in the blink of an eye, his open hand connecting with Robert's face and knocking him from his feet. Robert tripped over the brick hearth and fell hard. He lay on the floor, holding his reddening face, staring furiously at the ground.

"You and me are fixing to have a big problem, boy. If you know what's good for you, you'll stay out of my fucking sight for a long damn time."

Robert crawled from the room, down the hall, and into a bedroom where he shut the door softly behind him, making not another sound.

"You ought not treat him that way," Angie said. "He's your own flesh and blood. Your brother wouldn't like what you just did."

Charlie collapsed back in his chair. "Dammit, woman, my brother ain't here. I'm here. I'm bleeding and I'm tired of listening to your mouth. Patch me the fuck up. I don't give a shit about that boy right now."

Angie stared at him. "He ain't a boy, he's a man. And I give a shit about him. So did your brother."

Charlie had enough and a chill settled over him. He was near the place of unrepentant fury, the place where he could wipe all traces of his brother's family from this Godforsaken valley. "You're fixing to meet Jesus if you keep talking."

Angie bit her tongue. She had no doubt of Charlie's seriousness. "Take your shirt off."

Charlie pulled his shirt off over his head. His face and chest were bleeding from dozens of little wounds. Splinters protruded from many of them. Angie winced at the sight of it.

"All anybody in this family wants to do is run their mouth," Charlie continued, his voice beginning to slur from the pills he'd taken. "A man can only take so much."

Angie stood up. "I'll need tweezers."

She went to the bathroom and found some. In the cabinet she saw an old-fashioned straight razor sitting with a shaving brush in a mug. She considered taking the razor and slitting Charlie's throat right where he sat. She'd do it in front of God, her children, and everyone. She knew it would save her a lot of heartache to do it now and get it over with, but she didn't think she could. She'd never been a good decision-maker.

Maybe she'd have to, later. She grabbed the razor and tucked it into the pocket of her shorts.

Just in case.

*

After a few hours of sleep, Charlie woke up in the chair where he'd passed out. Everyone else was awake and was in a sour mood. They all seemed pissed at him but he wasn't sure what they thought he'd done. What the hell did those people expect, anyway? He went out and risked his life to try and find supplies for all of them and this was the thanks he got? He had to get out of there for the day. To hell with all of them.

He found a good pair of binoculars in Henry's bedroom closet. He looked through the guns he'd accumulated, searching for a replacement for the revolver he'd lost in his fight after getting shot last night. He ended up choosing a Winchester lever-action .30-.30. He'd always liked those, probably from so many fond memories of watching westerns on television when he was a kid. He worked the action, enjoying the mechanical clatter of it. There was a box of shells in the closet. It was a full box of twenty rounds and surely to God he'd not need more than that to get through the day.

He took his binoculars and rifle and went to the truck and drove away from the lot of them. They receded in his rear-view mirror like a headache responding to aspirin.

When he neared the house that he wanted to watch, he pulled the truck off the road. He opened an unlocked gate and pulled the truck through, leaving it parked in the weeds. He locked the truck and pocketed the keys. There were lots of son-of-a-bitches wandering around these days who'd steal your shit.

He walked along the fence line through the thick weeds, keeping an eye out for any people. He wanted to position himself across from the house where that woman and her kids lived. He had to know what they had. This was his mission now. He would hide in the weeds and keep an eye on them. He would get in that house at all costs. If he succeeded, he might just leave Angie and her kids where they were. He needed some space. He had a hard time thinking with the racket all those children made. Angie wasn't much better. She was so damn mopey anymore and always siding with that oldest boy of hers.

He dropped to his hands and knees and crawled when he came within sight of the house, staying close to the fence and then working his way into the ditch line. He had planted himself in the weeded ditch across from the gate when he heard a vehicle approaching. It was coming down the road from the house. He locked his binoculars onto them. It was an older man and woman. This was not the woman that lived here. He didn't know these people, but they must mean something to that woman or they wouldn't have been there. From their age, he wondered if they could be her parents. That would be nice. Charlie could do a lot with that scenario.

The man got out, opened the gate and drove through. For a moment, Charlie panicked, thinking the man might pull off the shoulder of the road and run over him, but he didn't. He was damn close, though. The man hopped out of the cab and began plodding back to close the gate. Through the open cab door, Charlie saw the woman was asleep now.

Charlie's brain was overloaded with possibilities. He could steal the truck. Maybe these people were going somewhere important. Someplace where they had supplies stashed. He didn't know, but thought maybe he should find out. With hardly a thought, he rose from his hiding place, put a foot on the truck tire, and soundlessly pulled himself into the tall bed. It was a heavy duty work truck that sat high off the ground. Charlie knew that unless the man lowered the tailgate he'd never see him. He did not even breathe again until he heard the truck door shut and the shifter move into gear.

He did not know where he was going. He had not thought this out completely; however, he had certainly taken bigger chances on less information than this. Maybe it would turn into something. Maybe it would give him some leverage.

*

The Russell County Medical Center was probably the largest building in the town of Lebanon, Virginia. Originally a small hospital started by two local doctors, it had grown steadily over the years. It was now a conglomeration of multiple additions and wings that made it pretty difficult to know where you were even supposed to enter the building. Pops had been on their Board of Directors for years and was on a first name basis with most of the doctors. As soon as he got within sight of the hospital, he could tell that it was sheer chaos there. The parking lots were overflowing and cars were parked along both sides of the road leading up to the hospital. Folks were walking back and forth to vehicles, some crying, some being carried.

Pops saw nothing blocking the ambulance bay doors at the ER, so he drove straight there. He could see that the Emergency Room was crammed with people. In fact, there was a line extending out the door. Two gurneys stood outside the ambulance bay. Blue sheets were stretched across what was obviously dead bodies. There were heavy blood stains on one of the sheets. Having no interest in waiting in that line, Pops parked at the swinging doors that were typically used to bring emergency patients in on stretchers. He barged through the doors into sheer pandemonium.

There were no lights and folks were using headlamps, flashlights, and battery lanterns to get around. There was screaming and crying. Three more bodies lay in the triage areas covered fully by sheets, obviously dead. With no functional instruments, the few nurses who were working were limited in what they could do. They could take temperatures, administer oxygen for as long as they had it, stitch and splint, but any advanced procedures were pretty much off the table for the immediate future. Pops wondered how long medications would hold out at this rate.

When no one noticed him, Pops bellowed. "Harrison? Where's Dr. Harrison?" His voice was so loud that there was no ignoring it.

A nurse trying to get an injection into an uncooperative woman looked at him with a glimmer of recognition, like she'd seen Pops before but she couldn't place him. "No one's seen him in days," she said. "We don't know where he is."

Pops frowned. "What about Nelson?"

The nurse shook her head. "He hasn't left here in a week. I'm not sure where he is at the moment."

"So who's working the ER? There has to be a doctor."

"I am," the nurse replied. "And Pam over there."

"That's it? With all these people out there?"

She nodded. "That line's not going down. It keeps getting longer."

Pops realized he'd better take advantage of what expertise he could get. He wasn't wasting any more time looking for a doctor. "My wife is sick – coughing, fever, kind of rattly."

"Have you started her on antibiotics?"

"Yes."

"She have cough medicine?"

"Yes."

The nurse finally landed her injection, tossed the empty syringe in a sharps container, and went to a cabinet on the wall. She pulled a key from around her neck and opened the cabinet, then removed a pre-loaded syringe and a white bottle. "Give her this injection in her arm and start her on the pills. Two pills, three times a day."

"I'll never remember that."

The nurse frowned, pulled a pen from her pocket, and scribbled a note on the side of the white bottle. She handed the items to Pops and he put them in his pocket. He started to thank the woman but when he looked up from his pocket she was gone. To his left there was a horrific wail and a woman holding a child began rocking the child back and forth, screaming. The child was dead.

Pops burst back through the doors he'd entered. He felt a rush of euphoria, feeling like he'd taken a significant step toward getting his wife back on track. He stopped dead in his tracks. His world collapsed around him.

His truck was gone.

He looked around, thinking maybe someone had moved it because of where he'd left it. He didn't see it. He saw a man smoking nearby. "You see what happened to my truck?" he demanded.

"Drove off."

Pops stepped up to the man and got in his face. Despite his age, he was intimidating. He stood a full six foot seven inches tall. "Who the hell drove it off?"

The man shrugged. "That feller that was in the back got out and drove it off."

"There wasn't anyone in the back."

The man nodded, his eyes wide with fear. "There was. He crawled right out of there and hopped in the front. Gave me a little wave as he was pulling out."

Pops roared with anger. He was frantic. He put his head in his hands and stood there. It was his fault. The day was hot and he'd left the keys in the truck, with the A/C running to keep Nana comfortable. Now she was gone. He had to do something.

He shoved his way back into the ER. "Call the police. Somebody stole my truck and kidnapped my wife."

Despite his volume and rage, no one responded. All he got was stares. He tried to tone it down a notch, to appear less threatening. "I need to call the police!"

Everyone continued to stare like he was losing his mind.

"Won't anyone help me?"

Silence.

Then it was broken by an overweight, toothless lady in her sixties wearing a tank-top and sweatpants. "There ain't no phones," she said.

"Dammit!"

Pops turned and kicked the door open, barging through. He started walking.

CHAPTER 23

The largest highway intersection in the region was at Claypool Hill, where Highways 19 and 460 either joined or diverged, depending on which way you were headed. From the Tazewell direction, a right at Claypool Hill led you to Grundy, Virginia, and then into Kentucky. Continuing straight on Route 19 South led you to Russell County and then into Tennessee. This would be where the group finally parted ways. Gary would continue another couple of miles with the family on the tractor until they discharged him at the town of Cedar Bluff. Randi and Jim would walk the remaining couple of miles to their office complex and find a place to stay for the night. Earlier in the day, Jim had hoped that by catching a ride they might make it down here early enough to walk on to his house. That had not happened. Although the tractor was faster and easier, it was not *significantly* faster. It was nearly 7 p.m. when they reached this point. The miles between them and the office were probably all that Jim and Randi could hope to cover this evening.

Riding those last few miles together on the wagon, the trio discussed how they might maintain contact once everyone reached their homes. After this much time together, each felt that they were somewhat invested in the others reaching home. Each wanted their companions to get home and find their family safely awaiting them. Jim wasn't the sort to get all sentimental about this kind of thing. He acknowledged that they had some sort of connection, perhaps the kind of connection that survivors of any life-threatening event experienced. Still, he wasn't ready to hold hands and sing Kumbaya. That was not his kind of thing.

"I tried for several years to get you to get your HAM license, Jim. If you'd done it, and bought the little Baofeng handheld that I recommended, this would be no issue. I'm certain that we could reach each other easily with those radios."

Jim had been kicking himself for this every time he thought about it on the walk home. As he saw it, there were two big failures in his preparations. He was certain there were probably several thousand small failures but only two big ones that gnawed at him over all the miles he'd walked. The first was that he hadn't replaced the family dogs who'd died this past year. They'd had two since purchasing their small farm. They got them around the same time. One was a German Shepard and coonhound mix that Jim had found in a dumpster while tossing in a bag of garbage. He named him Crow, because he was small, black, and eating garbage. The other was an Australian Shepard.

Both dogs had been getting older and Crow had died the past winter of old age. The Australian Shepard, Panda, had been killed in the spring when a group of coyotes came through. They killed Panda and ate five cats. The losses had been hard on the family and Jim hadn't been ready to replace them yet. Every farm needed a dog. They provided the best alarm system and were one of the first lines of defense on a homestead. Jim had kicked himself each day for not leaving his family with one good dog guarding the house.

The second thing that he was punishing himself over was for not obtaining the HAM radios that Gary had encouraged him to buy. It was possible that those radios would have allowed him to communicate with his family already. Even if he couldn't reach them directly, it was highly likely that he could have found another HAM operator who could have reached them and relayed a message.

Honestly, the only reason he didn't have the license was that he didn't want to go take the test. He had no doubt he could have passed it, he just didn't want to go take it. Even so, he should have bought the damn radio. The Chinese radios were cheap and at this point who was going to be checking for licenses anyway? If he owned it, he could be using it now regardless of whether he had a license or not. It only went to show that no matter how well one prepared, there were always gaps.

"Okay, I don't have the radio, we've established that. What now?"

"I'm about three miles' walk from the top of Kent's Ridge," Gary said after a moment of thought. "You're only a couple of miles from Clinch Mountain, right?"

"Just about one mile," Jim said.

"Then how about we say that three days from now I go to my high spot, you go to yours, and we try to reach each other with the radios that we got from the ranger station? Say about 8 p.m. or so."

Jim nodded. He had several sets of those family band radios at home, but the sets they'd taken from the ranger station at Mount Rogers were better than anything he had. "I think those have a 35 mile range. That should cover us if we can get above the hills."

"What channel?" Gary asked.

"How about Channel 10, set to privacy code 10 for starters. If someone is already on that channel and code, move down to Channel 10, privacy code 9, and so on until we find a good signal."

"What about you, Randi?" Gary asked.

"I live close to a hill and I'm about ten miles from Jim. I can give it a shot."

"Do you understand how to set the channel and privacy code?"

She nodded.

"If we can't reach each other, we try again the next night at the same time until we've linked up. Got it?" Gary said.

"Almost there," called the driver. "Coming up to the roadblock here in a minute. I can already see it."

"Roadblock?" Jim asked.

"Yes," the man's wife replied. "There's so many bad people out and about that they have put a couple of roadblocks in place to keep an eye on who's running the roads."

"We have guns," Gary said. "Will that be a problem? Cause if it is, I'm jumping off now."

"No, not at all – *everybody* has guns now. You'd have to be crazy to be out here without one." The woman opened her purse to show them a polished chrome Taurus automatic. "I shoot .40 cal, myself."

"After what we've seen, I feel a lot safer knowing that there are good people with guns, too, and not only the bad guys," Jim said.

Nearing the roadblock, they could see that the four lanes coming into the T-intersection from each direction had been narrowed down to two. Concrete jersey barriers acted as funnels. Deputies in orange safety vests and tactical gear manned the checkpoint. They appeared to only be checking the few vehicles that were moving. As this was a rural area, there was no use trying to check foot traffic because most people would not use the road. If they were on foot, they would use shortcuts, side roads, and hunting trails.

The big tractor pulled into the chute of concrete barriers, and a deputy held up his hand to stop them. His insignia indicated that he was a Tazewell County deputy. He held a full-auto H&K MP5. Jim always wondered how these small counties that could barely afford to pay and insure their teachers could afford such expensive weapons.

Their driver killed his engine. "Howdy boys, been to the flea market, and I'm heading back home now."

The deputy came closer and scanned the group on the trailer. "You got more folks now than when you left," he commented.

"We brought back some hitchhikers," the driver said. "One's going into town with us. The other two are headed into Russell County."

The deputy came closer, staring at the three. "You guys look like shit."

"We feel like shit, too," Jim said. "We walked all the way back from Richmond."

"Fair enough," the deputy replied. "What's Richmond like?"

"We got out of there pretty quickly," Gary said. "But the interstate is like a war zone."

The deputy assessed them. "You guys don't look that dangerous. How'd you make it through that?"

"The fact that we're here should tell you something," Randi replied.

The deputy considered this, then nodded and waved them through. "Take it easy, badasses. I ain't sure you'll find home any safer. Some places around here are turning into war zones."

That was not encouraging. The tractor pulled through the intersection, turned right, and then pulled over to the side of the road once they were clear of the barricades.

Jim shook Gary's hand. "Thanks, my friend. I couldn't have got this far without you."

"Same here," Gary said. "Thanks for everything."

Randi dropped her gear and came rolling in from the side. She hugged Gary, nearly knocking him over. "Thank you, Gary. You made it much easier to tolerate this guy," she said, gesturing toward Jim. "He can be a jerk."

"The meter is running," the driver reminded them. "I've got places to go and people to bother."

Gary jumped back on the wagon. "Let's go. Maybe I'll get home in time for dinner."

Jim and Randi thanked the driver as he drove away. As the tractor moved away from them, an odd feeling of loneliness crept over the pair. It was like separation anxiety. After an intense period on the road, sharing every moment together, losing one of their group was disturbing. The three becoming two would take some getting used to. They turned away from the receding tractor and shouldered their loads. It was quiet now, just the two of them and a pair of deputies manning the checkpoint. There were no more moving vehicles and no foot traffic. The sun was getting lower in the sky. They needed to move. They were racing daylight.

When they moved toward their road, one of the deputies called to them. "Where you guys headed right now? You ain't going to make it as far as Lebanon tonight, if that's what you're thinking."

"We're headed to the mental health agency by the college," Jim said. "We both work there. We thought we might find an office we could stay in for the night and then head to Lebanon in the morning."

The deputy walked closer to them. "Be careful down there. Any place that might have any type of drugs stored there has been broken into and looted. You all dispense meds, don't you?"

"Some," Randi replied.

"Doesn't matter," he said. "If it's a drug, people are stealing it. The college next door to your office has been turned into an emergency shelter. Things are a little crazy down there now. They don't really have much food or anything so people are living there and foraging for what they can find. We don't have enough cops to help out with it."

"The National Guard armory is by the college," Jim said. "Are they helping out?"

The cop shook his head. "No, every unit in Southwest Virginia got pulled out. They've all been deployed to Northern Virginia to help those folks out."

"What about *our* folks?" Randi asked.

The deputy slung his rifle over his shoulder and smiled. "We are the red-headed stepchild in this state. You guys should know that. Nobody cares what happens to the hillbillies in the coalfields."

"No shit," Randi said.

"Well, thanks for the information," Jim said.

"No problem. You all be safe."

Randi and Jim started walking. The five miles between them and the office seemed uneventful after the craziness of the past days. At times, the walk was even boring, but neither of them complained. They were in very familiar territory now. They passed the store where Randi bought cigarettes on her lunch break each day, the liquor store they both admitted to stopping at occasionally to buy a little something for the weekend. They passed the fast food joint where they bought lunch when they were in a hurry, the tractor dealership where Jim bought parts for his excavator and chains for his chainsaw. This wasn't yet home, but it was damn close. Familiarity was an energizing thing.

*

The sun was below the horizon by the time they finally reached their office complex. The mental health agency where they both worked was basically in the middle of nowhere, on the highway between two small towns. Besides their agency, there was a community college and a National Guard armory located adjacent to each other, making for a large cluster of buildings all merging into what looked like one large campus. Their agency was among the first set of buildings they came to. They stood at the intersection staring toward the nearest building. It was a single-story brick office building that housed clinic services for the mentally ill and for substance abusers. They could see that the glass storefront had been completely demolished. It looked like someone had driven a car through it to gain access. They experienced a mixture of relief and anxiety seeing a place so familiar, yet uncertain if it was safe to proceed or not.

Randi's office had been in this building. She shook her head as she stared at it. "I'm not going in there."

"Me neither."

One of the items under Jim's umbrella in the structure of this agency was supervision of construction and maintenance. He could only imagine the nightmare that the repair of this facility would be, if reopening was ever an option. Realistically, it might not be. There might not be the money in the government anymore to operate large agencies such as this. He wondered what would happen to the mentally ill. Those that survived would probably be locked up in facilities like they were forty years ago. He knew the facilities would eventually reopen. The state of Virginia had had the first mental health facilities in the nation, going all the way back to 1773 in Williamsburg. There were a lot of social programs society could do without, but if mentally ill people were running around without treatment, everyone paid the price.

Jim started walking. "Let's try the administrative building."

Randi hesitated, then started walking toward the entrance of the clinical building. There were benches outside for visitors waiting for their appointments. As Randi walked toward the bench, Jim noticed the still form laying in the tall grass. The typically well-manicured grounds were tipping toward overgrown and the weeds obscured the body. By the time Jim got there, Randi was backing up, her hand over her mouth. He stared down at what Randi had found.

At their feet lay the body of an overweight man with unkempt hair, his glasses askew on his face. He'd slit his wrists with a pocketknife. A bright orange appointment card lay beside him.

"This guy has been coming here for over twenty years," Randi said. "I remember him from back when I used to work clinics. He said we saved his life."

"I guess he couldn't face what was waiting for him when the meds ran out."

Randi shook her head, turned, and walked away.

They found the administrative building in no better shape. Even though no drugs were kept there, it appeared to have made no difference to the vandals. The front windows had all been knocked out and the glass doors shattered.

"Do you want to go in?" Randi asked.

"Yes. The second floor would have been harder to access with no power. The elevator would be dead so they couldn't get upstairs using it. The access control system is fail-secure, so the doors stays locked when the power goes off."

"There might be other places we could stay if this building has been trashed, places that haven't been broken into."

"It's not just about finding a safe place to hole up. We have a Continuity of Operations plan that requires us to store a few emergency supplies on site. I was responsible for buying and storing them. I know exactly what's in there and we need to get to it. They're stored in a locked cabinet behind a locked door. If that area is still secure, there will be some water and a few other supplies."

"Lead the way," Randi said.

Jim drew his pistol and held it ready. They carefully moved through the entrance area, crunching their way through granules of broken safety glass into the reception area. The sliding reception windows were also shattered. Jim stepped up to the counter and looked through the opening. Inside was chaos. Everything had been broken and vandalized.

"These weren't just people searching for stuff," Jim said. "These were just people breaking shit."

"The cop said people were using the college as a shelter. Maybe the bored teens paid us a visit to blow off some steam."

"You may be right. Or it may have been substance abusers pissed off about being court-ordered here for services."

Jim turned away from the window and walked toward the seating area. The soft drink vending machine was overturned, and the front of the snack machine was shattered.

"You must have family in the area," Randi jabbed. "The vending machine has been hit."

"Funny."

They walked the entire lower floor, which required headlamps after they left the windowed lobby area. The supply rooms and the break room, which were typically unlocked, were thoroughly ransacked. There were several offices that must have been unlocked because they were trashed as well. In the back of the building, they came upon an unmarked steel door in a dark corridor. Jim pushed on it, but it was locked. The door had a proximity reader beside it which required a person to hold their employee ID badge near the reader to unlock it. With the power dead, the door could only be unlocked with a key. Several dents in the door made it clear that someone had not been willing to accept this without a fight. It looked like the door had won. The lock had held.

"Don't tell me you still have your keys?"

"Of course," Jim said. "It's habit." He tucked his gun into his holster, reached into his pocket and withdrew a ring of keys. On the ring was the master key for the entire building. He slipped the key into the lock and turned it. The lock opened.

"Be very quiet in case someone's up there," Jim warned. "I don't want to make it this far to get beaned by a desk stapler."

They slipped through the door and Jim used the key to lock it back behind them. He drew his gun again and tracked his beam of light up the stairs. In contrast to the hallway they'd just left, there was no debris, which made Jim further certain that this floor might not have been breached. They carefully ascended the stairs and paused at the top landing. Jim listened but heard nothing. He used his key here, the door unlocked without a hitch, and they stepped through into the upper hallway.

They paused again, listening. Jim held his gun at the ready, still not ready to trust the feeling that they were the first to come up here since the disaster.

Randi leaned toward him. "This shit is spooky."

"It's only an office," he said. "I've been here at night a lot, coming back from a trip or after a late meeting."

Jim started walking, pausing frequently to listen for any sound. The upper hallway was a square, and they walked the entire perimeter, not seeing or hearing anything. Jim holstered his pistol.

"It looks like no one has been here," he said.

"It's getting dark. You think it's safe to stay here?"

"I'm not sure anywhere is safe, but I'd be willing to give it a shot."

They found an interior office that had no outside windows and dropped their gear. Jim spotted a scented candle and lighter on the desk. He lit it and the glow filled the room. "Alice must have missed this candle. It's clearly a violation of policy."

Randi sagged into the desk chair. "I'm starving. We didn't even eat lunch today."

"I know, but this floor is mostly women."

Randi looked offended. "What the hell does that have to do with anything?"

Jim smiled. "Open the bottom desk drawer next to you."

Randi leaned over and did as he asked. "Holy shit."

"What did you find?"

"Peanut butter, crackers, a can of soup, tuna." She placed each on the desk as she named them off.

"I bet you'll find more if you check every woman's office on this floor."

"Give me your master key."

"Let's go open the door to my emergency supply closet. I'll see what we can use out of there. While I'm going through it, you can use my key and check offices."

In an hour, they were both eating soup and crackers purloined from the desks of coworkers and drinking bottled water from the emergency supply cabinet. The cabinet had held a battery-powered lantern, and Jim substituted that for the scented candle since the smell of Gardenia Colada was becoming overpowering and starting to give him a headache.

"If this office ever opens back up, these people are going to be mad about their food," Randi said. "If they find out who ate it, I might not be able to set foot in this building again."

"They'll get over it. After all the crap that's gone on, this should be the least of anyone's problems."

Randi was eating tomato soup and slightly stale oyster crackers. Jim was eating a thick beef soup with slightly stale saltines.

"I still can't believe that you noticed all of these food stashes that people had in their desks."

"It really was part of my emergency plan. If I ran out of food getting home, I would look for offices because there might be less chance of them already being looted than stores and restaurants. I would check breakrooms and desks for food. You have to notice and remember all these secondary sources of food because the primary sources could be wiped out before you get to them."

They grew quiet as they finished their meals. Most evenings had been like this. There was a rush of activity when they reached where they were staying for the night as they attempted to set up a camp and get food in their bellies. With that done, there was nothing left to do but think, and that was always a black hole, sucking them down into darkness.

"You ever think about what happened to Alice and Rebecca?" Randi asked.

Jim set his bowl down beside him. "They made their decision, we made ours. They're grown women."

"I'm not talking about blame and decisions. I'm talking about what happened to them. Do you ever wonder if they've made it home already or if they're still out there on the road somewhere?"

Jim finished his water and tossed the empty toward the trashcan. He missed. "I do wonder. I was thinking about leaving them a message here, just in case they come by. If they're not home yet and they come down

460, they may stop here, like we did."

"You can do it if you want," Randi said. "I think I'm going to go clean up some. I don't want to reach home looking like ten miles of bad road."

"That's probably a good idea," Jim said. "We could pour some bottled water into the sink in the bathrooms. After days of creek baths, it will seem like five star accommodations."

Randi looked excited. "Is there enough water for that?"

"There's cases in the emergency cabinet. Way more than we could ever carry with us. There's also another of these lanterns. We could each take one. You'd be stuck with soap from the soap dispensers and drying with paper towels, but it's still the best we've had in a while."

"No shit," Randi said. "Sign me up."

They gathered their supplies and each of them headed to one of the staff restrooms. Despite the building being empty, habit drove each toward the bathroom of the appropriate gender – Jim to the men's, Randi to the women's. As office bathrooms typically did, theirs had a large wall-mounted mirror over the double sinks. When Jim placed his lantern on the vanity, he caught his reflection in the mirror and was stopped in his tracks. Although he had caught brief glances of his reflection in the shiny surface of car windows and other reflective materials over the past weeks, he had not been subjected to his current appearance in such stark detail as he was now.

They'd been on the road less than two weeks, but he appeared to have aged ten years in that time. He could not be sure if his appearance was really so different than it had been two weeks ago or if he just hadn't paid much attention to himself before since he was looking in the mirror every day. The first thing he noticed was his eyes. Not only did they show significant aging since he'd last seen them, but there was a look in them that he was not sure he recognized. Not exactly a haunted look, but a different look. Looking back over his journey, it was very likely that he was not the same man who had started this trip. Every experience changes you, some more than others.

His hair and beard appeared to have more gray. He thought of stories he'd heard growing up of people suffering severe traumas that made their hair whiten over very brief periods. He knew those stories were not true, or were at least exaggerated. Yet, unless he had forgotten what he looked like two weeks ago, he had significantly more white hair in his beard than he'd had before.

His skin had felt gritty when he'd wiped the sweat from it each day. He assumed that his constant sweating and wiping of his face had kept it reasonably clean but that was definitely not the case. He saw now that his face was streaked with a mixture of dust, dried sweat, and skin oils. In short, he was a filthy mess.

Too tired to continue this self-examination, Jim pulled the lever on the sink stopper to close the drain. He emptied three bottles of water into the sink, pumped his hand full of soap from the wall-mounted dispenser, and set about the task of de-crusting himself.

When he was done, he went to the supply room and got a Sharpie marker. He went to the stairwell door where they'd entered this floor. On the wall opposite the door to the stairwell, making it the first thing someone would see when coming through that door, Jim wrote: JIM, RANDI, AND GARY MADE IT THIS FAR. THERE'S FOOD AND WATER IN OFFICE 17. Writing on the wall was probably a violation of policy, but if Alice and Rebecca showed up here, tired and hungry, they might just find it in their hearts to forgive him.

CHAPTER 24

Route 460
Bluefield, Virginia

The trip from Narrows to the outskirts of Bluefield, Virginia, ranked as one of the worst experiences of Alice's life. After literally being chased out of town by kids throwing cans at her, Alice had run until she could run no further. When she finally stopped running, she finished another bottle from her dwindling water supply. She started walking again, eating a few bites on the run, drinking only when she had to. When she heard people approaching, she hid until they passed. She would not trust anyone on this road again. She walked all day and reached Princeton, West Virginia, that evening.

She had run out of water sometime that day. When thirst drove her completely beyond reason, she drank from a half-empty bottle that she found in the weeds. When that ran out, she filled her empty bottle from a creek beside the road. She didn't know what else to do. She knew she was dehydrated and suffering from heat exhaustion. She was afraid she was dying. Within hours of drinking from that creek, a dull pain grew in her stomach and her intestines cramped. At times, she walked nearly doubled over, clutching her abdomen.

The road appeared to be highly trafficked and was littered with abandoned cars and debris from looting. There appeared to be signs of criminal activity. There were cars riddled with bullet holes. She saw a broken beer bottle with what looked like dried blood on its sharp edges. She passed one car so full of flies and reeking of carrion that she did not dare approach it.

This section of populated highway did not look like a safe place at all, so Alice used her flashlight and walked for most of the night. By the time the sun came up, she was in a state of hallucinatory delirium that few ever experience. It was the domain of ultra-runners, drug users, and people on the cusp of death. It was not solely the product of exhaustion, but of pushing the body beyond the point of collapse until you entered a surreal and disassociated state. She could no longer feel her body. It had disappeared from her perception completely. All that remained was her will, unencumbered by the flesh but anchored still to the wide, black highway.

The nightscape was full of sounds. In her state, she did not so much hear the sounds as *experience* them. The city of Bluefield was below her and to the north. Were this several weeks ago, she would see lights and shopping centers in the distance. Instead, on this night, there were screams and gunfire. Occasionally there would be the sound of a car squealing its tires. Those sounds did not scare her nearly as much as the disembodied voices that came from the night. Those voices meant people were near her. When she heard them, she turned off her flashlight and hid.

"Come on out and play, little girl," a voice had once called to her. "We know you're here. We saw you."

"Yeah, we won't hurt you," another voice said. "We want to be friends. *Good* friends."

There was a laughter that conveyed anything but joy.

Alice bit her lip until she could taste the blood, stifling the panicked sob that threatened to burst from her throat. She did not trust that she could hold the scream in any other way, so she used that bite to physically lock her mouth closed against it.

When morning finally came, it was like no morning that she'd ever experienced. It may have been a morning like *no one* had ever experienced. The sun lightened the sky with a brilliant red orange, the colors so vivid that she felt they were attempting to swallow her. In her altered state, Alice thought she had walked so far that she'd ventured into Hell itself. The voices she'd heard last night were demons taunting her, welcoming her to Hell.

She should have known. She should have turned back. She'd crossed over, that was it. Boyd must have killed her, too, and she was so determined to reach home that she'd never noticed she was dead. Even in death, her soul kept walking home. Was this how people became ghosts?

Am I a ghost?

Her raw feet began to bleed through the heels of her yellow Nikes, staining them.

The sun, she thought. *My blood-stained shoes are the color of the sun here in Hell.*

She passed an old Mercury Cougar abandoned in the road. She stared at it for a long time.

My first car. My first car is in Hell, too. I loved that car. Why did it go to Hell?

She tried the door and found it unlocked. She opened it and climbed inside, closing the door behind her. Someone had been driving her car, maybe one of the demons, because the seat was not adjusted properly. She tried to adjust it but could not get it right. She accidentally hit the lever to recline the seat, then decided she liked that so she left it. She stared at the sky, watching it bleed upon the Earth, then she lost consciousness.

When Alice awoke hours later, the inside of the car was sweltering. She was soaked in sweat, her clothes saturated and stuck to her. She shoved the door open, panting, sucking in the fresh air that rolled across her body. The car had been so hot inside that even the hot summer air felt cool as it washed over her roasting body.

"I'm alive," she gasped. "I'm not in Hell."

She swung her feet out, resting them painfully on the pavement. The crusted blood had glued the shoes to her feet and there was a miserable tearing sensation when she stood. Despite the pain, she had slept comfortably, just like she had a time or two in that old Mercury of hers. It had the most comfortable seats of any vehicle she'd ever owned. She stretched. It was a new day and she was closer to home.

When she raised her arms above her head, she felt hands grab her ankles. She looked down in time to see the hands retract violently, yanking her feet from underneath her. She did not finish a thought before her forehead cracked against the pavement and she lost consciousness again.

CHAPTER 25

The Cave
Russell County, Virginia

Pete decided that he was beginning to enjoy his job more than he'd ever enjoyed his role in the world before the attacks. He had never felt so useful. He always heard people talking about how important it was to find your place in this world and he'd found his. His role was to guard his family. He imagined that even after his father's return home, this could still be his role.

Drawing on information he'd recalled from conversations with his dad and from books he'd been reading while at his outpost, he'd come up with a set of duties for himself. Each morning, he tried to be up here early, both monitoring his surroundings and working on improving his outpost. The original observation post had been a simple cluster of brush at the top of a hill that was a little higher than the surrounding hills. There was an old tree there that had fallen down and clusters of wild rose bushes grew around it. Pete had gone in with his machete and cleared the center out to give himself more room. Then he'd brought in more brush, piling it randomly around so that it looked like any old farmer's brush pile waiting to be burned off. In one of the storage buildings, he'd found an olive green tarp. He'd rigged that over his observation post, camouflaging it with branches, and now he could stay out there rain or shine.

Once he piled the brush thick enough that you couldn't easily see through it, he took cinderblocks from a pallet near the house and used old partial cans of spray paint to paint them in earth tones. He stacked the cinderblocks three high in a semi-circle around him. He didn't need them on the back side, which was protected by the downed tree. It would serve as sufficient cover on its own. The cinderblocks gave him an eighteen inch high wall that, after he packed the block cores with dirt, would stop a bullet.

He used pruning shears to trim the rose bushes at select locations, creating shooting lanes to points that he frequently observed. He had a clear lane to their empty house, to the gate, and to several other points that his family might have reason to visit. His dad had a laser rangefinder that he used to measure distances to shooting targets. Pete had found it, put fresh batteries in it, and used it for the same thing. He took a scrap of metal and used a Sharpie marker to write down the distances to the same landmarks he'd cleared shooting lanes to. He knew the exact distance to the house, the gate, to the barn, to the workshop, and to the woodpile. He also knew exactly how many clicks on his rifle scope it took to adjust the .270 rifle to zero for each of those target ranges.

While his initial forays up to his observation post had been disorganized and required several trips back and forth to the cave, he now had his own Bug Out Bag, just like his dad's, that contained the items he would need for the day. The bag contained his spotting scope and tripod, a set of binoculars, a notebook and pen, his radio, a machete, pruning shears, a folding camp shovel, spare ammunition, a cleaning kit for his weapons, water, and snacks. On his belt he carried the Smith & Wesson M&P22 pistol, with two spare magazines in a pants pocket, and his lucky knife. He owned several knives, but his lucky knife was the one that he and his dad had made together. They'd built a forge and used it to make the knife blank. For a handle, he'd used an antler that he'd found in the woods. Carrying that knife made him think of his dad. It made him feel connected to his dad. He thought his dad was a strong man, and through that knife he felt that strength.

Most days, he saw more wildlife than human activity. The road at the end of their driveway was a public road and did see some traffic, although it was very sporadic. One day, he saw two folks on bicycles go by. They were each wearing backpacks but didn't even slow down as they passed his gate. There were still other people living in the valley, too. He knew that because he saw them occasionally go by in one fashion or other – tractor, truck, horse, or on foot – conducting what farm activities they could manage to do. No one stopped.

He saw Henry's truck going by but he knew it could not be Henry driving it. He knew Henry was dead, and he knew his son was dead. He'd seen the bodies with his own eyes. He knew that the man driving Henry's truck had to be the bad man who'd killed them. One time the man had driven by as Pete was using his rifle scope to watch the road. As the man passed their driveway, he slowed, then stopped and stared at their house. For a long moment, Pete laid his crosshairs right across the bridge of the man's nose. It was contrary to everything he'd ever been taught about the safe use of a firearm, but he couldn't help it. He knew this man was not a nice person. Even as a young man, he understood that pulling the trigger and dropping the man where he stood would save his family a lot of suffering and hardship. They would butt heads one day. It was inevitable. He knew it the way you know that the dark clouds coming your way will bring rain.

As much as he wanted to, he couldn't shoot a man who was not threatening him or a member of his family. His thumb hovered over the safety, but did not release it. The man, perhaps sensing that his fate was balanced on a knife edge, hit the gas and accelerated away.

Sissy, Pete told himself. *You should have done it.*

*

The day that Pops had left had been sad for them all. Pete had a special bond with his grandparents. His Nana had babysat him as a child when his mother and father were at work. He worried about her being sick. He worried about them not being in the safety of the cave. He could not protect them if they were not here.

He sat his post all day. He noted a man on a horse, a man on a tractor, and two men walking by the gate in separate incidents. He recorded the time in his log. He saw nine deer, a fox, a coyote, and more squirrels and rabbits than he could count. He stared at the firewood pile through the scope, wondering if he should close up shop early and go bring down more firewood since Pops was not here to do it today. He would try to leave early enough before dark that he could get that done.

While Pete was beginning to think about lunch, he heard the distinctive roar of a diesel engine. Many of the trucks in farming communities were diesel so this in itself didn't mean much, even though the sound instantly made him think of Pops' truck. Pete adjusted the spotting scope toward the road, needing to know who was traveling his road. Even before he'd focused, he knew that he was seeing his grandfather's truck. The color, the cab, the toolbox, the spare tire mount – it all added up to Pops. He felt a surge of excitement.

When he finally got the spotting scope adjusted for the distance, he saw that, oddly, the truck was not slowing down for their gate.

He panned the scope along with the speed of the moving truck cab. He could see that the man driving was not Pops. In fact, it was the bad man – the killer –that was living in Henry's house. Pete's breathing stopped.

What had the man done with Pops? Was he dead? Had this man killed him?

Then the panic went full throttle and Pete's stomach rose into his throat. His Nana was still in the truck. He could see her sleeping next to the dangerous man. She looked the same as she had when she left that morning, except she was not with Pops.

Pete brushed the spotting scope out of the way with tears stinging his eyes. He grabbed his .270 and dropped the fore end across a stack of cinderblocks. He chambered a round and attempted to level his scope on the man, but he could not see through it. Pete nearly screamed in frustration. *Lens caps*. He'd left the lens caps on.

He tore them off and dropped them, reorienting himself to the rifle. He tried to get the driver in his crosshairs, thinking that if he could catch the man as he drove away, he could shoot him through the rear glass and not take a chance on hitting his Nana. The shot never presented itself. He hovered, thumb ready to flip the safety off, finger ready to wrap the trigger, but the shot was never there. The body pillar at the rear of the cab was always in the way. Pete did not know what the bullet would do if he fired into that steel. Would it punch through and slow the man or would it deflect right and hit his Nana? He couldn't take the chance.

Pete dropped his head and moaned, beating the earth-filled cinderblocks with his fist. How could this be happening? Where was his Pops? Had the man killed him? The thought hurt him like nothing had ever hurt him before.

Suddenly he knew what he had to do.

He grabbed his backpack and slung it onto his back. He slithered out of his hide, rifle in his hand. The truck was out of sight now. He could no longer even hear it. He thought he knew where it was going, though.

The same place he was going.

He tore off at a dead run.

*

It took Pete nearly a half hour to run the fields and game trails to Henry's farm. He was not used to running long distances and became winded several times, a combination of the terrain, exertion, and the gear he was carrying. Every time he had to stop running, he thought of his Nana waking up to find herself in the clutches of that man. He could not bear it. When he had to slow, tears filled his eyes, and he would allow himself a certain number of walking steps before he started running again. It was a mental game his dad had taught him.

I'll walk ten steps and then I have to run again.

I'm going to walk as far as that maple tree and then I'll start running again.

When I reach that blackberry bush I'll start running again.

It was the farthest he'd ever run in his life, but he could not let himself stop.

When he reached Henry's farm, he looked for the spot where he and his mother had observed the family previously. He dropped there, gasping for air, his lungs burning, and his legs so spent that they were wracked with cramps. He shrugged out of his pack and slid it around in front of him. He pulled the spotting scope from his bag. He didn't bother with the tripod, laying the scope right across his pack. He could instantly see that Henry's pickup truck was indeed there, just as he expected. It was pulled up to the barn, like it had been when he was here watching with his mother. He held his breath as he checked the bed of the truck with the scope, making sure there were no bodies there as there had been that previous time.

Maybe his Nana was still alive.

CHAPTER 26

The Cave
Russell County, Virginia

Ellen was working on dinner. When she could, she cooked on the woodstove to preserve the precious stove fuel that they might not easily be able to replace. She and Ariel had not seen Pete all afternoon but that was not unusual. When he was in his outpost, he focused on what he was doing. He would either be watching the grounds or improving his post. That's what he did all day. As it both served a function for the family and kept him busy, Ellen had no problem with it. She knew that he needed something like that to occupy him.

A banging on the steel door startled both of them. Ariel was instantly terrified and grabbed her mother tightly, a whimper escaping her lips.

After her immediate fear reaction had dissipated, Ellen began processing the situation. It couldn't be Pete. He had key to the door and he would have called out to them on the radio before he came down. They'd established that procedure on the first day to make sure nobody got shot by mistake. It shouldn't be a stranger, both because of Pete's over watch and because the cave was so well-hidden.

"Ellen!" came Pop's voice from outside. He sounded both weak and frantic.

"Oh my God," Ellen said, rushing to the door. Her first thought was that Nana must have passed away, judging by what she heard in Pops' voice. She threw the deadbolts and pulled the door open. Pops stood there breathing hard, tears in his eyes.

"Somebody took Nana," he said. It was all he got out before sobs overtook him.

Ellen grasped his arm and led him in, seating him at the table. "Ariel, get your Pops some water and get Pete on the radio. Tell him to get down here."

She sat down across from Pops. Ariel brought him a cup of water.

"Tell me what happened."

Pops took a deep breath. "I took Nana by the ER. It was sheer chaos there. It took a while, but I got her some meds. I had left her outside the ER door in the truck. I left the truck running so she could have some air conditioning. When I came out the truck was gone."

Ellen said the first thing that popped into her head. "Did you call the police?"

"There are no phones and I'm not sure there's even police anymore. There's no one to call."

"Did anyone see anything?"

Pops shook his head.

"How did you get here?"

"I started walking back here as fast as I could. I didn't know what else to do. After a little while, I came across a man I knew who was on a four-wheeler. He let me ride on the rack and he drove me as far as the gate."

Ellen looked at the ground. She had no clue what to do in a situation like this. Without police to call, how did they handle this? They might never get Nana back. How would they even find her?

"Mommy, Pete's not answering."

Ellen went to the door and looked up the hill toward Pete's observation post. She couldn't see anything, but that in itself wasn't unusual. It had become elaborate enough, and well-camouflaged enough, that it was impossible to see him when he was in there. She broke protocol and shouted to him.

"Pete!"

There was no answer.

"Pete!"

Nothing.

"You stay with Ariel," she ordered Pops.

Ellen tore up the hill, sensing that something was not right. Pete always answered. About halfway up she realized that, although she was wearing her sidearm, she'd not brought her rifle, but she was not going back for it. She needed to calm down. She could not panic. Panic got you killed.

Too late, I'm already panicked.

She tried to take a deep breath, but with the exertion of running straight uphill she could not do it.

"Pete," she gasped, getting closer.

Arriving at the top, Ellen forced her way through the wild roses. They tore at her skin, scraping and leaving pinpricks of blood on her arms and hands. When she was in far enough, she threw back the tarp and looked beneath it.

It was empty.

"PEEEEEEEETE!" she screamed.

They'd spent the entire period since this disaster began trying to be as low-key as possible, but Ellen threw all discipline out the window as she ran around the hilltop screaming Pete's name in all directions. He did not answer.

She forced herself to calm down. She collapsed to her knees in the grass and tried to think through things rationally. Maybe he was using the bathroom? Maybe he was at the house? Maybe he was getting firewood?

No, he would not have done any of those things without radioing her.

Yet again, she scanned the terrain before her for any sign of her child. "PEEEEEEEETE!"

Then she saw movement at their empty house. Two figures walked up the driveway and stood in front of it. They were too far away to distinguish anything about them.

Had they hurt her son? Was this the confrontation that had been looming over them since all of this happened? If so, she would kill them.

Ellen tore down the hill at a dead run. Nearly halfway down, her foot slid, the force of her step too much for the grade, and her leg went out from under her. She went down hard, rolling and tumbling over the hard ground, her elbow banging painfully off an exposed rock. When her fall stopped, she did not pause to assess for injuries. She got up and ran again.

When she reached the bottom of the hill she went straight for the cave. Pops and Ariel were standing at the door. Pops was hugging a terrified Ariel. Ellen ran right past them and grabbed Jim's M-4 carbine from where it hung inside the door. She grabbed the truck keys and a sling pack of spare M-4 magazines.

"What's going on, Ellen?" Pops asked.

"People at the house. Stay here with Ariel. Lock the door."

She ran past them, ignoring the questions that came from behind her, and climbed into the Suburban, cranking the engine and speeding away, grass and dirt slinging from beneath the spinning tires. When she topped the hill and came out of the little valley that held their cave, she saw the figures at the house react to the sound of her engine and turn toward her. She punched the gas to the floor. The vehicle accelerated so hard that it lost traction, the rear end fishtailing on the farm road. She let off the gas enough to correct the slip and aimed the vehicle for the house. She could see that the two figures had on packs. They made no effort to run or hide.

That was a mistake you'll live to regret, she thought.

She pulled the M-4 from the passenger seat in preparation for stopping. She would put the engine block between her and the strangers and question them. Maybe she would shoot one of them right now, to make it crystal clear that she wasn't fucking around.

Then one of the figures waved at her.

She could see it was a man now. She could see it was… *Jim.*

Her husband was home.

She slammed on the brakes less than fifty feet from them. She climbed out of the driver's door, M-4 still in hand, and stood. She couldn't believe her eyes. It was real. It was him.

The man dropped his pack to the dirt. His clothes were filthy and he'd lost a lot of weight, but it was her husband. He started toward her. She tossed the rifle onto the hood of the vehicle and willed her feet to move toward him. A few minutes ago she felt as if the weight of the entire world was crushing her. Now, when they embraced, she felt the lightness of the weight being lifting from her. She exploded into tears.

While her mind raced, wanting to explain the entirety of the situation to him right away, all she could say was his name. She said it over and over, as if seeking confirmation that this was indeed her husband, and that he was alive, and he was here. Her respite was brief. The absence of her son and the kidnapping of Jim's mother came slamming back onto her like a hammer blow. She tried explaining, her words a staccato burst that tumbled over each other. Jim could not understand her through the sobs.

"Easy, Ellen. Take deep breaths."

She forced herself to calm down even while everything inside her felt like exploding in all directions, like the Big Bang emerging from the heart of a single person. "Pops and Ariel are at the cave. Your mother has been… kidnapped, and I can't find Pete."

The wind left Jim's sails and he collapsed to his knees, too exhausted for the burden that he now bore. He had imagined this homecoming every day. It was his sole motivation. It was the light that drew him across the dark landscape of what America had become in a short period of time. He had expected unrest and maybe some conflict, but he had never in his worst nightmares expected to hear the words his wife had told him.

"Let's go back to the house," she said. "We'll figure out something."

The woman standing behind them had been silent up to this point, melting into the landscape, but she cleared her throat. Ellen turned and looked at her.

"This is Randi," Jim said. "She was on the trip with us. I've got to get her home."

Ellen frowned. "Where is everyone else? I thought there were several of you."

"That's a long story," Jim said. "And not as important right now as the one I need to hear from you."

*

The reunion at the cave was bittersweet. Jim didn't even really feel like he was home yet, instead feeling like he'd entered a new theater of war. This was the new battlefield and it was his own backyard.

Ellen made coffee for everyone and while they drank, she explained the day's events to the newcomers. She did not feel like she had time to update them on everything that had happened here – there was too much – so she only went into details of the previous days when it was required.

Ariel sat perched on her father's lap, the radio clutched determinedly in both hands. Every few minutes, she would hold the transmit button and say her brother's name. There was no response. Randi sat and drank her coffee, allowing the family to discuss their course of action. Jim's only idea for finding Pete was to arm up and go house-to-house asking about him. Ellen realized that Jim understood little about what their neighborhood had become. Approaching any homes could be life-threatening.

"Pete," Ariel said into the radio for what must have been the one hundredth time. "Where are you, Bubby?"

The conversation around the table fell into a frustrated silence. There was a crackle of static, then a voice.

"Sissy?"

The table exploded with activity. Ellen stood so quickly she nearly upset the table, knocking her coffee over. Jim took the radio from Ariel, although she did not appear anxious to give it up.

217

"Pete, it's your dad," Jim said into the radio.

There was a crackle again. "You guys have to listen carefully. I'm at Henry's farm. I can't talk long. They have Nana. I think she's in their barn."

"They have Nana?" Pops asked. "Who has Nana?"

Ellen looked at Pops. "The people who killed Henry."

Jim looked shocked. "Henry's dead?"

Ellen nodded. "Some lowlife moved into the trailer park a few days ago. He's been trying to run everyone out of the valley. He killed Henry and his wife and hung their bodies from our gate."

Jim recoiled in horror, unable to believe that his family had to deal with such things while he was gone. He felt a tremendous wave of guilt for not being here with them.

The radio crackled again. "Dad, I'm glad you're home. I've missed you. Did you guys hear what I said?"

Jim spoke into the radio. "I heard you, Pete. We're coming to you right now. Do not move. Do not try anything on your own. Do you hear me?"

"I hear you," Pete replied. "Now I'm going to turn my radio off so they don't hear it. Okay?"

"I love you, Pete," Jim said, his voice cracking. To be this close, to have made it only to find his son and mother in danger, was more than he could bear. That wave of self-pity was shoved to the side by a distant voice in his head. It was his grandfather again.

Harden the fuck up.

When Jim set the radio on the table, Ellen began hurriedly gathering gear. Jim went to her and put his hand on her shoulder.

"Ellen, you have to stay here."

A fire rose in Ellen's eyes. "The hell I will. I have fought this battle every day while you've been gone. I have held this family together. This is my fight and I will not sit it out just because you're home."

"You need to stay here with Pops and Ariel. What if this is only a diversion to get us out of the house so they can steal our supplies?"

"I'll stay with them," came a voice from across the room. It was Randi.

Ellen turned to her. "Thank you." She returned her gaze to Jim and waited to see if he had any reaction to that.

Jim knew when to fold. "You have my shotgun?"

She pointed to where it hung on the wall.

"Grab it and the bandoleer of spare shells," he said. "Get the night vision in case this gets drawn out. I see you're wearing your pistol. Make sure it's loaded and get some spare mags for it."

Ellen did as she was instructed. Jim took the M-4, the sling pack of spare magazines that Ellen had carried earlier, and got some extra clips for his Beretta from the supply that Ellen had brought from the house. He loaded every magazine. He got his night vision from his backpack and put fresh batteries in it.

"You ready?" Ellen asked him, already standing by the door.

Jim turned to Randi. "Make sure your weapon is loaded. There are more here if you need them. Do not open that door unless you know it's me."

Randi nodded. "Be careful."

Ellen and Jim left the cave, got in the Suburban, and drove off into the late evening light.

CHAPTER 27

Henry's Farm
Russell County, Virginia

Charlie put the woman in a horse stall, dumping her casually onto a pile of old hay. He didn't know what was wrong with her, but he figured she didn't have the strength to try and get away. From the heat he felt radiating from her body as he carried her, he figured she must have pneumonia or the flu. If that was the case, she probably wasn't long for this world, and he wanted to get some information from her before she died. There was a rain barrel outside the barn. He would get a bucket of water and toss it on her. Maybe she'd wake up and be able to talk. He had to get this show on the road. She wasn't any good to him dead.

When he turned to leave, he found Angie and Robert standing behind him. The suddenness of their appearance irritated him. He hated being startled.

"You all better be careful about sneaking up on people. That could get you killed around here."

They stared back at him like they didn't know what to make of him. He hoped they'd be afraid, but they didn't appear to be. He might just have to give them new reason to be.

"What you got in there?" Angie asked.

"Hopefully some information about what's in that house down the road."

Robert strode forward and peered through the stall gate. "That's an old lady you got there."

Charlie scowled at the young man. "You're about a damn genius, aren't you? Mind like that, it's a wonder you ain't made a fortune in the stock market."

Angie stepped toward the stall. "There ain't no call for you to talk that way to him. I've warned you about that."

She looked into the stall. Charlie felt a heat rising in his soul. He stepped up to Angie.

"First off, you need to be careful about who you're handing out warnings to," he said. "Second, I'm beginning to wonder what my brother saw in the lot of you. Y'all ain't nothing but a bunch of damn bother as far as I'm concerned."

"That's Mrs. Powell," Angie said, ignoring Charlie. "She was my music teacher in elementary school. She must be related to those folks down there. I never knew that."

"I don't give a damn who she is," Charlie said. "I want to know what they have in that house that they're not out having to scrounge for food like the rest of us. I also want to know what kind of guns they got in there. I might need some of them, too, for my own self."

Angie turned to Robert. "Sweetie, would you go outside for a second? Charlie and I need to talk about something."

Robert glared coldly at Charlie.

Charlie spat on the ground, the heat within him about to boil over. When it did, people would suffer. They'd be sorry. "Boy, you keep eye-fucking me like that and I'll give you an ass whooping that you won't get up from. You hear me?"

Robert didn't hurry, but he turned and went outside the barn.

*

Robert walked outside the wide sliding doors to the barn and sat down on a bucket of hydraulic oil. It had been a hot day and he was glad to see the sun starting to go down. Deer would be out soon. He scanned the fields around the house and saw nothing. He looked toward the taller hills, hoping he might find the silhouette of a deer foraging in the hay stubble. A flash of light caught his eyes. He turned back toward it and watched.

There it was again – a flicker. Charlie had once made him track down a flash like that and it had turned out to be the bottom of an aluminum drink can laying in the weeds. He decided he'd better check. You couldn't be too careful.

He didn't like that Charlie had the older woman locked up in the there. He didn't approve of tactics like that, but he wasn't sure he could do anything about it. Things between him and Charlie were about as bad as they could get without someone dying. Soon he knew the conflict between them would come to a head. When it did, one of them would die. That was all there was to it. He just hoped it wasn't him. He hoped that he could see it coming in time to make the first move.

Robert was hoping that his mom was in there telling Charlie to leave, but he didn't think she had it in her. Like the rest of them, she was afraid of Charlie. They'd all seen what he was capable of. He'd come in to their lives like he was the Lone Ranger, there to save them from this miserable world. Instead, he'd turned out to be a criminal like their dad, but with less regard for them. At least their dad was reasonably nice to them. This man needed to move on. Surely he didn't think they needed him that badly.

The flash came again and Robert rose from his bucket. He stuck his head around the corner to say something to his mom and Charlie, but they were involved in an intense exchange that he didn't want to interrupt. He'd check it out on his own. There was a .22 rifle leaning against the house and he grabbed it. Maybe he'd stir up a rabbit if nothing else. If he saw a deer, he'd shoot at that. Like Charlie said, there weren't any rules anymore. A man could do what he wanted. For Charlie, that meant breaking into houses, looting them, then burning them down. For Robert, it meant shooting a deer any damn time he wanted to.

223

CHAPTER 28

Henry's Farm
Russell County, Virginia

When Pete saw the older boy grab the rifle from the carport and start up the hill, he knew he'd been spotted. He knew exactly how it had happened. His dad had told him about positioning himself so that the sun didn't reflect from his scope, but in his intense desire to find his Nana he'd not paid any attention. He figured he had only minutes before he was discovered.

Pete dug furiously into his pack and found a green nylon backpacking tarp that he carried as an emergency rain shelter. He spread it on the ground about twenty feet from the spotting scope and his pack, then pulled handfuls of the straw-like broom sedge from the ground and arranged them on the tarp. In less than a minute, the tarp was nearly invisible unless you were standing right over it. Pete left his pack and spotting scope in plain sight. He took his rifle and slid it under the tarp. He unsheathed his knife, the one he'd made with his dad, and he crawled under the tarp. He positioned his head at the edge nearest his scope and pack. He raised the edge enough that he could watch his gear and see when someone approached it.

In the moments that he waited, he wondered if he was making the right choice. Should he have grabbed his gear and run? Maybe he should have. If he'd headed toward the road, he could have intercepted his dad, who was no doubt racing here right now in a vehicle. He would have been able to share what information he had about the man, his family, and the barn. If he got killed this way, they may never know what happened to him. He began to think that he should probably crawl out from under the tarp with his rifle and run for his life.

As all of this passed through his head, the young man walked into Pete's line of sight. Pete's heart began racing. His fear told him that he should draw his pistol and empty it into him. His head told him that the crazy man at the barn would hear the shots and might do something to his Nana. He could not make any noise. He had to resolve this up here and

225

without raising any alarm. His life and his Nana's depended on that.

When the young man came fully upon Pete's gear, he paused and looked around. He raised the .22 and scanned the horizon, seeming to assume that whomever had been here was long gone. After all, with the spotting scope still set up in a position to create the reflection, this gear could have been laying here for days. The young man obviously became curious about what could be seen through the spotting scope. He laid his rifle to the side, dropped to his belly, and peered through the scope.

"I'll be damned."

With the young man lying on his belly and facing the other direction, Pete realized that this may be his only opportunity to act. He folded the tarp back as quietly as possible and rose to his feet. He'd removed his boots before sliding under the tarp and in his socks he made no noise at all as he crept toward the man. Twenty feet became fifteen. Fifteen feet became ten. Ten became six.

And the man looked back.

When he saw Pete with his knife raised, his eyes filled with terror. Pete was filled with terror, too, but he shoved it out of his head, knowing that there was no room for it now. He had a job to do. The man quickly rolled onto his back, stretching an arm toward his rifle, but it was just beyond his fingertips. Pete fell onto him, all of his weight behind the knife, plunging it into his heart. The man had raised an arm to block Pete, but it could not stop the momentum of the falling boy. The knife plunged into his chest.

With more training, Pete may have chosen another target for his blade. The brachial artery, the carotid artery, the subclavian artery were all common targets. Sometimes a combatant would slit the throat to silence any scream. Pete only knew the location of one target – the heart. It was fortuitous for him that of all the possible targets, this one killed the quickest. Within three seconds, the man was dead. While three seconds seems like only the briefest of moments, it is not the case when you are laying across the body of the dying man, eye to eye, his rancid breath warm on your face. It felt like an eternity. Pete would remember the experience for the rest of his life.

When the man's breathing stopped, the muscles softened, and the eyes no longer had life remaining in them, Pete rolled to the side. He could finally breathe and he sucked in huge gulps of air. He listened but heard no one. He had not given away his position. He waited for tears to come, but they did not. Accepting that he had killed this man had been easier than accepting the last man he'd killed. He did not know if this was a good thing or not, but it meant that he was different than he had been mere days ago.

Had he used any other knife, he would have left it there sticking from the man's chest. He could not leave this one. He took the antler handle in his hand and pulled gently, not liking the sound that the knife made as it pulled free of the chest. The blade was covered in blood and Pete wiped it on the dead man's shirt, then shoved the knife back in its sheath.

He grabbed his boots and put them back on, tying them as fast as he could. Then he flattened out on the ground again and looked through the spotting scope. The woman, the mother of those children, was stomping out of the barn. He could tell by her quick pace that she was mad. His sister walked that way when she was mad at him. She walked over to the house where two of her kids sat in the dirt playing with plastic trucks and spoke to them.

She must have been asking where the young man went because the children both pointed up the hill toward Pete. The woman started walking toward him. Pete panicked. He did not want to have to kill this woman. He shoved the spotting scope in his pack and put it on. He slung the rifle over his shoulder. He looked at the tarp and thought about pulling it over the body. It might slow her down.

He ran to the tarp and grabbed an edge. He carefully dragged it over the dead body, then repositioned the grasses that covered it, hoping it would blend in. He knew he only had moments before she was up the hill. He ran as quickly and as quietly as he was able.

Pete's plan was to head south toward the road. He hoped he could intersect his parents, figuring they were already on their way here, probably by vehicle. Before he reached the bottom of the hill, he knew that his luck had run out. The calm of the twilight was shattered by a bloodcurdling scream. He knew exactly what that meant. That woman had found her son's body.

He froze, crouching in the tall grass. He could not see the barn from where he was but knew that he had to get eyes on it. He trotted toward Henry's driveway. He had a hill between him and the barn now, but hoped that by moving toward the driveway he could remain safe while gaining a view of the barn. That scream kept on going, like nails on a blackboard.

227

He wished she'd stop. He tried not to dwell on the fact that the scream was *his* fault, her pain *his* doing. He did not have room for that right now.

When he came around the base of the hill, he found cover behind a rusty hay baler and looked toward the barn. The man that had kidnapped his Nana came out of the barn to see what the screaming was about. He was yelling to the woman up the hill but she kept screaming. His shouted questions received no answers. He finally started trotting in her direction, up the hill, needing to see for himself what all the fuss was about.

Pete knew that this might be his only chance to get into the barn and save his Nana. He crossed Henry's driveway, crouched, and raced across the yard, hoping the weeds obscured him from their view. He assumed the barn would have a back entrance, so he aimed for that. Sure enough, as he got closer, he could see that there was a smaller door going in the back of the barn. An ancient door of gray poplar boards lay askew beside the opening. Pete ran into the barn and began frantically looking around.

There were heaped shelves and tottering piles, decrepit chairs with no seats, and rusting bottomless buckets. He noticed the stalls. Seeing very few other places to hide a person, he began checking stalls. The first was empty. With the second he got lucky. His Nana lay in a fetal position in dirty hay. She appeared so small and pitiful that his heart ached for her. Pete propped his rifle against the stall boards, unhooked the gate latch, and swung the stall door open.

"Oh Nana," he moaned. He crouched at her side and tried to lift her. Despite her small stature, he could not carry her. He was a big boy, but still a boy and not of the size that he could carry her out of the barn and to safety.

"We have to get out of here," he pleaded, trying to lift her to her feet. "You have to wake up. You have to walk."

She groaned and tried to answer him, but was too weak to stand. As much as he hated to, he might have to drag her out of here. If he could get her out of the barn, maybe he could hide her until help arrived. He could guard her and make sure that no one hurt her.

He closed his hand around her wrist. Her bones felt so thin that he worried he might break her arms trying to pull her out of here. As he pulled her toward the stall opening, a massive blow struck him in the back of the neck. He turned loose his Nana's arms and flew across the stall, falling headfirst into the barn siding and striking his head. He pushed himself back, staggering, blood running into his eyes, completely stunned. He put a hand to his head, unable to know what he should do next. His vision was darkening. He thought of his gun and tried to look for it, not even recalling that he wore one within reach on his hip. From the looming blackness, a fist emerged, striking the side of his head and knocking him out cold.

*

Pete regained consciousness when a bucket of nasty water was thrown in his face. It smelled like water that a dead rat had floated in for a week. He knew because he'd smelled that once and would never forget it. Either from that smell or from what water went into his open mouth, he started to gag. He tried to reach for his aching head but could not raise an arm. He tried to walk and found he couldn't do that either. He opened his eyes and raised his head from where it slumped on his chest. His vision was blurry, but two figures stood in front of him in the light of a propane lantern. He hoped that it was his parents come to help him, but it was not. He tried to move again and realized that he was tied to one of the poles that supported the barn, his hands behind his back.

"Bastard's waking up," the man said.

Pete now noticed that the woman emitted a steady moan. It would have reminded him of the cooing of a pigeon were it not so etched with pain.

The man stepped closer to Pete, leaned into his ear. He was so close that Pete could feel the warmth of the man's breath. "You kill my nephew, boy?"

Pete turned his head and tried to focus on the man but he was too close. His eyes were not cooperating. His head swayed. Vomit rose in his throat, then receded.

The man nodded his head toward the woman. "That woman is the boy's mother. The boy you killed. What do you think she wants to do to you right now?"

The man looked to the woman, then back at Pete. He got in close again. "I bet she'd like to stick her hand through that soft belly of yours and pull your guts right out. What do you think it would be like to watch that?"

Pete tried to focus on the words. He could imagine that this woman probably did want to kill him, he was aware enough to understand that. However, he did not answer, for fear of provoking the man's wrath.

"Tell me about your house, boy."

Pete tried to shake off the fog. The question about his house instantly raised a sobering red flag. "House?"

"Yeah, the house where you and your mommy live. Anything special about that house?"

"No. Not really. It's just our house." His words were thick and slow.

"Then why don't you all seem to be suffering like the rest of us?" the man asked. "It don't make sense to me."

Even through his cloudy thinking, Pete remembered what his dad had told him over and over. *Do not tell people about the preparations you make. In times of trouble, they may come for them.* "We can food from our garden. We've been eating last year's canning. It's almost gone, though."

The man slapped a hand hard against the support post, the blow barely missing Pete's head. He could feel the post reverberate against his throbbing skull. "Bull...shit."

Pete felt like he was going to throw up any minute. He could smell the dead animal water on his hair and clothes. He could taste it.

"What about those guns you all have?"

"We do have some guns," Pete said. "We like to hunt."

"You're lying to me, son," the man said in a sing-song voice. He smiled like a parent catching a child telling a cute fib. "Everyone who has seen them says you all have guns for killing men, not for killing animals."

Pete said nothing. He didn't know what to say to that.

"Where's your daddy?"

At the mention of his father, Pete perked up again. He began to recall more about the last hour. About why he was here. He hoped his parents came soon.

"We ain't seen a man up there, except for that old fellow. Where's your dad?" the man asked again.

Pete realized that he should continue to let them think his dad was gone. No need to put them on alert, thinking that his father would be here any minute. Pete hoped he would be. He did not want to die, nor did he want his Nana to die.

"My dad's out of town. For work."

The man smiled and stepped back triumphantly. "Oh now you're practically talking my damn ear off, boy. You wouldn't lie to ole Charlie now, would you?"

230

Pete shook his head. "Uh uh. No."

The man grabbed Pete by the face, forcing him to look up. The man held an axe in his other hand. He pressed the blade of the axe against Pete's face. "You feel that? Feel how sharp that is?"

Pete was afraid to nod, afraid that any motion would cause the axe to slice into his face.

"Do you feel it?" he asked louder.

"Yes."

The man let go and stepped back. He nodded toward the stall. "That your granny in there?"

"Yes."

"Angie here says she taught music."

Pete nodded. "She still does."

"She play piano?"

"Yeah."

"Think she could play without *hands*?"

Pete found the horror of this unthinkable. He recoiled against his ropes. He could not forget that this was the very man who had hung the bodies of Henry and his wife on his gate. This man was a monster. He was probably capable of anything. He could kill a boy. He could kill a grandmother. He could cut off someone's hands.

The man noticed Pete's thinking and smiled. "Of course, the question of whether she can or can't play without hands is only what they call a rhetorical question. If I cut her hands off, she'd never even see another piano. She'd probably bleed to death before anybody could stop the bleeding."

Pete looked the man in the eye. "Don't hurt my Nana."

The man smiled a wicked smile. He scanned the barn and found a shovel. He laid the shovel across a crude wooden bench. "I reckon that handle is about as thick as your Nana's wrist. What do you think?"

Pete stared at the handle, but did not answer.

The man drew back the axe, lined up his swing, and brought it down across the shovel handle. With a loud crack, the handle cut into two pieces. Pete flinched at both the sound and the mental picture it conjured. The man set down the axe, picked up the pieces, and studied the ends. "Not sure if it did more cutting or more breaking, but I guess it doesn't really matter as long as the result is the same, does it?"

Pete looked the man in the eye again. "Don't hurt my Nana," he repeated.

The man ignored Pete. "I'm thinking about a trade," the man said. "You and the woman for all of guns and food at your house. You all give me all your shit and you leave your house."

"We don't have much," Pete said. "I told you."

The man laughed. "You better fucking well hope they got something to trade for you, boy. I'm not giving you back for a bag of rice and a pat on the back. I want the serious shit. I know you all have something better than old canning jars of stewed tomatoes. You're not telling me the whole truth. I've known some good liars in my day and you sure as hell ain't one."

The woman put her hands to her ears and began screaming. The noise startled both Pete and the man interrogating him. They both flinched and turned to her.

"I can't stand this! Quit playing games, Charlie."

The man turned to her. "What do you want to do, honey?"

She looked Pete square in the eye and Pete did not see the hate he expected to see. "I'm not sure yet."

The man raised an eyebrow. "You want to kill him? The only problem with that idea is that we couldn't do much trading for a dead boy. They don't bring nearly as much."

She didn't respond, only stared Pete in the eye. He could not turn away from her. It was as if she was looking for something deep inside him. She finally spoke. "I didn't say I wanted to kill him. I said I didn't know what I wanted to do."

When Pete opened his mouth to speak, the woman flew from where she was sitting and slapped him so hard his ears rang. "You don't say a fucking word," she warned. She leaned over and picked up the axe, cocked it back over her shoulder like a batter ready to swing. "Not a fucking word or I will kill you right now."

He couldn't have said anything at that point anyway. Pete was more terrified than he'd ever been in his life. He was about to die. He and his Nana were both going to die. He might as well accept it. He hoped they didn't get the rest of his family.

The man considered Pete again. "Of course, maybe we'll just kill them and then go down there and take what we want. Shouldn't be anyone down there now but the woman and the little girl. I doubt they could put up much of a fight."

"I don't care," the woman said, her voice weak. Her outburst had drained what little she had left. "My boy won't be coming back either way. He's dead and gone."

"You see what you done here, don't you, boy?" the man said. "It ain't that I love her or anything, but you went and killed my brother's son, and your mommy probably killed my brother. Somebody needs to die for that. Surely you can understand."

Pete could see the furnace door opening in the man's eyes. A fire grew in the blackness of those eyes, his face tightened, and rage filled him. He was going to do it. The man was going to kill him. He took up the axe and fingered the blade, talking low to Pete in words that Pete could not hear anymore. It reminded him of when he watched someone butcher a chicken, how they spoke low and calming to it before they committed the act.

The man drew the axe back, opened his mouth to offer final validation, and all hell broke loose.

"Noooo!" Pete screamed.

There was an explosion and the man's head snapped back, blood erupting from a massive hole in the side of his skull. A mist of blood enveloped Pete, spraying his eyes and his mouth. Pete screamed again as the man's body toppled into the dirt, oozing blood into the thirsty dust of the barn floor.

The woman had no reaction. She looked as if nothing else that happened in the remainder of her life would ever cause her to so much as raise an eyebrow.

"Don't fucking move!" Jim crept in, M-4 held high, sighting the woman through the red dot. "Get your hands up! Get them up!"

The woman did not move, only stared at Jim.

"Don't shoot her, Dad," Pete said. "She has children in the house. They don't have anyone else."

Jim kept his gun on her.

Pete's mother was suddenly in front of him, cutting him loose.

With his hands free, there was nothing left holding his body upright. He staggered and nearly fell. "The stall," Pete croaked.

Jim nodded toward the woman on the stool. "Keep an eye on her," he told Ellen. "If she moves, kill her."

He found his mother where she lay in the straw. He knelt and put his ear to her mouth. "Thank God, she's still breathing. Randi is a nurse. Let's get her home now."

While Jim carried his mother to the truck, Ellen aimed her pistol at the woman's head and spoke quietly to her. "We'll be back tomorrow. You should be gone. Don't ever come back here."

Pete grabbed his gear and staggered out the door. Ellen backed behind him, pistol still aimed at the woman, and the family disappeared into the darkness.

CHAPTER 29

Jim's House
Russell County, Virginia

When Ellen and Jim had raced to Henry's farm earlier, she'd explained that they were living in the cave without really having any time to tell him why. As they returned to their farm, driving through the gate and weaving through the steel obstructions, Jim stopped in front of his house.

"Pete, I need you to help me get Nana into the house if you feel up to it. Ellen, get everyone at the cave and bring them back here. Bring back the medical totes and some food and drinks."

Pete took Ellen's house key, put on his headlamp, and ran to open the house. Jim followed, wearing his own headlamp and carrying his mother. He took her to his room and placed her on the bed. He noticed her high fever as he carried her, and was concerned that she was dehydrated.

At his father's side, Pete watched everything silently. With his mother settled, Jim turned to his son. "I am so proud of you, Pete. You helped keep everyone alive while I was gone. You went after your Nana all by yourself. You grew up while I was gone."

Pete started crying and grabbed his father, hugging him tightly. "I was so scared, Dad. I thought I was going to die."

Jim patted his son's damp hair, holding him. "I've been scared a lot lately, Pete. What's important is that you don't let being scared stop you from what you need to do." They didn't say anything else, just held each other. Jim could feel the void within him start to refill from the love and presence of his family. It recharged his battery.

It was only a few minutes before the entire family was crowded into the master bedroom watching Randi take Nana's vitals.

"I appreciate this, Randi," Jim said. "I know you want to get home."

"I only got this far because of you and Gary, Jim. I'm not going to run out on you now."

After a few moments, Randi corralled everyone out of the room and into the living room. They encircled her while she briefed them on Nana's condition. "She's dehydrated, malnourished, and needs IV antibiotics. We have to get that stuff."

"Shouldn't we take her to the hospital?" Pops asked.

Randi shook her head. "She'll be much better off here than in a hospital. They probably don't have enough staff on hand to take care of what they have. She'll get better care here with you all, but we need to get her hospital grade meds."

"That may not be easy," Pops said. "It was a madhouse when I was there earlier."

"Do you have any pain pills in that med kit?" Randi asked.

Jim nodded. "Hydrocodone from my hernia surgery."

"There's a nurse on the third floor that will probably be there. Her name is Claire. Offer her ten of those pills for the list of drugs I'm going to give you. Do *not* give her the drugs until you get your stuff."

"Thank God for drug addicts," Jim said sarcastically.

"Don't analyze the morality of the situation, Jim. Just go," Ellen said.

"I'll drive," Jim said. "Pops, come with me."

The pair headed out the front door to Jim's diesel truck, which had not been moved since he'd left on his trip. It started right up and had a full tank of fuel. "Nice to be driving," he remarked.

*

They were back in an hour with everything on Randi's list. Things had gone exactly as planned. Jim left Pops in the truck, armed with the tactical shotgun and instructions to shoot anyone who touched it. Jim had gone inside the hospital, lit now only with battery-powered lights, and found the nurse Randi had mentioned. When offered the pills, she did exactly as they'd been told she would. In mere minutes, he was back out the door and in his vehicle.

They were the only vehicle on the road that night but they passed several groups of pedestrians and a few ATVs moving about. There were bonfires in town with people standing around them socializing. In general, everything seemed more peaceful than the places Jim had been, but maybe that was simply the feeling of being home. He was glad his family was safe, but certain that the stories he would hear over the coming days would be very upsetting. He could tell his son was a different person now, more of a man than he'd been when Jim left. He was sure that there was a story behind that, and he was certain that it would be painful to hear.

With the medications in hand, Randi had an IV line in Nana in no time. In the glow of a battery lantern, she administered fluids and antibiotics. She also had steroids to be administered in the morning before she left. By the time everyone left Nana alone for the night, her color was better and she was resting peacefully. Randi wouldn't leave her side, so they all stepped out, shutting the door behind them.

Jim was not comfortable leaving the house unguarded and no one was ready to sleep, anyway, so they all moved to the front porch. They sat in the dark, eating a little, drinking, and enjoying the feeling of a family once again intact. Occasionally, Jim lifted the night vision and scanned the perimeter, but saw nothing. The only sound was the crickets and Jim even felt like they were welcoming him home.

All the little things that each party had experienced in the other's absence hung over the group like a cloud of insects, but no one was ready to tear into those wounds yet. Those stories would come out over days and weeks, sometimes when they sat together as a family, sometimes when they were together individually. Some stories would bring anger, others would bring tears.

When the kids began to fall asleep, Ellen offered to take first watch. They moved the kids inside, back into the beds they'd both missed during life in the cave. Pops agreed to take second watch, with Jim taking the last shift in the morning. He would stay up from there, then return Randi to her family.

*

As it happened, Ellen and Pops covered all the watch shifts that night and let Jim sleep. He was a little perturbed at this, but did not complain too much. He was never so happy to wake in his own house as he was that morning. Even though he slept on the couch, it was *his* couch in *his* living room and that was a damn fine place to be. He went to check on his mother first thing and found Randi already up and tending to her. She'd kept the fluid bags going all night and Nana was conscious now, though still weak. Jim kissed her on the cheek and she returned a weak hug.

"I thought we'd lost you," he said.

"We never thought we'd lost you. We knew you'd be back any day now."

He smiled at their confidence in him. It made him proud.

"I'm taking your nurse home," he said.

Randi placed a hand on Nana's arm. "I already told her that I'd be back in a few days to check on her. I intend to keep that promise, even if you have to come get me."

"It's a deal," Jim said. "Are you ready to go?"

Randi gave him a final explanation of the med regimen for his mother. She explained what complications to watch for, and that they should leave the IV in place until she returned to remove it.

"I almost didn't get that thing in her," Randi explained. "I don't want to give up that line until I'm sure she's on the mend."

Jim nodded, feeling a bit overloaded with information.

"I kind of like being the one with all the answers for a change," Randi said with a smile. "I felt pretty dumb out there on the road."

"You weren't dumb," Jim assured her. "You got back alive."

While Randi said her goodbyes to everyone and got an especially grateful hug from Pops, Jim grabbed his M-4, a dozen clips, and replenished the ammo for his pistol. He stuck the backpack he'd walked all these miles with in the bed of his truck. He hoped to God that he didn't have to walk home from wherever Randi's family lived, but he wanted to be prepared in case he did. If his bag had not saved his life, it had certainly made his journey home easier. He would never travel any distance without a similar bag for the rest of his life.

As he and Randi drove out of the valley, Jim noticed numerous houses and barns burned to the ground. From the brief information that he and Ellen shared, he assumed this was the work of the man he'd killed last night. He wondered if all of the burned-out houses meant that those families were dead. He did notice that there were still some people alive and moving about. The closer he got to town, the more people he saw. Perhaps their little valley was the only location to experience the fury of Charlie Rakes. He knew there would be other communities that would suffer the same from different oppressors. Other men, turned out from jail as Charlie was, had spread outward like the four horsemen of the apocalypse, delivering their own particular breed of pain, suffering, and criminality to the outer reaches of his community.

Randi lived in a little roadside community called Pumpkin Center about fifteen miles away from Jim's home. Halfway into their journey they encountered a police roadblock similar to the one they'd run into at Claypool Hill. Jim approached slowly, his windows down, keeping his hands in view. It would suck to make it all the way home only to get shot because a local cop got nervous. It turned out that Jim knew the man working the roadblock, a Virginia State Trooper that he'd gone to high school with. The man was carrying some type of bullpup automatic rifle. Another example of tax dollars being used to buy cops weapons that Jim himself could not afford. That still pissed him off.

The trooper was dressed in combat fatigues and studied Jim through his window. He appeared not to recognize Jim, but Jim knew that he probably still looked like shit from his time on the road.

"It's me, Travis. Jim Powell."

A light came on in the Trooper's brain and he nodded. "Oh, yeah, Jim. Sorry, I recognize you now. The last time I saw you I don't remember you looking like something the cat threw up."

"If you only fucking knew," Jim said. "I've had a rough couple of weeks."

"I think we all have," Travis replied ruefully. "Where you headed?"

"This is Randi. We were on a work trip when all this went down. I'm taking her back to her family over at Pumpkin Center."

Travis nodded. "Things aren't too bad over that way. You shouldn't run into trouble. There's another roadblock coming out of Honaker, but that should be all you need to look out for."

"Thanks for the information."

"You armed?"

Jim raised an eyebrow at the trooper. "Why are you asking?"

"Cause if you're not, you need to be," the Trooper said. "People are getting a little crazy."

"I've noticed, and I'm prepared," Jim said. That was all he planned on saying on the matter.

"They'll get worse, I'm afraid," Travis said.

Something about the way he said that made Jim think he may know something. Information was scarce these days. People knew nothing of what was going on anywhere outside their own immediate world.

"What are you hearing?"

"There's not much information getting through. It's all been passed through a lot of hands so it's not reliable. They're saying that the electrical grid problems are serious. Some of the transformers that were hit were critical ones. There may be some localized power back up and running eventually, but nationwide power could take years because of the transformers."

"We have coal-fired plants. We should get ours back, right?" Jim asked.

"The refinery issue is hurting us there. The strategic oil reserve is useless without the ability to refine. There are some working refineries but only small ones. All the big ones got hit. The fuel that's being made now isn't going very far. It's not making its way up here yet."

Jim sighed and looked at Randi. It was as if all the worst case scenarios that had played out in his head on the way home were becoming reality.

"We're expecting refugees to start showing up here," the trooper continued. "That'll be the icing on the cake."

"Refugees? From where?" Randi asked.

"Out west. There are some nuclear disasters unfolding out there. We're not getting much in the way of details, but I hear it's getting worse every day. People in the fallout zones are trying to clear out, most of them on foot since they can't get fuel."

"Most of those will probably die," Jim said. "The road is a hard, unforgiving place."

Travis nodded. "Sounds like you've been there."

"We have. By the way, what are you hearing about the FEMA camps?" Jim asked. "We had some co-workers who went to stay at one near Lexington. They didn't like my company."

Travis scratched his head under his riot helmet. "If they went to a FEMA camp, they're probably still there," he said. "That whole thing didn't work out as planned. Most of those camps are falling apart. What I'm hearing is that they won't be restocked when their supplies run out. They're going to turn the people out and tell them to get home as best they can."

"What about you cops? Everyone still showing up for work?"

The trooper laughed. "Hell no. Don't even get me started on that. There were probably sixty law enforcement officers in this county before. There's probably a dozen working now."

Jim shook his head. "They all just quit and go home?"

"Yep. We put cops on all the big gas stations when the order came down from the governor. It was made clear to us that the only fuel we'd get during this crisis would be the fuel we seized locally, so it was up to us to protect it. The deputies guarding those tanks had a hard time saying no to their friends so they started trading gas off for food, guns, ammunition, chickens, sex, whatever the hell they could get. Then when they realized how long this was going to last, they started carrying it off to their own homes. Now there's hardly any left at all."

"So how long are you going to keep working?" Jim asked.

"I love being a cop, but I'm about out of road flares and gas. I can't keep driving up here every damn day. In another week or two, folks will be on their own. There might not be any cops at all by then."

"What will you do then?" Randi asked.

"I'll go home and protect my family. Work in the garden. Cut firewood. I'll do all the stuff that needs doing, you know."

"Where do you live?" Jim asked.

Travis stared him down hard. "None of your damn business, Jim."

"Don't get all defensive, Travis, I was just asking," Jim said. "If things turn ugly and good people have to start enforcing the law on their own, I thought it might be good to know where to find an actual cop with a badge. Or at least a man who can handle a weapon."

The trooper looked Jim in the eye. He leaned closer conspiratorially and whispered, "Between you and me – fuck people. I'm sick of them. I took this job because I wanted to help people. These days, I could care less about them. You know what I mean?"

Jim smiled at that. "I know *exactly* what you mean."

The trooper smiled back. "All right then. You have a good day."

"I'll be coming back through later, Travis, if you're still here."

Travis nodded, then leaned up to Jim's window. "By the way, where do you live, Jim?"

Jim smiled. "None of your damn business."

CHAPTER 30

Pumpkin Center
Russell County, Virginia

The closer they got to Pumpkin Center, the more Randi squirmed in her seat. She couldn't sit still and she couldn't shut up. Nerves affected everyone differently. Both her body and her mouth were in constant motion.

Jim could only try to focus on the road and not pay attention to the chatter. He'd forgotten how confining the interior of a vehicle was. On the road, his personal space had expanded and he wasn't ready to give up the area he'd gained. Now, Randi was sitting right in the middle of his personal space and he couldn't do a damn thing about it.

"Seeing you in that state reminds me that I haven't seen you smoke a cigarette in days. Did you quit looking for them?"

"I quit."

"When?"

"I don't know. I just did."

"I wish to hell I had one to give you. It might calm you down some."

"I'm sorry."

"No need to apologize. How much farther? Not that you're getting on my nerves or anything."

She pointed. "The blue trailer."

They pulled off the main road onto a gravel driveway. In front of them was a mobile home with blue aluminum siding. The yard was full of children's toys – slides, sandboxes, little tables and chairs. It was a home that was all about children.

"No cars and the curtains are closed," Randi said. "Not good."

"Don't overreact," Jim said. "There's a note on the door. Go see what it says."

While Randi hopped out of the truck, Jim reached for his M-4 and pulled it across his lap. Better to have it within reach if something crazy happened. There could be squatters in the house watching them right now. There could be people wanting a fueled vehicle who saw him drive by and

243

were coming for him. In this world, those were the kinds of things you had to think about now. Not only what was going on in front of you, but all the possibilities of what could be coming up behind you.

Randi tore the note off the door and walked back. She stood in the open doorway and stared at him. "It says they went to my dad's house."

"See, nothing to worry about. Where's that?"

"Not far. Back a few miles, turn off the main road. He has a small farm with a few horses, and one of my brothers has a trailer on the farm."

"Then hop in. Let's go."

"I can walk, Jim," Randi said. "Really, you driving me here was a lot to ask. You've done enough."

"Don't be silly. Get in."

"It's okay, I—"

"Do I have to pull a fucking gun, Randi? Get in this truck *now*!"

"Alrighty then." She climbed into the truck and shut her door.

It was indeed merely a few minutes before they were pulling up in front of her dad's farm. The gate at the road was chained and padlocked.

"Honk the horn and I'll get out and wave," Randi said. "He has lots of guns and poor eyesight so stay on your toes."

"What a combination," Jim said, laying on the horn.

In a few minutes, a side-by-side ATV approached with two armed men riding in the back, weapons laid across the top of the cab and pointed in Jim's direction. As they got closer and the men saw Randi, the guns were lowered and one of the men called back toward the house. "It's Randi! She's home!"

At this, the door to the brick ranch opened and a small herd of people emerged.

"Oh my God!" Randi said. She started jumping up and down, unable to contain herself.

Jim took his eyes from the ATV and looked over at her standing in the open door of the truck. Tears were streaming down her face.

"They're all here," she said, counting. "They're safe." She bolted and ran to the gate. While her dad fumbled with a chain of keys, she got tired of waiting and climbed over the gate, jumping into the arms of a man I later learned was her brother. From there, she was swarmed and lost in a sea of ecstatic huggers and weepers.

Her dad, stoic and task-oriented, his eyes blurred with welling tears, continued to struggle with his keys until he finally had the gate open. He waved at Jim to drive in, but Jim declined, instead getting out and walking through the gate.

"That's Jim," Randi said, holding a grandchild in each arm. "He got us home from Richmond."

Randi's dad shook Jim's hand, then gave up and grabbed him tightly into a bear hug. When he was done, Randi's daughters swarmed Jim with their own hugs.

"You raised a tough and determined girl," Jim told her father. "She could have gotten herself home even without anyone's help."

"Either way, we're indebted to you," he said. "You ever need anything, you let us know."

Jim thanked him. "Now that you mention it, I will be needing your daughter back in a few days. My mom is sick and Randi needs to check in on her in a few days. I figured I'd come pick her back up the day after tomorrow about this same time if that's okay."

"Don't worry about it," her dad said. "We'll bring her to you. It's the least we can do for whatever role you played in helping her get home."

Jim shook his hand, waved to Randi, who was still being bombarded with kisses and hugs, and went to get Randi's pack from his truck. He handed it to her dad, then returned to his truck while the gate was shut and locked behind him. He backed out the driveway, watching the procession of Randi's family walk up the driveway in a staggering, multi-armed embrace.

CHAPTER 31

A Neighborhood
Bluefield, Virginia

In Bluefield, Virginia, cross streets cut into the steep hillsides. On one of these streets was a neighborhood of pre-World War II homes once occupied by Hungarian coal miners. Once bustling with those large immigrant families, the houses were now showing their age, their small yards wrapped in rusting chain-link fence. Steps of hand-cut stone were slewing awkwardly. Wrought iron railings rattled loosely, balusters missing, ornamentation long savaged by neighborhood vandals.

Most of the residents on the street were older, the children of those long-dead Hungarian miners. They watched the news too much, as the elderly are prone to do, worrying as the newscasters turned the tension up one notch at a time. When the power failed, most had no idea what to do. They tried calling children or grandchildren but landlines were not working any longer. The steep hills of the city did not allow cell signals to reach them. They sat in the dark, watching their neighbors through curtained windows, afraid to leave. Most would slowly starve to death rather than leave the house.

One nondescript house, with dingy white siding and aluminum awnings over each window, housed a younger resident. While not exactly young, he was younger than the neighborhood average of seventy-two years. For the majority of his life, the young man had been in and out of institutions. The newer generation of antipsychotic medications worked for his symptoms most of the time. When they didn't, his mother had him committed against his will. He resented those commitments, feeling that she sent him away every time he was beginning to enjoy life again, every time the veil of depression was lifted. He did not see that he ever did anything that bad. Nothing *really* bad, anyway.

With each commitment, a med regimen would finally be settled upon and he would stabilize. If that stability continued and he displayed the blunted, cooperative personality that was expected of him, he would eventually be released. He had been sent away on an inpatient commitment again several weeks ago, before the terror attacks, but had responded favorably to treatment. Ideally, he would have remained for several more weeks to make sure all of his symptoms were alleviated, but he'd been discharged on the morning of the attacks. He was on his way home when his bus ran out of fuel, could not obtain more, and had ended up in a FEMA camp.

He had finally arrived home in Bluefield last night. He'd brought a guest. His mother was not glad to see him. Had the phones been working, it was likely that she would have called her boyfriend to come throw him out. Since the phones weren't working, he and his mother worked things out between themselves.

*

In a dark, cold basement of cut stone, Alice began to stir. Her head throbbed. Her broken nose lay pressed against the gritty concrete floor. She went to touch it but her hands would not move. She rolled onto her back and found her numb hands trapped behind her. Craning her neck, she could see they were zip tied, with a tie around each wrist and one connecting her two wrists.

She tried to think back. She had a hazy memory of waking up in a car. She remembered being excited after being close to home, the prospect of being only days from her family. Then she remembered being yanked from her feet and hitting her head on the pavement. There was nothing else beyond that point.

She was badly dehydrated and could feel that blood had crusted around her mouth. She could taste it. When she blinked, she could feel that her face seemed swollen. She struggled to sit upright. A dim light came in through filthy hopper windows, too small for her to climb out of even if her hands were free. She looked around but her mobility was limited. She was too foggy to look for anything that might help her cut her bonds.

To her left she saw a shape. As her eyes adjusted, she could see that it was a woman. A blanket was thrown over her head and there was no sign of breathing. Cold chills ran through Alice.

A door opened above her in the darkness. The sound of a solid wood door and an old lock reminded her of her grandmother's house. Then there was the sound of creaking stairs and slow, cautious steps.

She twisted her body but could not get a good look. The pale light did not reach the foot of the stairs. The sound of the steps changed when the person reached the bottom. There was a gritty sound, smooth soles on dirty concrete. The steps were coming toward her. Alice panicked but there was nothing she could do. She could not get up, she could not fight back. She tried to scream but the pain of opening her mouth was excruciating.

The figure stepped into the light and smiled down at her.

"Hello, Alice," the man said.

Alice's heart sank. Tears welled in her eyes.

"Boyd," she whispered.

CHAPTER 32

Jim's Home
Russell County, Virginia

Two hours prior to the appointed time, Jim gathered his gear into a small daypack. It was a hot, sunny day and he packed four bottles of cold spring water, his radio, and a spare set of batteries for the trip. It was the same radio he'd taken from the ranger station on Mount Rogers. It seemed like years ago that they'd made that journey, although only a few days had passed. He took his spotting scope because he wanted to examine their valley from higher ground. When he'd driven Randi home, he'd seen indications of what had gone on in his absence, but he'd not gone out again since; there had been too much to do at home. The most important thing being simply basking in the love of his family. It was what he had walked hundreds of miles for. It was what he'd killed for.

The final gear he gathered was his weapons. He could not imagine that in the immediate future he and his weapons would be far apart. The world was too violent now, the personal risk too high, to be unable to defend yourself. He took the M-4, his Beretta pistol, the SOG Twitch pocketknife, and a Gerber fixed-blade knife taped to the strap of his pack. In the back of his mind, he thought that he was going to need to have a conversation with his wife about weapons in the future. Like many men, he loved guns and knives. Like many men, he sometimes bought more of them than he actually told his wife about. While she and Pete had done such a good job of transporting the weapons to the cave for safety, they had only taken the weapons they knew about. Jim had other guns stored in various locations. Those guns were going to have to come out of hiding and then Jim would have some explaining to do. Somehow, with the current state of the world, Jim didn't anticipate too much argument about having a few extra guns and a few extra cases of ammunition.

Pete had asked to come along on this short trip, and Jim saw no problem with that. Things at the house had been quiet since they'd dealt with Charlie Rakes. They'd seen people on the road occasionally but there'd been no trouble. The trailer park that had been such a source of worry now sat empty, home to only a few feral cats and a herd of rats.

Jim had walked to Henry's house the day after he'd dropped Randi off and found it abandoned, as he'd hoped. Henry's truck was gone and the house had been ransacked of all useful items, but the body of Charlie Rakes lay where Jim had dropped him. He was now in a condition offensive to both eye and nose, bloated and gnawed upon. Jim assumed that if he gave it a week under these warm and humid circumstances, there would be nothing left but a blackened crust on the dirt floor. Maybe he would come back then and see if he could find any remaining diesel fuel for his truck. He knew that Henry would not have minded. When Jim had left Henry's barn that day, he'd left the doors wide open to give coyotes easier access the decaying corpse.

Jim and Pete climbed the steep shoulder of Clinch Mountain using logging roads, eventually reaching the rocky crest near the old fire tower. It was an area now known as The Channels, named for the polished stone passages cut by ancient seas hundreds of millions of years ago. To walk through The Channels was like walking through a cave with no roof. When you climbed to the top of the rocks, you could see for hundreds of miles. People had once come from all over the country to hike there and see this geological feature. Now, with recreational walking probably a thing of the past, this scene would be a rare treat reserved for the strong hunter or explorer who came upon this trail and wondered where it led. It may even become the lodge of some half-crazed man of the mountains, unable to accept the world as he now found it, determined to discover a burrow where he might live out his days in separateness.

Jim and Pete climbed a rock perch near the decaying fire warden's shack. The disintegrating shack had once been the summer duty station of a young man named Jack Kestner, who would go on to become a newspaper reporter. His articles about Clinch Mountain and his love for The Channels would become a driving force for its preservation. Jim could not visit the site without thinking of the teenage fire warden spending his summer in such isolation, braving intense summer thunderstorms alone on this mountain peak. Children these days, and most adults, were not cut from that same stuff.

From the rocks where they sat, Jim and Pete could see Beartown Mountain, Paintlick Mountain, and House and Barn Mountain. Hopefully, somewhere among all those peaks, Gary sat with his radio.

"Gary, this is Jim, do you copy?"

The reply came almost immediately. "Jim, it's Gary. Reading you loud and clear."

Jim grinned. "I won't say I missed you guys, but it's damn good to hear your voice."

"Randi, you with us?" Gary asked.

"I'm here," Randi said. "There's a little static, but I'm getting most of it."

"Gary, I know Randi's doing okay because I dropped her off, how are things up your way?"

There was a hesitation. "Tolerable, Jim, but far from ideal."

"Was everyone okay when you got home?" Randi asked.

"Everyone's fine," Gary said. "We're too darn close to town. There was a lot that went on while I was gone."

"Problems with the neighbors?" Jim asked. "We had a few of those as well."

"Definitely," Gary said. "I'm right next door to a public housing complex and it's been a constant problem. My son-in-law kept everyone safe while I was gone, but our gardens were raided and my outbuildings have been broken into. I lost my generator, my solar equipment, my chainsaw, and most of my tools. There was no way they could watch everything."

Jim knew that one of Gary's three daughters lived next door. That would mean one large family trying to guard two properties, not an easy proposition.

"Are things safe, Gary?"

There was a long pause.

"For now."

"Do you need help?" Jim asked.

There was another pause.

"My plan had always been to bug *in* instead of bug *out*," Gary said. "I'm having second thoughts, now. The problem is my location. I don't think we can bug in here. It will be a constant battle and we don't have the numbers to keep a constant patrol. I bought this place before I became interested in preparedness. If I knew then what I know now, I would have kept looking."

"We might need to look at joining our groups," Jim offered. "There are a lot of empty houses in my valley. I'll try to speak with what neighbors are left. I'm sure we can come up with something."

"Give me some time to talk to my family, Jim. Can we do this again forty-eight hours from now?"

"We can," Jim said. "All good with you Randi?"

"We're fine, Jim. My dad is going to bring me down there tomorrow to check on your mom."

"Good. I'll see you then. Be careful."

They all signed off and Jim stowed his radio in his pack. The whole time that Jim was on the radio, Pete sat on a tall rock, reclined against his pack, staring out at the hills that surrounded them. A favorite writer of Jim's had once described the Appalachian Mountains as looking like a rug that had been kicked up. Jim had always thought that to be about as accurate a description as he'd ever heard.

"What are you looking at, Pete?"

"The hills," he said. "It's amazing to think of all the things that have gone on down there in that valley. There was probably a day when you could sit in this same spot and see wooly mammoths walking in those fields and drinking from our creek. Then one day they were gone and it was the Native Americans living down there in their villages. Then it was us, riding tractors and raising cows and living in houses. I was just imagining what would be next."

Jim smiled. He had sat on that same rock and thought those same thoughts. There must be something about that spot that invited reflection, or maybe it just stood as a balcony overlooking this borrowed world, allowing you to look down on the stage of man and see all the possibilities.

ABOUT THE AUTHOR

Franklin Horton lives and writes in the mountains of southwestern Virginia. He attended Virginia Intermont College and Virginia Commonwealth University. He holds a B.A. in English. In his spare time he pursues outdoor adventures with his wife and two children, including camping, kayaking, backpacking, mountain biking, and shooting. His first published novel, *The Borrowed World*, was published in May of 2015 and quickly became an Amazon bestseller. You can follow him online at www.franklinhorton.com.